'If poetry was the supreme literary form of the First World War then, as if in riposte, in the Second World War, the English novel came of age. This wonderful series is an exemplary reminder of that fact. Great novels were written about the Second World War and we should not forget them.'

WILLIAM BOYD

'It's wonderful to see these books given a new lease of life [...] classic novels from the Second World War written by those who were there, experienced the fear, anguish, pain and excitement first-hand and whose writings really do shine an incredibly vivid light onto what it was like to live and fight through that terrible conflict.'

JAMES HOLLAND, Historian, author and TV presenter

'The Imperial War Museum has performed a valuable public service by reissuing these absolutely superb novels.'

ANDREW ROBERTS, author of *Churchill: Walking with Destiny*

MAILED
FIST

John Foley

IMPERIAL WAR MUSEUMS

First published in Great Britain in 1957

First published in this format in 2022 by IWM, Lambeth Road, London SE1 6HZ
iwm.org.uk

© The Estate of John Foley, 2022

About the Author and Introduction © The Trustees of the Imperial War Museum, 2022

This edition printed 2024

2

ISBN 978-1-912423-49-1

A catalogue record for this book is available from the British Library.

Printed and bound by CPI Group (UK) Ltd, Croydon CR0 4YY

Every effort has been made to contact all copyright holders. The publishers will be glad to make good in future editions any error or omissions brought to their attention.

Cover illustration by Bill Bragg

Design by Clare Skeats

Series Editor Madeleine James

About the Author

John Foley (1917 – 1974)

MAJOR JOHN FOLEY (1917–1974) served in the British Army from 1936 until 1954. He attended the Royal Military Academy, Sandhurst, and passed out from officer training in 1943. Subsequently, Foley became a troop commander in the 107th Regiment, Royal Armoured Corps (King's Own). He was awarded an MBE for his service with the unit during the North-West Europe campaign. He then became a military reporter and later worked in the Directorate of Public Relations at the War Office. After leaving the army, he continued to work in public relations as well as becoming an author, broadcaster and scriptwriter. His books include *The Boilerplate War* (1963), an exploration of armoured warfare, as well as *Bull and Brass* (1958) and *Death of a Regiment* (1959), the latter of which is based on the experience of the 153rd (Essex) Regiment, Royal Armoured Corps. *Mailed Fist*, meanwhile, represents his fictionalised memoir, covering April 1943 until the end of the war in Europe.

Introduction

One of the literary legacies of the First World War was the proliferation of war novels, with an explosion of the genre in the late 1920s and 1930s. Erich Maria Remarque's *All Quiet on the Western Front* was a bestseller and was made into a Hollywood film in 1930. In the same year, Siegfried Sassoon's *Memoirs of an Infantry Officer* sold 24,000 copies. Generations of school children have grown up on a diet of Wilfred Owen's poetry and the novels of Sassoon.

In contrast to the First World War, the novels of the Second World War are often overlooked – John Foley's *Mailed Fist* is one such novel. It is a lightly fictionalised account of the author's own wartime experience, reminiscent of *Sword of Bone* by Anthony Rhodes (also reprinted in the IWM Wartime Classics series). *Mailed Fist* is a gripping depiction of commanding a tank troop, as well as that unit's inner life. Foley clearly states in the text: 'If this book can be said to be a history of anything, it is a history of Five Troop. Not of the squadron, or of the regiment. If anybody wants to know what happened in other troops, or in other squadrons, it's all recorded painstakingly in the War Diaries and lodged in a Records Office somewhere'. There are also many parallels between *Mailed Fist* and another book in the Wartime Classics series, Peter Elstob's *Warriors for the Working Day*. Indeed, both authors wrote fiction and military history after their military service in tanks.

Foley, a regular soldier before the war, became an officer during the Second World War, passing out from officer training at Sandhurst in 1943. As a result, he was able to wear two rank pips as a Lieutenant rather than the usual one pip as a Second Lieutenant, as he explains to his unconvinced commanding officer, 'because I've had more than six years in the ranks, sir!'. However, Foley ruminates, one thing is made paramount in his officer training:

> *At Sandhurst they held as their objective that every Troop Leader should be able to do every job in the troop better than*

the crewman who was supposed to do it. He should, according to the pundits, be a better driver than any of the three drivers; be a more accurate gunner than any of the gunners; and be able to operate the tank wireless better than any of the operators.

Foley does manage to impress his new troop, which has 'no officer and only one tank', with his driving skills: 'Five Troop had a Troop Leader – more by luck than anything else!'

Five Troop as described in the text was part of A Squadron, 107th Regiment, Royal Armoured Corps (RAC). The unit is initially equipped with Churchill Mark (Mk) II tanks with 6-pounder guns, these are soon replaced by later Churchill variants, mostly Mk VII with 75mm guns. During the war Churchill tanks were developed and built as infantry support tanks. Their role was to work alongside infantry with good cross-country performance, which was seen as more important than speed. Thus, at 12-15 miles per hour (mph) they were relatively slow moving. Sherman tanks by contrast travelled at 24mph, they were cruiser tanks that could exploit the advance once the enemy's defences had been breached. Foley himself became rather an expert on armoured warfare. He describes the different role of tanks in the novel:

At the risk of this sounding like a military textbook (which Heaven forbid) it would be as well if I explained that there are two jobs for which tanks are considered to be the right tools. One is the short, set-piece attack, in which you are given an objective not very far away but pretty heavily defended. The other is the disorganising, long sweeps behind the enemy lines, playing havoc with his bases and lines of communication and generally getting as far as you can, as fast as you can.

The first of these jobs was the sort of thing we liked, because each of these tasks requires a different technique, different equipment and, I maintain, a different personality on the part of the tank crews.

Personally, I would much rather be shown a hill, say, a thousand yards away, and told that once I'd reached the top of that hill the job was over – although the ground between was stiff with defence works and hateful devices to stop us reaching that hill.

I have an inherent loathing of dashing madly through enemy-held territory for mile after mile, never knowing which bend in the road conceals an anti-tank ambush, and expecting any moment to hear that you've been cut off from your own supplies and the enemy were just sitting back waiting for you to run out of petrol.

This is a gross case of over-simplification, I know. But it will give you the rough idea.

And, of course, it's only fair to tell you that I've met lots of chaps in Armoured Divisions who take exactly the opposite view, and who would much rather do a mad dash across Europe than plough their way slowly and steadily through a heavily defended locality.

Churchill tank regiments all had three tanks per troop, five (sometimes six) troops per squadron, and four squadrons to a regiment. In the case of Five Troop the three tanks are *Avenger*, *Alert* and *Angler*. The crew comprises five men: driver, co-driver, wireless operator, gunner and tank commander. Tank crews became very used to each other, living in prolonged, cramped conditions together, and it could be difficult for newcomers to fit in. Derek Hunter takes over as the new co-driver for Foley's tank *Avenger*, Foley describing him as 'a nice boy […] an only child, he had all the benefits (and disadvantages) of being carefully brought up and given a good education. He was like a fish out of water with the other earthy members of Five Troop and my main worry during the first few days was that the others would bully him'. Foley's concerns prove correct as 'the troop didn't accept him'. They call him Hunter rather than any sort of nickname ('Mac, or Henry, or "Bing" or Smudger, or something'). Hunter makes all the 'new boy's mistakes', culminating in blowing off the waterproof sealing on the Churchill, which was in place for landing on the Normandy beaches. However, he stays up all night to re-seal and re-waterproof *Avenger* by himself. After which he is accepted by the crew:

Sandy-haired Lance-Corporal Westham pushed himself forward.

'Th'art a moog, Derek,' he said roughly, in his broadest accent. 'But tha'll do. C'mon, lad, I'll buy thee a pint soon as they're open.'

Trooper Derek Hunter was in Five Troop.

The regiment trains in England for the fighting in Normandy and goes ashore after D-Day. Fifty-eight Churchill tanks are taken over in an American Landing Ship Tank (LST). The remaining six, including Five Troop, travel in a small Landing Craft, Tank (LCT). Foley compares notes with one of his fellow officers:

'Superior sort of trip,' he said. 'Shower baths, stacks of tinned fruit, ice-cream.' He went on, his eyes twinkling wickedly. 'The only pity was that being an American ship it was strictly teetotal. Very dry indeed. But very luxurious. What sort of a trip did you have in that little packet of yours?'

'We had a bottle of gin,' I said simply.

The unit then spends the first couple of weeks parked up in a field before their first battle experience in Operation 'Greenline', on 15 July 1944. The objective is the capture of the hamlet of Bon Repos: 'We hoped the Brigadier hadn't paid a lot of money for that battle because as battles go, it wasn't an awful lot of good. But we didn't have any other battles by which to measure it, so far as we were concerned it ranked with Malplaquet, Waterloo, and the Second Battle of Mons'. There are a number of strong, detailed descriptions of action in the novel, from this first battle in Normandy until the Ardennes in Germany. One such description arises from the Troop's first encounter with a German Tiger tank:

Through the fog of self-analysis my brain picked up the conversation behind me and when I looked around I saw the pocket-sized McGinty trudging along with his hands thrust deep into his pockets. He was talking to 'Bing' Crosby.

'Bouncing off, they were,' he said bitterly. 'Bouncing off like peas off a flippin' drum!'

It seemed to me that Five Troop morale was in danger of sinking to an all-time low, so I dropped back and joined in the conversation.

'What's the matter, McGinty?' I said.

He kicked a stone idly and muttered under his breath. Then he said: 'Didn't somebody in Parliament the other day say that our tanks were every bit as good as the Germans?'

'I believe he did,' I said. 'But it's not the sort of thing you can generalise about like that. Some of our tanks are better in some respect than some of the German tanks, and vice versa.'

'What have we got that will knock out a Tiger?' he said.

'The seventeen-pounder Sherman,' I said. 'And the Firefly SP gun. Besides, we've got the RAF on our side with their rocket-firing Typhoons. They make a hell of a mess of a Tiger.'

But he wasn't convinced.

Foley reflects: 'I racked my brains but couldn't think of anything off-hand, and I wished I had one of those clever articles from the 'ARMY QUARTERLY' in which ballistic experts proved by numbers that we had better tanks and guns than the enemy' (indeed, another officer of 107 Regiment, RAC is told by his crew that the 75mm guns are as much good as a peashooter). The problem was that these British tank guns still fired an effective high explosive (HE) shell, particularly useful in the unit's main role of infantry support, but as an anti-tank gun it had become obsolete by 1944.

In *Mailed Fist*, one of Foley's fellow officers suggests that there will be little interest in the story of Five Troop, remarking that the 'British public is fed up with war and talk of war. Wait until it's history'. This Foley did, with his very readable account of fighting in North-West Europe not being published until 1957. It proved popular and was reprinted numerous times. Nevertheless, more recently it has become a much sought-after novel due to its scarcity. This welcome reprint makes it widely available again for a new generation of readers.

Alan Jeffreys
2022

ONE

WHEN I FIRST met Five Troop there was nothing about our meeting to signify that our acquaintance would last for over two years and extend to well beyond the Siegfried Line.

My battledress still bore the creases of the Quartermaster's store and was hung about with that peculiar camphorated odour which was supposed by some people to give protection against gas, and by others to provide immunity to lice. Happily I never had the opportunity of disproving either of these contentions.

The two yellow pips on my shoulder gleamed like stars in the night as I made my way to 'A' Squadron Headquarters for the first time.

Westgate-on-Sea in April, 1943, was not a bit like the popular holiday resort it is now or, for that matter, like it was before the war.

A tangle of barbed wire festooned the sea front and the promenade was set with concrete pyramids called, hopefully, Dragon's Teeth. The tall boarding houses and residential hotels were bare of curtains and furnishings and the wooden floorboards echoed to the clump of Boots, Ankle, Infantry Pattern.

The morning had been filled with interviews and what the army euphemistically calls 'Documentation', and the most memorable of these was the interview with the Second-in-Command, who was later to be the Commanding Officer.

I was frankly foxed by this business of who salutes who in the commissioned ranks, but my Sandhurst notebooks were stuffed full of well-meant guidance and one thing they were clear about was that you saluted when you went into anyone's office.

That's fine, I thought, and gave the second-in-command a magnificent salute, crashing my heels together with a bang that shook the window-frame.

The balding major behind the desk winced.

'There's no need to stamp your feet quite so hard, Foley,' he said coldly. 'That's the sort of thing I expect from NCOs – not officers.'

But he didn't say anything about the salute so I took it that was all right. He then proceeded to question me pretty closely about where I'd been and what I'd been and what I'd done, and my answers must have satisfied him because he unbent slightly, to give me some words of kindly advice and guidance. But the business of the stamping feet still rankled slightly and for the life of me I can't remember any of the kindly advice now. But I'm sure it was useful.

The interview ended with the information that I was posted to 'A' Squadron and in my best Royal Military Academy manner I threw up a vibrating salute and – just in time I halted my bent knee in mid-air. A split-second decision had averted another window-shaking crash and for a brief instant I stood there on one leg like a dog torn between two trees.

Then I smiled weakly and *clicked* my heels together and somehow extricated myself from the presence.

I was halfway down the road from Regimental Headquarters before I realised that I hadn't the vaguest notion where 'A' Squadron was. So I did a smart About Turn and retraced my steps.

In the Orderly Room one of the clerks momentarily raised his eyes from his typewriter and then to my surprise he stood up. I was still at the stage where I had constantly to remind myself that I was an officer now and people did stand up when I came into a room.

'Whereabouts is "A" Squadron?' I asked.

'Up at Dandelion, sir,' replied the clerk.

'Up at where?'

'Dandelion!'

He looked at me as if he had made himself abundantly clear and then seeing the look of complete mystification on my face he reached down a map and stabbed an inky finger at a rectangular patch of green.

'Dent-de-Lion,' I read aloud.

'That's right, sir. Dandelion.'

'Oh,' I said, studying the map. 'About a mile and a half. Well, that shouldn't take long to walk.'

'Why don't you take the duty truck, sir,' said the clerk. And I thought I detected a pitying note in his voice.

'Of course,' I said. 'The duty truck.' Now I was an officer I could ride in trucks without anybody's say so. My chest began to expand and my voice took on a ring of self-confidence. And then I had a niggling doubt.

'Oughtn't I to ask the Adjutant?' I said.

The clerk pursed his lips knowingly and shook his head.

'I don't think so, sir,' he said. 'The Adjutant has gone off to Brigade and won't be back for an hour or two.'

Five minutes later I was sitting in the front of a fifteen-hundredweight truck being driven in style to my new Squadron. And what's more I had an easy conscience for the first time since I put up my two new pips.

I discovered later that the Assistant Adjutant nearly went berserk trying to discover who had pinched the duty truck. The Adjutant's car had broken down on the way back from Brigade, and he was fuming by the roadside waiting for a vehicle.

I shall always be grateful to the unknown driver who somehow squared things without mentioning my name.

The Major in charge of 'A' Squadron in those days was a dapper little man with gleaming teeth and a pencil-thin moustache. With his glossy hair brushed back and clipped short at the sides he looked as if he had been a Regular Officer since the kindergarten passing out parade. I found out afterwards that he had been a bus conductor before the war; but come to think of it that's as good a prelude to military service as anything else.

One of the things on which I pride myself is my ability to learn quickly. I gave the Squadron Leader a magnificent salute and placed my heels gently together.

'Don't they teach you to come to attention better than that at Sandhurst?' he snapped.

'Well, sir,' I said. 'I... ' My voice trailed away. It didn't seem much use trying to explain, but I made a mental note that from there on I would classify senior officers into two categories: those who liked stamping feet and those who didn't.

'How long have you been commissioned?' was the next question.

'Since – since just the other day,' I said, not quite clear what he was getting at.

'Then why are you wearing two pips instead of one?' he said, pouncing on the point like an eagle on a rabbit. But I was all ready for this.

'Because I've had more than six years' service in the ranks, sir!'

And sucks to you, I thought. But he shook his head doubtfully.

'I'll want to see that in writing,' he said. 'I think you're improperly dressed. Everybody I've known from Sandhurst has come as a Second-Lieutenant. Why, this makes you senior to officers who had been here five months or more!'

He leaned back in his chair as if he had produced the unanswerable argument.

I don't suppose it was a very good move on my part to lean forward and pick up his copy of ROYAL WARRANT FOR PAY, PROMOTION, AND NON-EFFECTIVE PAY OF OUR ARMY, but years of training as a chief clerk rose up within me. My knowledge of regulations was being doubted and it was with a certain amount of untactful emphasis that I slapped the book down on his table, open at the appropriate paragraph.

I have only the vaguest memories of the rest of that interview, but I know it was slightly painful and I walked out of the office secure in the knowledge that the impregnated battle-dress was no protection against fleas in the ear.

On the office steps a chubby, brown-faced Captain caught me up.

'By the way,' he said. 'The Squadron Leader forgot to tell you you've got to go and take over Five Troop.'

It was Jim Steward, and thus began an acquaintance which was to last long after Five Troop and, indeed, the whole regiment, had passed into the pages of history.

Jim had obviously been as embarrassed by the painful interview as I had. He fell in step with me for a little way and told me something about the Squadron set-up.

'You'll find Five Troop down there,' he said at last. 'And don't worry too much about the Squadron Leader; his bark is worse than his bite.'

'Thanks very much,' I said. 'I'll make do with his bark for the time being.'

Dent-de-Lion was a creeper-covered red brick building set in a large wooded patch of ground some way back from the main road. The patch itself held the squadron offices and stores and some of the men lived there.

Between the road and the house a concrete road had been laid, and branching off this road at intervals were concrete bays, each one big enough to provide a firm standing for a Churchill tank.

This concrete road led past the squadron office and on into the wooded scrub, and the Troops were parked in numerical order starting from the road. Thus No.1 Troop was next to the main road and No.5 was somewhere in the dark green hinterland beyond the red brick house.

I marched briskly along the concrete road drinking in the strange scene. Overhead the May sunshine filtered through the leafy trees, throwing a mottled pattern of light and shade on the ungainly shapes of the Churchills. Birds were competing shrilly with the bumbling of tank engines turning over, and every now and then a resonant clang betokened the dropping of an engine hatch or the sudden closing of a cupola lid.

As I walked between the tank bays I realised that the squadron symbol was a yellow triangle, painted on the side of each turret. Inside the triangle a numeral indicated which troop the tank belonged to.

'Easy,' I thought. 'I've only got to look for three tanks carrying a number five inside their yellow triangle.'

I studied all the tank names and found, not surprisingly, that they all began with the letter A. There was *Archer*, *Angry*, and *Arkholme*; *Archilles*, *Albion*, and *Acanthus*; and many others. I wouldn't have thought it possible to find so many tank names beginning with A.

In my mind's eye I started to sort out three suitable names for Five Troop. I didn't doubt they already had names, but I was going to change all that. Boy, the things I was going to do with that troop.

I felt a momentary twinge of sympathy for the Troop Leader I was replacing; it must be a bitter blow. I thought, to be replaced by a brand-new boy straight out of stores. But maybe the present Troop Leader was going away on promotion, I thought. That wouldn't be too bad for him.

I surreptitiously ticked off on my fingers all the things I had been taught at Sandhurst about taking and handing over tanks: Vehicle Inspection Reports, Wireless Log Books, Gun History Sheets. See the Squadron-Sergeant-Major about the two NCOs and find out if they are any good. Check the men's Conduct Sheets and discover the habitual wrongdoers amongst them.

Quite a job; but I still felt sorry for the man I was going to replace.

The tanks I was passing bore a number four in their squadron triangle so I slowed my pace a bit. I wanted to weigh up the troop from a distance before introducing myself and breaking the news to the Troop Leader.

The concrete here was cracked and unswept, and already the undergrowth from the woods had begun to encroach again on man's intrusion. Two or three empty oil drums lay about and a large splodge of khaki paint lay in the middle of the road like a relief map of Australia.

There were two empty bays and in the third was a single, solitary, rather rusty tank bearing a yellow triangle surrounding a number five.

Just one tank. And very much Mark II, too, mounting a pip-squeak of a two-pounder gun instead of the big business-like six-pounders I had seen in the other troops.

A tall, spare sergeant was addressing a heterogeneous group of soldiers who were staring woodenly down at a Besa machine gun resting on an inverted petrol tin.

On the back of the tank a rotund, red-faced, ginger-haired trooper was struggling with one end of the engine cover hatch. The other end was being manoeuvred by a long, thin man with bony wrists and protruding teeth.

The job of replacing the engine hatches of a Churchill is one that calls for a certain amount of brute strength (since they are fairly thick armour-plate) and also a certain amount of precision, for the bolt holes in the hatch must match up exactly with the holes in the tank hull, if the holding-down bolts are to be got in without tears and bloodshed.

'To me a bit,' said Fatty.

'Right!' said Thinny. 'Now to your left, Henry.'

'Aye, that's about arf an inch too much, lad. Back to thee. Steady! Reight. 'Ow is it yon end?'

Thinny straightened up and eased his stiff shoulders.

'That's near enough,' he said.

'Near enough won't do!' exploded the puce-complexioned Fatty. 'It's got to be *reight*!'

'Well, it's right, then,' said his helper.

Fatty considered this for a bit, and then he said: 'Well that's near enough.'

Thus was my introduction to Trooper Henry Westham, grocer and saxophonist from Lancashire; Troop comedian and tower of strength in emergencies, and wireless operator *par excellence*.

I've forgotten the thin man's name, but he didn't last long after that.

I turned my attention to the sergeant, and, the first thing I noticed about him was his brisk, decisive voice. He was obviously fairly young and strictly not a pre-war soldier. His eyes sparkled blackly and the questions which shot out from his rat-trap mouth left no doubt as to the answers he wanted.

This was Sergeant Atkins and I knew instinctively that I wouldn't need to check up on him with the Squadron-Sergeant-Major.

There didn't seem to be any sign of an officer so I thought I had better make myself known.

'Stand at ease, please, sergeant,' I said as Sergeant Atkins called the dishevelled group up to attention. 'Where's your Troop Leader?' I asked.

He looked at me incredulously.

'This is Five Troop!' he said.

'I know,' I said. 'And I'd like to see Five Troop Leader.'

'Five Troop 'asn't ever 'ad a Troop Leader, sir,' said a small dark-faced trooper, whom I came to know as Farrell.

'No, sir,' confirmed Sergeant Atkins. 'No officer and only one tank – that's Five Troop.'

I drew a deep breath. This was going to be better than I thought.

'Well,' I said, looking around. 'You've got a Troop Leader now. And I'm it.'

I had a busy time for the rest of that day. At Sandhurst they held as their objective the ideal that every Troop Leader should be able to do every job in the troop better than the crewman who was supposed to do it. He should, according to the pundits, be a better driver than any of the three drivers; be a more accurate gunner than any of the gunners; and be able to operate the tank wireless better than any of the operators.

This is a fine idea, but I never happened to meet any superman who measured up to it.

But by and large I managed to keep up a pretence of being an expert in the ways and habits of Churchill tanks, and I spent the rest of that morning dodging highly technical questions and taking surreptitious peeks into the many Sandhurst notebooks with which my pockets were stuffed.

Great things, those notebooks. Compiled in the sweat of my trunk over a gruelling nine-months' course they contained beautifully coloured diagrams showing the cooling system of the tank, carefully-drawn sketches showing the disposition of a troop in defence, hurriedly scribbled lectures on Duties in Aid of the Civil Power, and a chart showing the badges of rank in the German Army. Sandwiched between all this was a mass of other information of varying degrees of usefulness.

Well, there I was as a Troop Leader, the sun was still shining, I had managed to answer all the posers the cunning soldiers had thrust at me and it looked as if all was right with the world.

I might have known.

With a look of angelic innocence in his baby-blue eyes Trooper 'Bing' Crosby stood respectfully in front of me.

'We've finished that oil change, zur,' he drawled. 'Would you loike to take un out for a test run.'

He nodded towards the tank and stood waiting.

This was it, I thought. This was where I make a complete hash of things and provide the troop with enough material for hours of hilarious reminiscence. My driving had been the despair of my instructor during training, and the country around Camberley is, to this day, scattered with iron filings and whole sets of teeth from tank gear-boxes. Once I sit in the driving seat of a tank a horde of Gremlins post themselves from the RAF and squabble to have first go at the control rods and engines.

But the troop was waiting, looking at me expectantly.

'All right,' I said, hastily swallowing my Adam's apple again. 'I'll take her out for a test run.'

I don't know if you have ever tried to start an engine with crossed fingers, but it is jolly difficult. From the sounds of scraping on the hull of the tank I gathered that practically every man in the troop was coming along for the ride. It showed a touching faith in my ability to avoid accidents, I thought; but it wasn't till afterwards that I realised they were all on the outside of the tank, from where they could easily jump to safety if the need arose.

The engine burst into life and effectively drowned any other noise. I licked my lips nervously, adjusted a pair of driving goggles, secured the intercom headphones over my beret – and reached for the gear lever.

Life's full of little surprises. Do you know that gear lever moved into first gear as smoothly as if there was nothing in the gear box but oil. My relief and amazement increased as the huge machine lumbered obediently out of the concrete bay and swung towards the open country with hardly a murmur of protest. The speed of the tank increased with my confidence and soon we were belting along at a fine lick, the rattle of the steel tracks sounding through the headphones like an overgrown lawnmower.

A brisk voice came over the intercom, and I guessed it to be Sergeant Atkins.

'We usually turn left here, sir,' he crackled. 'Take a couple of turns around the field and then go back home.'

I swung the tiller bar to the left and saw we were heading down a short but steep incline. Nothing to it, I thought, and I savoured to the full the wonderful exhilaration of rushing madly downhill with the wind tearing at my goggles and trying to get underneath my beret.

We reached the bottom in safety and I was just chuckling at the thought of the men standing on the back of the tank waiting for me to do something wrong – and then I realised that I would have to get the tank back up the hill again, and that's where the trouble would really start.

All too soon I found myself at the bottom of the short hill once more, and the nose of the tank started to rise. As it did so the roar of the engine grew more laboured and the black apple-like knob on the gear lever grew in my anxious eye until it almost filled the driving compartment.

I knew that it was a safe bet I would muff a normal change down, but if I didn't do something quickly the overworked engine would stall and I'd be in an even worse mess.

And then in a flash of inspiration I saw a picture of a hard-bitten, long serving Tanks Corps Private. Many years before the war he had taught me to drive one of the old Medium Mark II tanks, and I could almost hear his sandpaper voice teaching me the unofficial way to change down.

'Keep yer foot 'ard down on that throttle, Foley boy,' he said. 'Then bang the old clutch out twice, but quickly; and at the same time whip the old gear lever across the gate. Yer can't go wrong.'

The engine note had now dropped so low that even through the headphones I could hear sarcastic laughter from the troops standing on the back of the tank.

I breathed a prayer of hope to ex-Private Johnny Walker and closed my eyes. Twice in rapid succession I slammed down the clutch pedal, at the same time thrusting the gear lever into third gear.

The sarcastic laughter stopped instantly; the engine burst into a full-throated roar once more, and with never a falter or a jerk the tank swept smoothly up the rest of the hill and on to level ground.

When we got back to Dent-de-Lion I was the centre of an admiring throng. Nobody actually referred to the magical gear change, least of all me.

With my most nonchalant air I handed the goggles to Crosby and said: 'Seems to be all right. Could pull a bit better on hills, perhaps, but nothing to worry about.'

'Yes, zur,' said Crosby deferentially. But there was a friendly note in his voice and I knew that from then on I was accepted.

Five Troop had a Troop Leader – more by luck than anything else!

I felt very pleased with life as I made my way back to the squadron office at tea time. And then I saw a familiar hawk-nosed, black-moustached figure coming towards me. It was the Regimental Second-in-Command.

Now what did it say in my Sandhurst notebook about saluting? Oh yes, I salute Majors first time I see them each day, and thereafter only if I go into their offices. Fine, I'd seen this Major once that day, so that let me out.

We drew level and I smiled affably.

'Nice day, sir,' I said cheerfully.

He allowed me to walk on about six paces and then he barked: 'Come here, Foley!'

I doubled back and stood to attention, remembering in the nick of time that he was in the 'No Stamping' category.

'What about saluting?' he coldly enquired.

'Saluting, sir?' I said. 'But at Sandhurst they told us only to salute Majors first time each morning and in offices. I thought… '

'Rubbish!' he said. 'I cannot believe they taught you any such thing. Absolute nonsense.'

I half-heartedly reached for one of my notebooks, and then I remembered the business in the squadron office with the Royal Warrant for Pay.

I dropped my hand, said I was sorry and was prepared to let it go at that. But he wasn't. I got a five-minute lecture, most of which was taken up with pointed remarks indicating that I would salute him on every conceivable occasion.

So that gave me a flea in the other ear. But it couldn't detract from the wonderful sense of well-being I'd had ever since I had made the magical gear change.

And after tea I carefully removed my Sandhurst notebooks from my various pockets and stowed them away in my suitcase. I was always prepared to learn again.

Before we finally left Westgate Five Troop had acquired three tanks and a Troop Corporal. I breezed into the squadron office with my three suggested names and came out with another flea to add to my collection and the names *Avenger*, *Alert*, and *Angler* as the registered titles of the vehicles of Five Troop.

I liked the look of Corporal Robinson as soon as I saw him. He was the only man in the Troop with more service than myself and he gave me an instant impression of rocklike steadiness. He was a short, squat man with a bullet head and close-cropped hair. He had what Smith 161 described as a 'dark brown voice' and his battle-dress always looked as if he had been poured into it.

Somewhere Corporal Robinson had a secret. It was just not possible that a man of his service and experience could only have reached the rank of corporal. I had a shrewd idea that somewhere in his past there had been a court martial; I suppose I could easily have found out by asking the Orderly Room to produce his Regimental Conduct Sheet. I thought about this for a bit and then decided against it. As far as I was concerned he was making a new start with Five Troop and I would judge him by his behaviour and not on his record.

From Westgate we went to Stone Street, that old Roman road which runs straight as an arrow due south from Canterbury. And it was here that we began training in earnest for the battles which lay ahead.

Until then we had been road-bound. If we wanted to get from A to B we got out the maps and followed the roads exactly as if we were using a family saloon car. Somebody with a shrewd understanding of human nature had decided that if we went on that way there was a distinct danger that when we went to war we would still instinctively use the roads. This would put us at a considerable disadvantage in trying to fight an enemy who had no such inhibitions.

So it was ruled that, as from a certain date, tanks would at all times move cross country regardless of obstructions. The only places out of bounds were buildings, orchards and sheep-pens.

I was a bit doubtful how this would work, but it made a nice change to be able to get out the map, draw a straight line from A to B, and head along it with a happy disregard for road and tracks.

The first time we tried this we were doing one of our periodic attacks on the windmill at Stelling Minnis. For most of the way our route lay down Stone Street itself, so there was no need to go charging across country. Then the windmill came in sight and I decided to head straight for it.

'Driver left,' I said over the intercom.

The tank slowed down as 'Bing' took his foot off the throttle, and after a while his plaintive voice came through my headset.

'Turn left where, zur?'

'Anywhere here, but you'd better turn off soon or it'll be too late.'

'What, straight through this noicely laid 'edge, zur?'

'Yes! Go on, man. Driver left.'

Obediently 'Bing' swung the tank. It nosed its way up the bank, hawthorn branches snapping and crunching beneath the tracks. For a few seconds the tracks skidded in the loose earth of the bank and then we were over the top. And instantly *Avenger* shuddered to a halt.

'Driver advance,' I said. 'Go on, what's the matter with you?'

'But is this all right, zur?' protested Crosby. 'This yer is winter wheat. We can't go chargin' across 'ere loike a mad un. Farmer 'd be arter us wi' a twelve-bore soon as look at us.'

'Stop worrying,' I said into my microphone. 'The farmers have all been warned. And they'll get stacks of compensation.'

But he didn't like it. Although I never heard him say anything complimentary about farming or the agricultural life, it went against his inborn breeding deliberately to churn up growing crops.

I could see Sergeant Atkins and Corporal Robinson having just the same trouble behind me. After years of carefully avoiding damage with their tanks, they were now being ordered to smash things. Overcoming this psychological barrier was quite an effort but it was, of course, the very reason why we were ordered to do it.

Over the 'B' set I told Sergeant Atkins and Corporal Robinson to deploy behind me, and in arrowhead formation we crashed through the next hedge and sent a storm of cabbage leaves sailing into the air as we ploughed through serried green ranksof these vegetables.

Needless to say, we captured the windmill, but I came in for some very hurt looks from the three drivers.

I keep talking about the intercom and the 'B' set so how would it be if I gave a brief description of these things?

There were three different systems in the tank: there was the 'A' set, used for longish range speech and morse back to squadron headquarters or further if necessary. There was the 'B' set, a very short-range radio used by the Troop Leader for talking to his other two tanks, and the intercom which simply allowed the tank commander to talk to the crew of his own tank.

Of course, with three microphones hanging around his neck the unfortunate Troop Leader would be in a bigger tangle than he usually is, so the back room boys thought up the bright idea of having just one microphone and a simple control box on the turret wall near the Commander's pedestal.

The control box consists of a simple three-way pointer which can be moved until it points, appropriately enough, to either 'A', 'B', or 'IC'. And according to which way the pointer is pointing, so the microphone is in that particular circuit.

Sounds simple, doesn't it? But many a well-meaning Troop Leader has dictated a model Situation Report to his Squadron Leader, only to receive a courteous acknowledgement from his driver together with the suggestion that he tries again, this time on the 'A' Set.

The opposite, of course, can sometimes have drastic results.

Like the time we were taking part in a Squadron mock attack across country. Things were going too well and I was just beginning to wonder where the snag was when I heard Corporal Robinson's voice coming over the 'A' set.

'Driver, slow down.'

A pregnant pause.

'Driver slow down, I said. Take it easy going through this hedge.'

Desperately I tried to call him on the 'B' set to tell him to alter his control switch, but of course he couldn't hear me.

'Smith! Slow down!' Corporal Robinson, his dark brown voice rising to bright blue. 'Are you mad? There's a damn chalk pit just the other side of this hedge. *Driver halt!*'

I closed my eyes and removed my headset in order to hear the crash, but just as the phones touched the turret roof I heard:

'Oh Christ!'

It was followed by an aggressive 'click' and I knew that Corporal Robinson had spotted his mistake in what they call the nick of time.

Trouble was, the Squadron Leader had also heard that broadcast and I received a shrill rebuke and a lecture about NCOs who couldn't work a simple three-way switch.

So it was with some gratification that on a gunnery exercise the next day I heard the familiar voice of the Squadron Leader coming over the air saying:

'Six-pounder traverse left. Traverse left, I said! Come on Jones. What the hell's the matter with you? Get that gun moving! Traverse… oh!'

So summer passed into autumn and in turn into winter. Stone Street began to lose a lot of its rural attractiveness and we received orders to move into winter quarters at Folkestone. But all this time we were learning more and more about each other and learning more and more about our jobs. There was a quickening in the tempo of each day, and certain changes were made.

For one thing, we lost a lot of our 6-pounder tanks and received instead tanks armed with 75mm guns, capable of firing a high-explosive shell. Prior to this our main armament would fire only a solid armour-piercing shell – pretty useful when taking on enemy tanks, but calling for hair-splitting accuracy when taking on a spread-out target like an anti-tank post.

And talking of high explosive shells…

Folkestone turned out to be a very pleasant station despite being in what the papers called 'Hell Fire Corner'. The troops just loved being able to bring out their best battle-dresses and parade in the town – though not 'parade' in its military connotation, of course.

There were WAAF from a nearby airfield, the cinemas were open, and so were the pubs. I began to see very little of Five Troop once the daily chores were over, which was probably just as well. Stone Street had almost been a twenty-four-hour tour of duty, and now it was nice to get into civilisation again.

But the shelling was a nuisance.

Somewhere behind the town a battery of Long Range Artillery used, from time to time, to engage in cross-Channel duels with their German opposite numbers across the water. This was all very well in its way, but sometimes we used to get mixed up in what we felt was a Gunner private war.

We had been in Folkestone about three days, I think, and I was enjoying the evening air in the High Street. From time to time the general atmosphere of peace would be rudely shattered by an enormous bang. It would come quite suddenly, without any warning whistle or shriek and didn't sound at all like the crump of landing shells which we had heard on the firing ranges.

So when I bumped into half a dozen men of Five Troop I was able to reassure them about these mysterious explosions.

'Are they our guns going off, or their shells landing, sir?' said Trooper Worrall looking anxiously over his shoulder.

'They're ours,' I said confidently, just as another crash devastated the nocturnal silence.

'You sure, sir?' said his driving-seat friend Trooper Johnson.

'Of course I'm sure,' I said with some asperity, and there and then, in the middle of the street, I gave them a short lecture on elementary ballistics and the speed of sound.

I believe I had a piece of chalk in my pocket and using the pavement as blackboard I demonstrated how it was absolutely impossible for those bangs to be enemy shells. If they were, I explained patiently, we would be bound to hear the sound of them rushing through the air.

Unfortunately the lecture was interrupted by the disintegration of a shop-front across the road, and when the dust and debris had cleared away they weren't interested any longer.

I found out afterwards that those Long Range shells had to climb to a terrific altitude to get across the Channel, and they came down at such a rate that they easily exceeded the speed of sound. But that's what I call learning the hard way.

The only fly in the ointment of life at Folkestone was a small question of Squadron Orderly Officers, a duty imposed on us by the Squadron Leader. And the orders for the SOO took up three foolscap sheets, most of which were sentences beginning with the words HE WILL, in blocks just like that. There were fire buckets to be inspected, cookhouses to be examined, men to be paraded for the Medical Officer and goodness knows what else. We Troop Leaders didn't mind – after all, what's one more inspection amongst so many? – but what caused more heart-burning than anything else was the business of making out a report at the end of the day.

We couldn't just say 'Please, sir, I was Orderly Officer and the squadron's still right there.' Oh, no! The SOO's report had to contain a lengthy sentence for each of those HE WILL's on the orders.

Some of the Troop Leaders tried to slide out of it by just forgetting to complete a report; but as sure as eggs next morning, probably just when they were in the middle of changing a track, along would come Lance-Corporal Willings on his bicycle.

'Please, sir, could you come and see the Major straight away. And bring your Orderly Officer's Report with you, sir.'

All of which was a bit hard, especially if you hadn't completed a report.

So we decided to revolt.

We held a Troop Leader's Meeting in one of the local pubs, sang a few bars of *The Red Flag* just to get the right atmosphere, and then we got down to planning the Big Insurrection.

There was a great deal of dark mutterings and finally we hit upon what we thought was a corker of a plan. All it consisted of was carrying out orders better than intended.

I believe the Trade Unions have now pinched the idea and call it working to rule, or something, but we thought of it all by ourselves in that little pub in Folkestone.

As we planned it, the great catch was going to be in the Orderly Officer's Report for the next day. It was to be almost book length, contain long-winded reports about every laughable little detail and was to be so absurdly verbose that even the Squadron Leader would see the folly of his ways and produce a more sensible routine for the future.

'That's the idea!' I said enthusiastically. 'Now, who's going to write the report.'

They all looked at me.

'Oh no,' I said, putting down my pint with a bang. 'Nothing on this earth is going to persuade me to write this immortal document.'

Well, I borrowed Lance-Corporal Willings' typewriter and as far as I remember the great document went something like this:

> *Sir,*
> *I have the honour to report that I was Squadron Orderly Officer from Reveille Thursday 10 December, 1943 to Reveille Friday 11 December 1943. During that time I inspected the*

Squadron Area and have to report as follows. The fifth fire bucket on the left as you come out of the Squadron Office has a slight dent in the lip. This may well result in the water being diverted from its legitimate target during an emergency.

Some person or persons unknown have altered the F in the word FIRE on the next bucket and I suggest this be remedied forthwith. At present it looks like an E – a procedure which may well result in the appliance being claimed as the property of the Irish Republic.

There is a slight crack in the lower left-hand window of No. 2 Troop's billet, caused, it is believed, by vibration from the nearby Long Range Artillery…

This went on for page after page; it was a document of which I was richly proud and when I produced it in the Officer's Mess that evening it drew shrieks of appreciative laughter and at least three free drinks. It was probably under the influence of the latter that I signed my name with an imperial flourish and placed the report on the Squadron Leader's table ready for the next morning.

Came the dawn, and with it alcoholic remorse. Would the Major take it as a joke? Or would I be for the High Jump? Or, worst of all, would he realise it was a combined effort from all his Troop Leaders and make life hell for us?

After breakfast I really began to fear the worst, for the ubiquitous Lance-Corporal Willings appeared to say that the Squadron Leader would like to see all officers, but at once.

We stood in a line in front of his desk and my heart dropped into my boots as I saw my facetious report four-square in the middle of his blotting pad.

He waited until we had finished shuffling our feet and then he said:

'I've called you gentlemen together about this Squadron Orderly Officer duty. I'm sick and tired and fed up with the miserable bits of paper I've been getting from you in the past. I know you don't like writing out these reports, but you're going to. I've told you and told you and told you what I want from you, and now… '

He picked up my report and waved it dramatically in the air.

'…This has come in from Mister Foley. I'm going to pin it up on the notice board where you can all see it. It is a model of a report and in future I want to get one from each of you on exactly the same lines. Now let this report be an example to you in future.'

He turned to me and said: 'Thank you, John.'

And there wasn't even the ghost of a twinkle in his eye.

TWO

PEOPLE ARE FOND of telling me that the trouble with me is I talk too much. And there are times when I'm inclined to agree with them. If only I'd learned when to keep my big mouth shut there wouldn't have been any mushroom trouble at Goodnestone – at least, not for Five Troop.

Goodnestone was a bit like Dent-de-Lion; a camp of Nissen huts in a wood split by a concrete road with bays for tank standings. It was early in 1944 and the ground between the tank standings was alive with the coming of daffodils. Crocuses (or croci?) danced between the trees and the air was heavy with fertility of spring.

Perhaps it was all this nature activity which turned the Squadron Leader's thoughts to gardening, but one day in the middle of a discussion about soldiers' socks he suddenly looked up and said: 'Has anybody got a gardener in their troop?'

For some inexplicable reason I said, 'I have'. The Squadron Leader said 'Who?'

This was just fine; I had now committed myself to having a gardener, and I racked my brains to think which of my twelve bodies looked most like a gardening body. Crosby, I knew, had some country background but if I put him on gardening he'd never forgive me. And then I had a flash of inspiration. Trooper Cooper (Cpl. Robinson's gunner) had been a garden sundries salesman in one of the big multiple stores. That was near enough.

'Cooper,' I said. '*Angler*'s gunner.'

'Right,' said the Squadron Leader. 'We've got a spare Nissen hut with a stove in it. Get him on to growing some mushrooms.'

'Yes, sir.' I said. 'Nothing to it. Five Troop will produce the finest mushrooms you ever saw.'

I shall never forget the look on Cooper's face when I told him. He put down the Besa barrel he was cleaning and his eyebrows started to climb up his forehead.

'Me, sir? Grow mushrooms, sir? I couldn't grow a toenail!' he said in a shocked whisper.

There was only one thing for it; I called a Troop Conference and asked if anybody knew anything about growing mushrooms. But my troop were wiser than their Troop Leader; they knew when to keep their mouths shut.

In the end it was Lance-Corporal Westham who produced the too-simple answer. 'There's a champion library in t'education hut,' he said. 'Appen they'll 'ave a book about it.'

Of course they had, an enormous great tome which gave explicit instructions about how to grow magnificent mushrooms. So we set to work.

The Squadron Welfare Account provided funds for buying compost and spawn, and the corporal in the Technical Stores coughed up with several cases, wood, packing, GS, which we soon converted into racks and trays.

And thus the great experiment began.

In the book of words there was a lovely full-colour art plate showing trays of compost simply bristling with pearly-white mushrooms. We hung this in the Nissen hut to inspire the mushrooms to come, and from time to time one or the other of us would stand over the compost beds and harangue the lumps dormant below the surface.

A thermometer was scrounged from somewhere so that we could keep the room at exactly the right temperature. Analytical tests were made to ensure that the humidity was just right, and every now and again with tremendous ceremonial we would lift a piece of compost and breathe entreaties direct on to the spawn.

According to the expert in the book, little luminous streaks should have sprouted from the spawn, like bits of silver cotton. And we always searched eagerly for these. But nary a sign did we see.

Smith 161 put forward the horrid suggestion that perhaps the mushroom were coming up during the night and being filched the next morning by unscrupulous people from another squadron. So we put a lock on the door and bribed the sentries on the tank bays to slip across every now and then to keep an eye on the mushroom hut.

I even kept watch once myself, armed with a twelve-bore shot gun, but only succeeded in catching Trooper Johnson creeping into the camp long after Lights Out having, he said, been explaining to one of the land girls all the finer points of an internal combustion engine.

All this time the Squadron Leader was getting more and more sarcastic. Where, he wanted to know, were the famous Five Troop mushrooms? Reinforcements were beginning to come in and that Nissen hut was wanted for troops to live in.

One by one the Troop lost faith in the project until there was only Cooper and myself who professed to believe that our mushrooms would one morning see the light of day.

But it was no use. Eventually the Squadron Leader gave me withering orders to clear the mess out of the hut and restore it to its original bareness. Disheartened, Cooper and I went to work one Sunday afternoon when the camp was wrapped in slumber and there was no one to witness our shame. The trays we broke up into firewood for the stoves in the living huts, and the compost we distributed about the daffodils, where the manure content might do the flowers a bit of good.

Yet we had our mushrooms; lovely, big, saucer-like growths; soft but firm and with an ambrosial flavour which blended superbly with fried bacon.

The only unhappy person was the Squadron Leader. He complained they shouldn't have been growing in amongst the daffodils like that.

This was about the time when regiments like ours, who had yet to go into action, received replacement officers home from the campaigns in Africa and Italy. The idea was that they would be able to pass on to us greenhorns the lessons they had learned during their battles, and a good idea it was, too.

And the upshot of it all was that we got a new Squadron Leader.

I couldn't believe my ears when Tony Cunningham broke the news.

'Of course, it may be a case of out of the frying-pan into the fire,' he said.

'I'm half afraid you're right,' I said. 'Here's dear Lance-Corporal Willings now.'

The squadron clerk on his green bicycle was pedalling slowly round the camp telling all Troop Leaders to report to the squadron office.

'Well, let's go and get the worst over,' I said to Tony, and we made our way to the end of the camp. We got there in time to find the other three Troop Leaders just about to go in.

'All present?' said Mike Carter, the senior of us. 'Right, in we go.'

We marched in, halted in front of the desk, turned smartly to face it and came up to the salute in unison – as had been insisted upon by the late martinet.

'Christ!' said a little fat man, sitting behind the desk. 'What on earth's all this?'

A look of absolute horror was written over his round face as he lit a cigarette and stood up.

'For goodness sake, chaps, relax,' he said. 'I asked you to come along for a drink so we can get to know one another. My name's Alan Biddulph. Shove that junk off the table and sit on it if you can't find enough chairs.'

'The "junk", sir, is the Orders for the Squadron Orderly Officers, Orders for the Fire Picquet, Orders for the Duty Storeman, Orders for the Sanitary Orderly, Orders for the... ' I said.

'Then it's about time it was cleared out,' he said, producing a bottle of gin from his brief-case. 'And for God's sake stop calling me sir. I know I can trust you to address me properly on parade; off parade my name's Alan.'

And all this was within twenty seconds of making his acquaintance.

Half an hour and three gins later we emerged from the office and looked at one another,

'Hasn't the sky gone blue all of a sudden,' said Mike Carter.

'Yes,' said Tony, rubbing his long-fingered hands together. 'Right now I'm seeing the future through rose coloured glasses.'

'That rose colour is pink gin,' I told him. 'Let us now go and offer up a few prayers that Alan Biddulph stays with us.'

He stayed all right, and a new era started in 'A' Squadron.

The new Squadron Leader could seldom be found in his office, more often than not he was bouncing around the camp giving impromptu lectures on the more effective ways of street fighting, or flat on his rotund belly underneath a tank, helping his crew to change a track plate.

He took us out on realistic exercises, rolling over the green Kent countryside. And the first time he took us out he threw consternation into the hearts of everyone with a peremptory order for a General Post change round. Troop Sergeants commanded troops, wireless operators were ordered into driving seats, yawning gunners were rudely awakened and told to work the radio; and then with a fat chuckle he told us to advance.

I found that Pickford, away from his beloved wireless set, suddenly acquired two left hands and two right feet. I spent half that day with my eyes shut waiting for the crash which somehow never came. Churchill tanks blundered about the countryside missing one another by hairs' breadths. I never did find out what Sgt Robinson, temporarily in charge of the troop, wanted me to do as his Troop Sergeant. I patiently waited for orders over the 'B' set, but none ever came. I don't think it was that he never sent any; if anything, the silence was due to driver Johnson getting hopelessly tangled up in the controls of the radio.

'Bing' Crosby's rich, rural accents on the ether didn't do much to restore order out of chaos, either.

'Hullo, King Five,' he drawled into his microphone. 'Report my zignals – 'ere, zur, this yer microphone ain't workin'. 'Tis a blarsted muck-up if yew arsk me. What's this yer switch for, zur?'

And all this going out over the air.

When we staggered back to Goodnestone, Alan addressed us thus:

'Well, chaps, the object of that exercise was to prove that in an emergency you want to be able to swop your crews around. Everybody has got to be able to do everybody else's job, after a fashion anyway.'

We conceded his point, and threw ourselves into a frantic training spell teaching drivers to improve their performance on the 75mm gun, and gunners how to get the tank from one place to another with a minimum amount of damage.

So the next time we went out on a squadron exercise we were all ready for a rapid change round. But it didn't come. Instead Alan had another unpleasant surprise up his sleeve for us.

It was a depressing day, with a steady downfall of rain from a leaden sky. Maps became a useless tangle of sodden paper and water trickled down the sides of the periscopes to drip remorselessly on to our necks.

We were taking part in a long attack, about three miles across country finishing on top of a bare hill we could see on the skyline.

From the moment we crossed the start line I knew this was not going to be one of Five Troop's better days. Engines stalled as we tried to surmount the short, steep banks which bordered the narrow country roads. *Alert* shed a track just as we were lurching and skidding around the shoulder of a hill and Sergeant Robinson's crew gave vent to their feelings in an unmistakable manner.

The tank tracks piled up thick wads of wet earth against the red-hot exhaust pipes, and as the earth had been richly laced with manure the smell of it drying out was hardly conducive to placid thought.

We came to the final assault on the hill and as we nosed through a hedge I told Pickford to fire three rounds of smoke from the little two-inch mortar on his side of the turret. I saw his hand reach for the pistol-grip, and then I was flung sideways as the end of our gun barrel hit a fairly stout tree trunk hidden in the hedge. The tree swung the turret around and to my horror I saw a smoke bomb go sailing off to our left – leaving behind it a trail of burning phosphorous as it headed straight for a haystack.

Setting fire to haystacks was one of the things we were not allowed to do. But strictly. I had visions of trying to do some rapid explaining to an irate farmer, and an even more irate Commanding Officer, and then to my huge relief the little bomb fell short and sent up its smoke screen harmlessly from a small paddock.

We reached the top of the hill and halted. One by one the engines were shut off and the only sound to interrupt the steady patter of the rain was the crackling of the cooling exhaust pipes, and tiny explosive hisses as the raindrops fell on them.

I climbed wetly out of the turret and dropped down on to some of the stickiest ploughland I ever hope to meet. It was a black, glutinous mass and before I'd taken a couple of paces my boots had quintupled their weight.

Alan Biddulph was waiting for us, sitting on the side of his tank and smoking the inevitable cigarette.

We squelched towards him and waited.

'That wasn't a very good show, chaps,' he said at last.

We murmured our agreement. It wasn't a very good show, whichever way you looked at it.

Another period of silence. I reached for a damp cigarette and wondered what was coming next. My feet were slowly turning to ice in the black mud and I inwardly vowed to break all speed limits getting back to a hot bath and change of clothing at Goodnestone.

Alan took off his beret and allowed the rain to fall on his balding head.

'Take a look at this field,' he said after a while. 'Take a good look at it. Sticky, isn't it? A nasty, horrible mess?'

We looked, and we agreed. A more uninviting field I have yet to see.

'Well,' went on our Squadron Leader gently. 'If that had been a real battle, and this was over the other side of the water, you would now be making what arrangements you could to sleep here. You would be trying to find a corner of this mud where you could curl in a blanket and close your eyes.'

It was a horrid prospect; in fact, it brought home the horrors of war more effectively than any training film we had ever seen.

'But this isn't a real battle,' Alan was saying. 'We can go back to Goodnestone and find warm huts waiting for us and what Rupert Brooke calls "the benison of hot water". You'll be dry, and warm and well fed tonight, instead of wet and cold and probably hungry.'

We brightened visibly.

'And so, for the good of your souls,' he said, 'we'll go back to the Start Line and do the whole thing all over again.'

Five young officers groaned in unison, and when I broke the news to Five Troop not one of them said what a splendid Squadron Leader they had.

But we did the attack again.

And when we got back to Goodnestone, Alan Biddulph gave the squadron a half-holiday next day and bought the Troop Leaders a double Scotch each to keep out the cold.

April, 1944, found us living in a world of increasing tension. We were ready for war in every respect. We were well trained, our tanks were in first-class condition, reinforcements were standing by to fill any gaps in the ranks, and our battle kit was issued and properly stowed away.

Because our corner of Kent was required for the troops who were massing for the initial assault on the beaches of Europe, we moved back to the little Hampshire village of Headley.

We had been told that other troops, and other tanks, would establish a bridgehead somewhere on the continent. Our job was going to be to burst out of that bridgehead and clear the way for the lighter, faster Sherman tanks to fan out across the country.

We could only wait. And to pass the time of waiting we water-proofed our tanks against the necessity of having to wade ashore.

This was a tedious and back-breaking job, and took us best part of six weeks.

Every rivet in the belly of the tank had to be rasped clean and painted with waterproof paint. Inspection plates had to be sealed with a rubbery solution; extension funnels had to be fitted to the tank exhaust pipes and the air inlet louvres. Yards of balloon fabric were pasted in position around the turret ring, the driver's visor, and gun mounting.

But because it might be necessary to go into action immediately upon emerging from the water, most of the balloon fabric had sealed under it a length of explosive Cordtex. This was wired through an electric detonator and taken to one of the headlamp sockets on the tank. Thus, as soon as the headlight switch was turned the sealing was blown to smithereens and the tank was ready for action.

Ah, I thought; I can just see some brainless member of Five Troop turning that switch by accident and blowing all our careful work to blazes. So I issued orders that the headlight switch should be stuck down with insulating tape, just to be on the safe side.

One by one the tanks were sealed and made ready for our journey, and then we waited, passing the time as best we could.

It seemed at one stage as if we'd been forgotten. We watched the zebra-striped planes and gliders soaring over our heads on D-Day, broke open our sealed boxes of Maps of Normandy and followed the course of the fighting from the reports on the BBC. But still we sat at Headley.

'Maybe they won't need us after all, sir,' said Farrell, my co-driver. I thought I detected a hopeful note in his voice, and this surprised me because until then ex-barrow boy Farrell had been almost relishing the idea of using the Besa machine gun he had so lovingly cleaned and cherished for the past year.

'What's up, Farrell?' I said.

I remember we were standing in the middle of a sandy rectangle which did duty for a tank park at Headley. Grass had started to grow up between the tank tracks, where they had stood idle so long.

'I'm all right, sir,' said Farrell, with a ghost of his usual Cockney grin. 'I'm stickin' wiv Five Troop, no matter what.'

This seemed a very odd sort of conversation to me.

'Of course you are,' I said. 'Why? Who said you weren't?'

'Oh, no one.'

'Well, then. Do you feel a bit off-colour, or something?'

He denied this so vehemently that I knew my remark had been pretty near the target. I looked at him more closely and saw that his normally pale face was even paler. His sharp, foxy features seemed pinched and drawn and there were tell-tale dark patches below his damson-like eyes.

I sent him off to bed and made a mental note to tell Sergeant Atkins first thing in the morning to keep an eye on him.

But it wasn't necessary. After dinner that evening a waiter interrupted our poker school to tell me that Sergeant Atkins was outside the Mess and please could he have a word with me.

'It's Farrell, sir,' said Sergeant Atkins as I joined him in the moonlight. 'He's come over queer. Laying in bed drenched with sweat, shivering, and delirious. I've rung up RHQ and they're sending the MO down in the ambulance, sir.'

'Let's have a look at him,' I said. And we set off together for the troop billet.

In the blacked-out room where the troop lived the air was blue with cigarette smoke. The naked electric lamp sent feeble yellow beams down to where Farrell was writhing in a mountain of grey blankets. Beads of perspiration stood out on his forehead, and in between fits of shivering he babbled deliriously.

'He seemed cold, sir, so we've put our blankets on un,' whispered Crosby. 'Doan't like the look of un, either.'

I knelt beside the sick co-driver and spoke to him.

'It's nae guid, sirr,' said Smith 053. 'He'll no' recognise ye.'

But to everybody's surprise (mine more than anyone's) he did recognise me. He turned a pain-seared face towards me and said: 'Ain't goin' yet, are yer, sir?'

'Course not,' I said. 'Wouldn't dream of going without you, would we, lads?'

A chorus of agreement greeted this somewhat trite remark, because the ready-tongued Farrell was one of the most popular men in the troop.

'Where's the pain, Farrell?' I said.

'Ain't got any pain, sir,' he said weakly. 'Fit as a flippin' flea, I am!'

'Sure you are,' I said.

I didn't really know what to say next and was glad when the door burst open to admit the MO and a couple of stretcher-bearers.

The Medical Officer, a brisk, friendly Canadian, gave Farrell a brief examination and then signalled to the two orderlies to put him on the stretcher.

'Appendicitis,' he whispered to me.

'Ere, wot's all this?' said Farrell, from the stretcher.

'Just for a couple of days, old man,' said the MO. 'You'll be in great shape before the end of the week.'

'Don't you b——s go without me!' called Farrell, as he was carried through the door. 'I'll be back.'

There didn't seem anything to say to that, so we watched him go in silence. 'Great pity,' I said to Sergeant Atkins. 'He was a good lad and could drive nearly as well as Crosby.'

'Yes sir,' said Sergeant Atkins. 'We'll be getting a replacement, I suppose?'

'Yes,' I said, and sighed heavily. I would probably get some half-trained clot who wouldn't speak the same language as the rest of the troop and wouldn't be able to join in those interminable conversations which begin 'Do you remember – ?'

'I'll see Major Biddulph about it first thing tomorrow,' I said, as I bade Sergeant Atkins good night.

I almost dreaded the arrival of my new co-driver. But I didn't dread it half enough.

Trooper Derek Hunter was a nice boy – and then you've said everything. An only child, he had had all the benefits (and disadvantages) of being carefully brought up and given a good education. He was like a fish out of water with the other earthy members of Five Troop and my main worry during the first few days was that the others would bully him.

He had an immature, schoolboy face and wore his hair in a carefully brushed quiff. His blue eyes were alight with enthusiasm and he was wildly delighted to be a fully-fledged member of a first-line tank crew.

But the troop didn't accept him. For one thing, they couldn't help remembering that he was sitting where the well-liked Farrell should have been, and for another they couldn't get used to his well-modulated voice. They called him 'Hunter', which was significant. Everybody else in the troop was Mac, or Henry, or 'Bing' or Smudger, or something. But the new boy was coldly called by his surname.

And of course he made all the new boy's mistakes.

Just to prove we could still do it, Alan ordered a 'spit and polish' parade. He made it a troop competition with a week's 'Excused Guards' for the best turned-out troop.

There was nobody better than Sergeant Atkins at this sort of thing. The night before the competition he alternately encouraged and blasted the troop. He produced magic potions for removing tank park oil from toecaps; worked wonders with blanco so that it didn't cake and drop off; scrounged wire wool from somewhere, the better to burnish cap-badges, and generally seemed to be in six places at once.

In the Officers' Mess the batmen were being driven insane as various Troop Leaders brow-beat them into ironing uniforms and polishing brassware. One way and another the rivalry was quite intense.

The next morning dawned bright and clear and, together with Alan Biddulph, we Troop Leaders marched down the road to where the squadron was drawn up on parade. Even from a distance I could see that Five Troop was out and away the best.

Badges glistened like chromium in carefully-brushed berets. Boots reflected the sunlight like pools of black ink. And anybody going too near Five Troop would have been in dire danger of slicing their calves on the trouser creases.

It was with a smug smile that I accompanied Alan down the ranks of Five Troop. And then he stopped and pointed wordlessly.

Whereas everybody else on parade was wearing their revolver holster on the left side, Trooper Derek Hunter was standing there quivering with excitement and wearing his on the right.

That didn't raise his status in the troop, either.

When we got back to the Mess I was all ready to sit down and have a first class sulk, but Jim Steward put his head round the ante-room door and said: 'We're off!'

'When?' I said, spilling coffee all over my beautiful battle-dress and not caring a damn.

'Tomorrow,' he said. 'We move on our own tracks to Lee-on-Solent. God knows how long we'll wait there before embarking, but it's a start.'

It was a start all right. And making the initial journey on our own tracks added a spice of enjoyment to it. We had half-expected to be moved to our embarkation port by rail, or else on gigantic tank transporting trucks. But we were going under our own steam, which was a big improvement.

Gleefully we ripped the sealing off the drivers' visors. We knew we'd have time to fix back that little bit of fabric either on the boat or at Lee-on-Solent.

Gladly we flung ourselves into the last-minute tasks, anxious to hasten the moment of our departure.

Maybe if we'd known what lay ahead we wouldn't have been so anxious.

The journey to Lee-on-Solent was long and dusty. We set off at dawn in numerical order, which meant that Five Troop was at the back of the column.

There is some mysterious rule of higher mathematics which explains the proportionate increase of speed in relation to the length of a column of vehicles, but I have never been able to understand it. All I know is that Squadron Headquarters at the head of the column were able to bumble along at a steady ten miles per hour, while Five Troop at the back had to go like the hammers of hell to keep the rest of the squadron in sight.

Crosby, Johnson, and Smith 161 did wonders with their unwieldy vehicles; skidding madly along village cobbled streets; thundering at full throttle down steep, narrow lanes sign-posted 'DANGEROUS HILL'; and belting a couple of extra miles an hour out of their tanks whenever the road was straight and clear.

And thus we moved nearer and nearer to the coast.

We came at last to a wide, straight stretch of road somewhere about ten miles from Lee-on-Solent. Here we stopped while the cooks' truck made its way down the column dispensing heavenly nectar which they called tea. We sucked it down gratefully, and then I noticed Crosby's bright blue eyes were red-rimmed and sore. The hand holding his enamel mug shook visibly, and I knew that strain of our headlong pursuit was beginning to tell on him.

Johnson and Smith 161 were just as bad, so I told Sergeant Robinson that from then on co-drivers would drive. After all, that's what they were for – to give the drivers a rest on long approach marches.

It was with considerable reluctance that Crosby handed over his driving seat to the sparkling-eyed Hunter.

'Now look, Hunter,' I said to our new recruit. 'This tank is worth thirty thousand pounds. But I value my life even more than that. So take it easy, for goodness sake. Never mind if you lose sight of the tank in front. I've got a map and, believe it or not, I know where we are.'

'Yes, sir,' said Hunter, in his cultured voice, 'I'll be most careful, sir. Golly! Wait till I tell Mum about this.'

He received a withering look from McGinty, and we took our places in *Avenger* once more.

I adjusted the head set and picked up the microphone.

'Driver, start up!' I commanded.

Nothing happened for a few seconds and then a thunderous explosion ripped the silence of the afternoon. I ducked instinctively into the turret, wondering what the hell had gone wrong. I hadn't seen any enemy aircraft, and I didn't think the cross-Channel guns could reach that far.

Gingerly I poked my head outside again, to find our precious sealing blown over half the county of Hampshire.

'Please sir, I turned the wrong switch,' was all the explanation I could get out of young Hunter. Three bitter voices tried to tell him why the switch was fixed down with insulating tape, and it looked as if our well-meaning co-driver was going to burst into tears. So I bundled them all back into the tank and we set off after the rest of the squadron. Hunter was still at the tiller bar; but I noticed a distinct absence of conversation from the driving compartment.

We reached Lee-on-Solent that evening, and I paraded the whole troop and told them what had happened.

'I don't suppose we'll embark tomorrow,' I said. 'And if every man jack of us works like stink we can get that sealing replaced in time. I know it took us six weeks to do last time, but this time it will be done in a day, simply because I can't give you any longer than that.'

Somebody must have foreseen this sort of thing would happen, because in Lee-on Solent a Sealing Store had been set up containing kits of waterproofing material.

That same night we drew the necessary gear, ready to start work first thing the next day.

But it wasn't necessary.

When I got down there early next morning I found the place abuzz with conversation and *Avenger* securely sealed and waterproofed.

A bleary-eyed Trooper Hunter was explaining to Sergeant Atkins what he'd done.

'He's done it, sir,' said Sergeant Atkins unbelievingly. 'Stayed up all night and did the job by himself; done it well, too.'

'Well, you're a little idiot, Hunter,' I said gruffly. 'There's no need to knock yourself up like that. Maybe you'll need all your wits about you tomorrow. Still, I like your spirit.'

Sandy-haired Lance-Corporal Westham pushed himself forward.

'Th'art a moog, Derek,' he said roughly, in his broadest accent. 'But tha'll do. C'mon, lad, I'll buy thee a pint soon as they're open.'

Trooper Derek Hunter was in Five Troop.

And a week later we sailed for Normandy.

THREE

IT WASN'T A bit as we imagined it was going to be.

The air should have been full of flying shells and the armour-plated hull of the LCT should have been ringing with the impact of small-arms fire. The Normandy coast, grey and uninviting in the morning light, should have been dotted with saffron flashes and overhung with a black pall of smoke.

But it wasn't.

It might almost have been a Combined Services Exercise, except that the train-like roar of the *Rodney*'s salvoes rushing overhead couldn't have been copied by any Battle Simulation Team.

The horizon rose and fell steadily and the Channel waves beat themselves against the square prow of the LCT as we ploughed steadily nearer the deceptively quiet beaches.

'How long?' I said to the skipper.

He shifted his weight thoughtfully from one foot to another and gave a professional throat-clearing.

'Bout an hour, I think,' he said.

I nodded and looked at Tony Cunningham. We were both thinking the same thing; we could do with a drink.

As if reading our thoughts the skipper turned and nodded towards the tiny hutch at the stern of the boat.

'In the wardroom you'll find a gin bottle with a drop left in,' he said. 'You can finish it off, if you like. Sorry we haven't any tonic or anything.'

Even neat gin sounded attractive just then. My stomach was still undecided about whether or not I was a good sailor, and the gradually approaching coastline did little to pacify the butterflies in my intestines.

'Aren't you going to join us?' I said.

The skipper shook his head.

'No, thanks,' he said. 'I had a couple earlier on. Besides, they might put us on to one of these floating pier things and I shall want to be moderately sober then.'

'Aren't they any good, then?'

He shrugged his shoulders.

'Not bad,' he said grudgingly. 'A bit bloody Mark One, though.'

He was interrupted by a steadily increasing whine somewhere above the grey clouds. It was a sound we had grown to know well during our brief stay in Lee-on-Solent; the sound of a fighter-bomber in a power dive.

Tony and I looked at one another again, and we both looked at the red-faced skipper. He was staring stolidly at the beach, not even bothering to look upwards.

'Sounds like trouble for someone,' said Tony, jerking his thumb towards the clouds.

The skipper pursed his lips and shook his head.

'Right over the other end of the beach,' he said. 'Oh, it's as quiet as Liverpool on a wet Sunday afternoon now. You should have seen it on D-Day.'

'Er... yes,' coughed Tony. 'Still, we can't all be in the assault wave can we?'

The sailor grinned.

'I'm not worried,' he said. 'I'll be back in Pompey tonight! Now you'd better see if you can locate that gin bottle. Give me a yell if you want another.'

We took this as a signal for us to leave the bridge and after a last apprehensive look at the Normandy coast we hurried down to his wardroom.

On the way we passed Sergeant Atkins, still with his overcoat buttoned smartly up to the neck and his collar neatly turned down.

'Everything all right, Sergeant Atkins?' I said.

'Yes, sir!' he replied in his clipped, monosyllabic speech. 'Smith 161 has been sea-sick all night and I wondered if Smith 053 could drive ashore.'

I bit my lip thoughtfully. Smith 053, the co-driver on *Angler*, was a good enough driver in his way. I never saw this dour Scotsman flustered or disturbed by anything; but he wasn't as good a driver as his namesake.

Smith 161 could turn a Churchill on a sixpence, and put the thirty-odd tons over a steep bank so that it came down on the far side like a piece of eiderdown.

Sergeant Atkins was waiting; I had to say something.

'Well, it all depends,' I said lamely. 'If the beach is as quiet as it looks now, Smith 053 would be perfectly OK. But if it suddenly turns nasty – though there's no reason why it should – then I'd like to think the other Smith was at the tiller-bar.'

'Yes, sir,' said Sergeant Atkins, which didn't help much.

I decided to stall this one for a bit.

'We'll see how he is just before we disembark,' I said. 'If he's still groggy we'll put 053 in.'

And then I remembered my duties as a Troop Leader, charged with the life and liberty of fourteen men and three tanks. I ought to see Smith 161 for myself.

'Where is he?' I asked.

Sergeant Atkins indicated a tall figure hanging over the rail, and I walked across.

'Not so good, eh, Smith?' I said.

He turned towards me and I saw that his blue-chinned face was faintly tinged with green. His expressive eyes were clouded and troubled and he was obviously worried about more than seasickness, At first I thought it was just pre-action nerves, but his first words dispelled that idea.

'Not to worry, eh, sir?' he said weakly. 'Something I ate, I think. They don't half give you some greasy food on this line don't they, sir?'

He pointed to the shrouded outline of *Angler*.

'I'll take 'er shore, sir,' he said urgently. 'Jus' let me put 'er on the flippin' beach, that's all. Then old Jock can drive all the way to Berlin if 'e likes.'

I punched him gently in the chest.

'All right, Smith,' I grinned. 'We'll prop you up with a cleaning rod or something.'

And then I noticed that, having been so preoccupied with the butterflies in Smith's stomach, I had quite forgotten my own collection. But that drop of gin was still a good idea.

I found Tony Cunningham occupying half the wardroom and staring in some bewilderment at a square, green bottle, sitting in the middle of a scrap of a table.

'That's it all right,' I said. 'Much left?'

'Well, the seal's broken,' said Tony in a dazed voice. 'But that's about all. I swear it hasn't had a thimbleful out!'

'But it's the only gin in sight.'

'I know. And he said finish it off,' Tony said.

We found two glasses from somewhere and, breathing thanks for the traditional hospitality of the Royal Navy, we commenced to lower the level in the green bottle.

Some three-quarters of an hour later we were thrown violently off the little bench (which formed the only seating accommodation in the tiny room) and landed in a heap on the floor.

'This is it,' I said to Tony. 'I feel we've arrived.'

The gin made us feel surprisingly good. I had to fight down a temptation to rush on deck brandishing my revolver and shouting 'Where's the enemy?' But we picked ourselves up rather sheepishly and went on deck, to stare in amazement at the change which had taken place while we had been down below.

No longer were we in the middle of a vast expanse of coldly hostile grey water; instead, the place looked like the Pool of London just after a dock strike. Craft of all sizes chugged busily between the beach and the long lines of sea-going vessels at anchor in deeper water. Barrage balloons swung lazily in the sky, and the superstructure of the sunken caisson ships stuck out above the waves like milk bars in a forest of umbrella skeletons.

The beach was a hive of activity as bulldozers and graders scraped and levelled the sand and shingle. Huge multi-coloured notices proclaimed a series of mysterious initials to the beaching craft.

'HQ 3 DIV BEACH OFP.'

'RAF RGT POST.'

'159 BDE STRAGGLERS.'

Feverishly I searched the beach through my binoculars looking for some sign which would indicate where I was to go with my three Churchills. For the hundredth time I cursed the luck which had decreed that Tony Cunningham and I should travel separately, away from the comforting bulk of the rest of the regiment. For of the 58 Churchill tanks in our regiment, the mammoth American Landing Ship Tank could accommodate 52. The remaining six were shunted on to a small LCT to make the crossing as best they could.

Disembarking with the rest of the regiment would have been too easy; simply a case of following the tank in front. Somebody, somewhere at the front of the column, would have known where we were supposed to go, and how we were supposed to get there. Perhaps there had even been someone from the Advance Party to meet them and guide them in.

But the rest of the regiment had landed some hours before, and it was up to Tony and I to catch them as best we could.

Vaguely I noticed that the LCT was backing away from the beach, but I was still scanning the shore for some sign of the passage of the regiment.

And then I saw it; large and comforting in huge white letters on a black board.

'ALL TRACKED VEHICLES THIS WAY, FOLLOW ARROWS.'

'Well, that seems to settle it,' I said to Tony, indicating the sign.

'Looks like it,' he replied. 'But what the hell are we going backwards for? Has someone called it all off?'

'I dunno,' I said. 'Let's ask the Navy.'

On the bridge the skipper looked as if he had been down with the green bottle, not us. His grey eyes sparkled mischievously and he hummed a little song under his breath.

'Going home?' I said.

He winked, and spoke into a voice tube at his side.

'Full ahead both,' he roared. Then he turned to us and added. 'There's a sand bar about fifty yards out from the beach, and we keep grounding on it.'

'Well, fancy choosing such a spot for a landing,' protested Tony, breathing indignant gin all over the bridge.

'It wasn't like it when we chose it,' said the sailor. 'The sand bar has been formed by LCTs keeping their engines running while they're beached. They have to, though, to stop drifting backwards.'

'How deep is it beyond the sand bar?' I asked.

'About four feet,' said the skipper.

'Well,' I said airily. 'Put us down in that. We're sealed to wade in seven foot of water!'

The skipper thrust out his pendulous lower lip.

'No,' he said flatly. 'I've landed every load dry-shod so far, and I'm damned if I'm going to put your lot in the drink.'

By now the little craft had reached quite a rate of knots. Vibrating to the roar of its twin engines it thundered straight for the beach, throwing up a bow wave which brought indignant yells from sappers and Ordnance characters wrestling with pontoons and floatation equipment nearby.

'Hadn't you pongoes better get into your sardine tins?' said the skipper. 'The others did.'

Tony and I looked at one another in alarm. Of course! Landing Drill seemed to have been pushing into the background somehow. Perhaps it was the gin, perhaps it was the worry of wondering where to go from the beach; but with one accord we turned from the bridge and fled for our tanks.

But the skipper hadn't finished with us.

'And hang on tight,' he roared gleefully. 'This time I'm going to take this old tub right up to Paris!'

The LCT was still racing flat out for the beach, with no sign of the engines slackening speed.

I jumped down into the hold, noting with a sigh of vast relief that the Churchills had been unsheeted.

'Mount!' I yelled, looking wildly around.

A stony silence greeted my command. And then I saw why. Every man of the troop was at his action station, helmets fastened over earphones, binoculars strapped to chests, engines ticking over. In short, the excellent Sergeant Atkins had seen to things in his own excellent way.

'Oh,' I said.

I felt them looking at me, waiting for me to say something. But I put on a bold front, clambered up on to *Avenger* and dropped down on to the commander's pedestal.

Lance-Corporal Pickford handed me the headset without a word and equally silently I put it on. And then I had a brainwave.

Hurriedly plugging in my microphone I switched the selector knob to 'B' and brought forth my excuse.

'Hullo all stations Fox Five,' I said, calling Sergeant Atkins and Corporal Robinson. 'I've just been getting the latest dope from the bridge. There's a sand bar about fifty yards from the beach and we're going to charge through it. So hold tight!'

I switched off with a satisfied smirk. My absence was justified.

But the smirk didn't last long. I reached up for my map, from the rack above the 75-millimetre gun, and was instantly thrown forward off my pedestal.

'Christ!' yelled McGinty, as my swinging binoculars caught him in the back of the neck.

Hurriedly I switched the selector knob to 'IC'.

'Sorry, McGinty,' I said. 'That was that sand bar I told you about.'

He looked around and up at me, a pained expression in his eyes. I saw his lips move but because he didn't use his microphone I couldn't hear what he said. Which is probably just as well.

By the time I got my head out of the turret again the beach was hardly a dozen yards away, with the LCT going as fast as ever. And then, as if some gigantic hand had grabbed the stern of the craft, we were dragged remorselessly to a halt.

With a loud clatter the armour-plated ramp dropped on to the shingle and the Petty Officer in the prow waved us forward.

'Driver advance!' I said into the microphone.

I turned for a valedictory wave to the skipper of the LCT, but he was already lighting his pipe. For him another 'milk run' had finished.

Avenger lurched forward and clattered over the ramp on to the soil of France.

I looked down at the beach. The skipper had kept his promise; we had landed dry-shod.

In a way it was almost annoying. Those weary hours spent in the dusty tank park at Headley, chipping rust away from the suspension blots and painstakingly filling the seams with 'Bostik'. The back-splitting task of laying supine under the belly of the tank, laboriously painting each rivet with bitumastic paint. The perspiring struggles with the iron extensions for the air louvres and exhausts – to say nothing of young Hunter's epic all-night replacement of the blown waterproofing – and we had landed without even getting seawater on the tracks.

But there was no time for reminiscing. Already the huge black and white sign was looming nearer, and I spoke to Crosby in the driving seat.

'Driver left. Follow those white arrows on black discs.'

'OK, sir,' came Bing Crosby's reply.

I looked around to reassure myself that Sergeant Atkins and Corporal Robinson were following. They were, and through the driving window of *Angler* I saw a self-satisfied smile on the face of Smith 161. He had driven ashore and achieved at least one small ambition.

'No sign of the enemy anyway, sir!' said Lance-Corporal Pickford, with a nervous laugh.

The words were hardly out of his mouth before we lurched over the top of a sandhill to see before us a nice level stretch of grassland. It was bounded by a single-strand wire fence, on which at intervals hung ominous notices in Germanic printing.

ACHTUNG – MINEN.

A skull and crossbones decorated each notice and although I had been taught what to expect, my heart gave an involuntary leap. These signs were real; they hadn't been prepared by an RE Instruction Team; they weren't part of any Battle Familiarisation Course; they had been put up by Germans, clad in field-grey just like we had seen in the Identification Manuals, and they guarded sudden death.

I looked hastily around for the white arrows, and saw to my relief that they pointed down a wide lane between two long strips of white tape. I breathed a prayer of thanks to all sappers and guided 'Bing' towards the swept lane.

Beyond the minefield a battery of anti-tank guns were dug in, their long barrels reaching over the tops of their sandy pits. Unshaven soldiers, grubby hands clutching stubs of cigarettes, watched us go by with unseeing eyes. I didn't know then that they had had no sleep for three days and nights, and that they had been sent back to the beach for the sole purpose of getting some sleep.

But it was all very new to me and Five Troop. As we clattered along the faithful trail of the white arrows we stared in fascination at the inverted rifles stuck into significant mounds of earth, each balancing a tin hat on the butt.

And we gazed with curious interest at the straggling line of bare-headed soldiers walking towards us; and then realised with a jolt that these were German prisoners, in the charge of a coldly indifferent Private in the Dorsetshire Regiment.

So this was the *Herrenvolk*! But where were the blond and arrogant supermen we had heard about? These were just ordinary soldiers, albeit rather scruffy ones, and looking a bit archaic in their ankle-length greatcoats. As they went by some of them gazed insolently at us, leaning out of the turrets of our tanks. Some of them just stared, as if their minds were too stunned to absorb any more impressions. One cheerful, imp-faced man – obviously the Platoon Jester – gave a Nazi salute and grinned broadly as he turned it into a mime of pulling a lavatory chain. And at the end of the column came a boy, he looked about thirteen years old and as he stumbled past he used the sleeve of his grey greatcoat to wipe the tears from his eyes.

'There's the enemy,' I said to Lance-Corporal Pickford.

But he didn't answer.

After a while I thought our six tanks were getting a bit spread out, so I halted to allow the others to catch up. I gave the signal to switch off the engines, and climbed out of the turret.

In the silence that followed I heard an unfamiliar noise. A rapid calico-tearing, Brrrrrp! Brrrrrp! Brrrrrrrp!

'What's that?' I said to Tony, as he came to meet me.

'Mice,' he said drily.

But we listened to it and shook our heads doubtfully. The noise was some distance away, and behind it we could hear the rumble of artillery fire and the intermittent staccato firing of Bren guns.

An infantry sergeant came running out of an orchard towards us, and immediately I thought he was coming to warn us of something. Had we strayed into a minefield? Or were we going too far forward? No; he simply held out an empty water bottle and asked if we could fill it for him.

'Yes, of course, sergeant,' said Tony. 'Ask one of the drivers; they're nearest to the freshwater tanks.'

'By the way,' I said, as the sergeant turned away. 'What's that burping noise?'

The sergeant listened for a while and then his dusty grey face split in a knowing grin.

'That? That's a Spandau,' he said. 'You'll hear plenty of them before we've finished with this little lot.'

'Tony,' I said solemnly. 'We've found the war.'

'Yes,' sighed Tony. 'But we haven't found the regiment. I wish we'd asked that sailor for that gin bottle. We didn't finish it for him, then.'

I wasn't listening. Ahead of us I could see a post standing some twelve feet high and completely covered with coloured signs.

'Come on,' I said. 'I'll bet the regimental signal is in that lot.'

Anxiously we scanned the multiplicity of signs on the post. And there, to our indescribable joy, was the familiar white '53' on a green square, with a movable arrow pointing along a Normandy lane.

'We're home,' I said. 'It can't be far now.'

'Blow me down!' cried Tony. 'Here's old Mike.'

Strolling down the lane to meet us, his handlebar moustache hardly hiding his enormous grin, came Mike Carter.

'Oh, so you thought you'd take part after all, did you?' he bellowed, in his bull-like voice.

We shook hands and asked him what sort of crossing he had had in the enormous American LST.

'Superior sort of trip,' he said. 'Shower baths, stacks of tinned fruit, ice-cream.' He went on, his eyes twinkling wickedly. 'The only pity was that being an American ship it was strictly teetotal. Very dry indeed. But very luxurious. What sort of a trip did you have in that little packet of yours?'

'We had a bottle of gin,' I said simply.

I think we rather expected to be hurled headlong at the enemy without even getting out of our tanks. But it was not to be. In fact we spent almost a fortnight in a pleasant rectangular field surrounded on three sides by woods.

Each day we expected to receive orders for battle. But they seemed to be getting on all right without us. So instead we learned a little about a lot of things.

For example, it was here that we first started living in bivouacs.

Happily no special training was necessary in order to erect those splendid dwelling places. A far-sighted designer had fitted alternate sets of lashings to the tank cover sheet so that it could also be used as a makeshift lean-to tent, one wall of which was formed by the side of the tank itself.

In this canvas-covered space it was just possible to get five rolls of bedding, but with a little ingenuity Five Troop managed to fix up electric light and dance music via the tank battery and radio set.

The ground had been baked hard by the summer sun and it wasn't until I had acquired a bruised hip that young Hunter showed me his Boy Scout trick of scooping out a little hollow in the ground just where the hipbone comes.

We learned too, to do our own laundry. At least some of us did.

Later on during the campaign we had the services of some splendid outfits calling themselves Mobile Laundry and Bath Units, but in the early days there couldn't have been enough of these to go round because Five Troop were suddenly smitten with the idea of doing their own laundry.

I watched this process with some fascination and then, having decided that I couldn't show myself to be less clean than my men, I thought I would have to have a go as well.

This instantly aroused a great deal of interest and for the first time since I took over the troop I had their undivided attention.

I got some water boiling in an old petrol tin on one of the tank pressure stoves, and into this I flaked shavings of toilet soap until I had what the copywriters call 'rich sudsy lather'.

And into this went vest, pants, shirt and towel.

'Ah, no!' I said to the grinning troop. 'Not socks! Socks, my lads, should be squeezed gently through warm soapy water; wrung out with only a slight amount of pressure, rinsed and hung up to dry.'

I was much impressed by the roar of appreciative laughter this remark drew. At least, I was impressed until I found that Westham had chalked on the back of *Avenger*.

FIVE TROOP LAUNDRY – MODERATE CHARGES DRESS SHIRTS OUR SPECIALITY

Even then I didn't see any significance in the mention of dress shirts.

But I did later.

After my laundry had been boiling for some time Dick Richards strolled across.

'Is that your washing?' he said, peering suspiciously into the seething mass of bubbles.

'It is,' I said proudly.

'Strewth, you must be a dirty individual. Look at the colour of the water. It's almost khaki!'

I looked closer. It was khaki. My shirt had been too.

I poured away the water and examined the results.

The Troop were now quite helpless with hilarity. Rolling over and over on the grass they howled delightedly as I slowly picked up my vest, pants and towel. They were covered in large khaki splodges, and my shirt had gone all piebald.

For a few minutes I tried to tell them that I had deliberately tried for that camouflage effect, but I couldn't make myself heard above the shrieks of merriment.

If a German platoon had come round the corner then they could have captured the lot of us without firing a shot.

But I was not to be beaten. This seemed to me to be an admirable opportunity of proving to Five Troop that obstacles are made to be overcome.

I racked my brains to think what my wife did to remove obstinate stains from her snow-white washing, and vaguely I recollected the word bleach.

That rang a bell. On the back of each tank was a bin containing equipment to be used in the event of a gas attack. And it contained a tin of bleach paste.

'Break open the anti-gas kit,' I said to McGinty. 'I'll show you how to get this washing white.'

While McGinty was getting the bleach paste, I put on some fresh water and shaved up some more soap. Soon it was boiling briskly and beneath the interested gaze of my fourteen morons I dumped in the stained underclothing and a good dollop of bleach paste.

The smell was indescribable!

Spectators from other troops hurried away, holding their noses in disdain. But Five Troop were made of sterner stuff. They wiped their streaming eyes and settled down grimly to watch.

From time to time I stirred the boiling mixture, but after a few minutes I noticed that it was becoming easier and easier to stir. But the washing couldn't be any worse, I thought.

How little I knew.

Five minutes later I decided the treatment had gone on long enough, and I started to pour away the water.

I poured... and I poured... and I poured.

Soon the tin was nearly empty, and nary a sign of my vest, pants, and towel.

I eyed the troop sternly.

'Any of you blighters been lifting it when my back was turned?'

To a man they denied this base charge, so I just kept on pouring. Eventually all the water ran away and I was left staring into a petrol tin containing nothing but the three bone buttons off my pants.

'And that,' I said with what I felt was considerable aplomb, 'demonstrates the dissolving power of Bleach Paste'.

Even a year later, if a dry wind was blowing, one of the troop would turn an innocent face towards me and say: 'Nice day for washing, sir.'

Now and then we had visitors from other armoured regiments who had been in action. I dare say they had fought only one battle, but they behaved towards us with that air of pompous superiority which seems automatically to envelope those people who have been through an experience you haven't.

They explained with relish just how easily a German 88-millimetre gun could penetrate the front of a Churchill, and they dictatorially advised us to paint out the names on our tanks.

Looking back on it they were quite right, of course. Our tank names were painted in large, yellow letters bright enough to be seen ten miles away by an enemy gunner whose pay book wasn't in Braille. But there seemed to be something slightly shameful about painting out those names; rather like 'casting away his arms in the face of the enemy', as the Manual of Military Law puts it.

So we put on sulky expressions and said to hell with it; the tank names would stay on. But after that we didn't bother much about cleaning them when they got dirty.

One sunny day when the tank names seemed their brightest we received a sudden call to arms. A big battle was to be fought for Caen, and we were to be in reserve ready to be hurled in should the need arise.

Full of expectancy we pulled down our bivouacs and prepared the tanks for action. Across the dusty fields of Normandy we motored to the place where we were to hold ourselves in readiness.

In mounting excitement we watched wave after wave of heavy bombers of the RAF soar above our heads and release their loads on the unhappy Caen. Black puffs of flak burst amongst them, and one we saw go down in flames followed by three doll-like figures swinging on the ends of parachute harnesses.

We brewed up tea and broke open our composite rations – which include everything for a day's living, not forgetting cigarettes, matches, and toilet paper – and for the thousandth time we checked the ammunition, petrol, oil, drinking water, and brake fluid. And we waited.

With a keen sense of what was fitting the sun was blood red as it sank on our right, and then a dusty despatch rider drove up through the evening mist with the news that our services would not be required. With hardly a word we drove back to our field in the woods not knowing whether to feel disappointed or relieved.

I don't think any of us were looking forward to being shot at by angry Germans, but it was rather like having sat in the dentist's waiting room all day, hoisted yourself into his operating chair, and then being told to come back tomorrow.

However, back to the field and the bivouac and the compo rations.

One of the things which surprised me most was the speed with which Five Troop acquired a degree of fluency in Norman French.

Westham and Hunter (between whom a surprisingly cordial friendship had sprung up) would go off with a couple of tins of date pudding. At the first farmhouse Hunter would address Madame in passable Grammar School French, only to receive a curt shake of the head. But Henry Westham would proffer one of the tins with a broad smile and something that sounded like 'Aavezz voo dayz erf, silver plate?' and at once be inundated with fresh eggs and delicious Camembert cheeses.

Funny thing, none of the troop liked the peculiar tang of the fluid Camembert cheese, but they never returned from one of their foraging expeditions without bringing one for me.

Usually it was handed over with some touching little speech like: 'You 'ave this. Then there'll be more eggs for us.'

The other thing which helped to prove the old saw about Life being full of Little Surprises, was the Love Affairs of Trooper Cooper.

For some time Troop Leaders had had the distasteful job of censoring the men's mail. We had to cut out any reference to future moves or plans (just as if we knew any!) and also any other information which might have been helpful to the enemy. To do this we had to read every letter through from beginning to end. The letters were, of course, treated as highly confidential and it was an unwritten law that we would take no action on anything uncensorable which came to our notice via these letters.

But Trooper Cooper wrote violent protestations of undying affection to women in ten different towns in the United Kingdom. Including Lee-on-Solent. And to look at him he was a most unimpressive man – slightly built, round shouldered, almost bald, and with a voice which was hardly ever raised above a whisper. All of which should prove something, but I'm not sure what.

I was frankly worried about these love affairs of *Angler*'s gunner. In at least three of the letters he said how much he was looking forward to seeing the little one again, and I had visions of his entire pay being split up to meet a sheaf of Affiliation Orders.

So one night when it was his turn to act as sentry I strolled across and started talking to him. I talked at first about the war and about *Angler* and then said:

'Oh, well. I'll be glad when it's all over and I can go home to my wife, won't you?'

'Yes, sir,' he said. And waited for me to go on.

'Fulham you come from, don't you?'

'Yes, sir.'

'Let me see, haven't your children been evacuated?'

48

'No, sir. The missus wouldn't have it. And so far they've escaped unhurt.'

'That's good,' I said. 'Well if anything should happen to them, you let me know. After all, I'm here to help you. You know that, don't you?'

'Oh, yes, sir' he said cheerfully.

'If ever you're in any trouble at all, come and tell me about it. Two heads are always better than one.'

'I will sir,' he said. But he was obviously puzzled by the conversation. 'But I'm not in any trouble, sir. Can't see myself getting into any either.'

So I gave it up.

And next day I had to read a letter to Mrs Cooper in Fulham in which her husband said he feared the war was getting his Troop Leader down. Proper funny he'd been lately, he said.

After nearly a fortnight the little field was showing signs of having been very much lived in. The grass was almost worn away and in the surrounding woods it was difficult to walk without bumping into notices which said 'FOUL GROUND'. Manuals on Sanitation in the Field were being dragged out into the light of day and worried Troop Leaders were beginning to recite in their sleep an alphabetical list of fly-borne diseases.

And then one afternoon the buzz of the flies was shattered by the high-pitched scream of a scout car being driven much too fast.

We stopped in our various tasks to watch a little four-wheeled, armour-plated vehicle roar into the middle of our field and skid to a halt in a cloud of dust. It bore the markings of Brigade Headquarters and we wondered who from that exalted level had come to visit us.

The dusty driver stood up revealing red gorget patches on his battledress. It was the Brigadier himself, and he pushed back his goggles, and beamed benevolently at us.

'You lucky people!' he bawled delightedly. 'I've bought you a battle! Where's yer Commanding Officer?'

Dumbly we directed him to RHQ, and then we looked at one another. Somehow this didn't sound like a 'waiting in reserve' job; somehow this sounded as though we really were going to be shot at.

FOUR

WE HOPED THE Brigadier hadn't paid a lot of money for that battle because, as battles go, it wasn't an awful lot of good. But we didn't have any other battles by which to measure it, so as far as we were concerned that night it ranked with Malplaquet, Waterloo, and the Second Battle of Mons.

Out from our little field we moved and turned the noses of our tanks towards the front line. This was going to be it; this was to be the testing ground for all the long and patient training and exercises in England. Now we would know whether or not the sacrifice of the Kent crops had been worthwhile.

There is nothing worse than a Churchill tank for throwing up dust. Its tracks, admirably designed to give a good grip on the worst of terrains, act as scoops in powdery soil, and send to the high heavens an unmistakable token of their passage.

The trees gradually became leafless skeletons, turning bare, shattered arms towards the darkening sky. Rusty, burned-out tanks dotted the flattened cornfields as sombre reminders of what might lay in store for us. And dead cattle, their bellies unbelievably distended by the gases of decomposition, lay in stiff-legged profusion in the shell-torn meadows.

Nose to tail we trundled slowly forward towards the place where we were to meet our Infantry – Hill 112. We passed thundering gun positions, where the bare-chested gunners paused in their sweaty labours to look at us and point indignantly to a large notice which proclaimed:

TAKE IT EASY. DUST BRINGS SHELLS
    – AND WE LIVE HERE!

We shrugged our shoulders apologetically. No use trying to explain to them that however slowly we went we would still send up clouds of tell-tale dust. But they were right.

With headsets clamped over our ears it was impossible to hear many extraneous noises. But to my sudden surprise I saw a black fountain of dirt erupt from a field on our left and a violent blast set my eardrums ringing. Circumspectly I dropped down into the turret and looked at Lance-Corporal Pickford. Immersed in the intricacies of keeping his

50

radio in tune despite the hundreds of other stations transmitting on frequencies quite close to ours, he hadn't heard a thing.

'We're being shelled,' I said over the IC. 'But keep going.'

Come to think of it, that was a fairly fatuous remark; there wasn't anything else we could do except keep going. And after a while the shelling seemed just a part of the landscape.

From time to time I stuck my head out of the turret just to make sure that *Alert* and *Angler* were coming on all right behind me, and that we were keeping in touch with the last tank of Duncan Watson's Troop, just in front of us. But most of the time I spent inside the turret, peering through the periscope now and again and talking quietly to the crew over the IC.

Satisfied that his set was receiving as well as possible Lance-Corporal Pickford leaned back against the side of the turret and grinned at me as he wiped the beads of sweat from his face. He looked almost demoniac in a way – in a friendly Christmas-pantomime demon sort of way. The ruby glow from the indicator light on the radio shone redly on one side of his face while the other side took on the yellow reflection of the turret festoon light. From behind his radio set he picked up one of the round tins of cigarettes which came in the compo rations. He held it in his hand and looked at me with raised eyebrows.

I nodded. Smoking was allowed in action, and this was as near as made no odds. I told the two in the driving compartment that they could smoke too, and soon the smell of burning tobacco was blending with the constant tang of engine fumes and the rich, greasiness of gun oil.

Avenger gave a couple of short, sharp bumps and I knew we were passing over the Bayeux-Caen railway line. Hurriedly I consulted my map and plotted our position.

'Won't be long now,' I told the crew, and hoisted my head and shoulders out of the turret.

The shelling had died away and we were fanning out on to a muddy stretch of ground which sloped upwards away from us.

This was Hill 112, and a pretty grim place it looked, at that.

A shell-battered copse lay on each side of the hill, bordered by slit trenches in which we could see our infantry waiting for us.

There were one or two things I wanted to sort out with the Infantry Company Commander I was supposed to be supporting, but somehow I didn't relish the idea of leaving the comfortable security of *Avenger* and walking across that treacherous open ground.

And then I saw Alan Biddulph. He was standing almost on the skyline with Jim Steward and roaring with fat laughter at some remark of Jim's. His map was in his hand and, in complete defiance of his own orders about steel helmets being *de rigeur,* he was wearing his familiar beret.

That gave me great heart, and I clambered out of the tank, and strolled (yes, deliberately strolled) across to *Alert*.

With a forced air of unconcern I called up to Sergeant Atkins in the turret.

'All right, Sergeant Atkins?'

I do wish my voice wouldn't squeak like that without warning.

'Yes, sir,' he said, looking at his watch. 'Move off in ten minutes?'

'That's right,' I said, and forcing myself to slow down to a a walk I went across to speak to the Company Commander.

About a mile beyond the crest of Hill 112 lay a little hamlet known as Bon Repos. Hunter translated this for the rest of the troop and they wouldn't believe him. Well, the idea was to capture this hamlet and just so we wouldn't get lost the Normandy authorities at some time or other had constructed a little road leading straight from Hill 112 to Bon Repos. So all we had to do was follow the road until we got there.

That's what we thought.

In order to baffle the enemy gunners on the hills overlooking our first battleground, lots and lots of smoke screens were put down. Perhaps the wind changed, perhaps some gunner added the date into his range calculations, perhaps – and this is more likely – the wily enemy added a few smoke concentrations of his own. But the result was a thick, impenetrable fog over the entire landscape just as we crossed the Start Line.

'Action!' I said, giving the command in earnest for the first time; and with the smooth precision of a drill many times carried out to the point of boredom Pickford fed a shell into the 75-millimetre gun and the breech-block clanged shut. McGinty loaded the turret machine gun and hitching his seat a bit higher he dug his forehead into the sponge-rubber brow-pad and wriggled his eyes more comfortably into the padded end of the telescopic sight.

Like khaki ghosts the infantry rose from the slit trenches and swept over the crest of the hill.

'Driver advance!' I said. And *Avenger* rolled forward into battle.

I was lucky; my line of advance lay just to the right of the little road. All I had to do was keep that road on my left and I couldn't go wrong.

On my right, 'Hobby' Hobson with No.4 Troop was without any such guide, and when the smoke lifted a little I saw to my horror that he was swinging out far too much to the right. I told Alan Biddulph, who tried to get him on the 'A' set, but Hobby was in full cry after his infantry, and faced with the prospect of sticking to them or getting back on his right course. He decided to stick with his infantry and, as far as I know, fought a very good infantry/tank attack on a Spandau post. It had nothing to do with our objective, of course, and I should think the German machine-gunners were pretty indignant at being dragged into what wasn't their battle.

But my infantry company, helped no doubt by that admirable road, were pushing steadily on towards Bon Repos.

Beside the road, an isolated cottage made an excellent half-way mark and nobody was more surprised than Five Troop when a heap of rubble and torn trees loomed up through the thinning smoke. We were half-way there without firing a shot.

Also taking part in the battle were some flame-throwing tanks from another regiment, and after pushing *Alert* out to the right a bit to fill the gap left by Hobby's departure I halted the troop while the flame-throwers squirted their frightening cargoes at the remains of this cottage.

The infantry were silhouetted against the flickering billows of flame, moving purposely about with fixed bayonets. Then I saw them regrouping for the second half of the attack.

I took off my headset and listened to the noises. A fierce crackling came from the burning ruins where the flame-throwers had somehow found some unburned debris; a cacophony of small arms fire came rattling from all directions. A whining thunderclap sounded over our heads – a noise which I grew to recognise later as an armour-piercing shell in full flight.

McGinty, I knew, was itching to fire his first shot. But never a target could I see. Nothing but shell holes, shattered trees, black mud and the narrow, pavé road.

The infantry moved off again, and I followed them telling McGinty to see if he could pick up any targets in his telescope. Questingly he swung the turret from side to side; but the guns remained silent.

There was nothing I could do but follow the infantry, tell Alan over the 'A' set what was going on, and keep a look out.

And then I saw some figures approaching down the middle of the road. They came out of the smoke like images on a photograph in the developing tray, and they were Germans.

'Co-ax, traverse left!' I said, trying to keep the quiver out of my voice. In one swift movement McGinty swung the turret round and out of the corner of my eye I saw his hand drop on to the pistol-grip of the turret machine gun.

'As you were,' I said. 'They're prisoners.'

They were, too. And they were coming from Bon Repos.

Our job was not to go into the hamlet; we were to stand off from a distance and see the infantry safely in. So I halted the troop and looked about me.

By now it was quite dark and the only illumination came from the flame-throwers still squirting fire all over the place, and the occasional shell-burst in the mud.

Across the road I could see 'B' Squadron coming up. They were five minutes late and I made a note to pull Tommy Tucker's leg about this. I knew his troop was supposed to be just the other side of the road from me.

I've often read that phrase about time passing on leaden feet, but I never knew how true it was until that night standing off from Bon Repos; then I realised just how much lead there could be in those feet of time.

The radio wasn't much help, either. Scores of voices crackled from the ether; orders to the flame-throwers; orders to the artillery; Alan vainly striving to re-establish contact with Hobby; and Troop Leaders plaintively asking how much longer they were going to sit out there like practice targets on the anti-tank range.

But eventually the infantry released us and the artillery began to put down smoke to cover the withdrawal of the tanks. This should have been the easiest part of the whole show. Just a case of traversing our guns over our tails and going flat out back to Hill 112. And then I noticed *Angler* wasn't with us.

Frantic calls on the 'B' set elicited no response and Sergeant Atkins said he thought he saw them going off to the left, but it might have been a Churchill from another troop.

There was nothing else for it; we had to swing around and cast about looking for my missing Troop Corporal. Luckily we didn't have to search for long; looming out of the smoke came *Angler* with Smith 161 breathing fire and slaughter from the driving seat. The engine had stalled and, in *Angler*'s own inexplicable way, had refused to start again for five minutes.

I heaved a sigh of relief and looked around for the way back to Hill 112.

And then I realised we were lost.

Gone were the comforting cobblestones of the little road, gone were the tumbling outlines of Bon Repos; we were plunging slowly through a pall of ever-increasing smoke in a completely unknown direction.

I switched the selector knob to 'A'.

'Hullo, Peter Five,' I called. 'I've temporarily lost my bearings. Can you send up a white Verey light to guide me back.'

Promptly a white signal flare burst in the sky behind my right shoulder, and I whistled appreciatively at Alan's promptness.

'Hullo, Peter Five,' came Alan's voice out of my earphones. 'That light you just saw was sent up by the enemy – well, you asked for it, didn't you, making a request like that over the air?'

I hoped the crew couldn't see me blushing and, for want of something better to do, I halted the troop and we sat there in the smoke while I tried to reconcile my map with the contours of the ground and the few stars I could see.

To help matters along a few stray shells started bursting amongst us, but I was hugely comforted to hear other Troop Leaders complaining on the air that they, too, were lost in the smoke.

And then a broad finger of light stabbed up into the clouds from somewhere on the horizon.

'Hullo, all stations Peter,' said Alan's voice. 'Head for that searchlight and you'll soon be home.'

Almost instantly another searchlight soared up into the night sky – a German one. I gave the enemy full marks for prompt action, but headed determinedly towards the first light. Other people did the same, and somewhere on the return journey the ether was enlivened by a rollicking chorus of 'Lead Kindly Light'. Nobody would admit to this afterwards, so we put it down to German interference; but it sounded awfully like a dark brown baritone to me.

Once we were reassembled at Hill 112 we switched off our engines and counted turrets. Only one tank was missing – Hobby's Troop Sergeant who had somehow wandered on to one of our own minefields during his troop's private war. None of the crew was injured, and as far as I remember, they successfully mended their broken track and limped back to 112 just before dawn.

I thought I detected a look of wistfulness on McGinty's face as he unloaded his guns, so I tried to explain how we came to win our first battle without firing a shot.

'The mere presence of tanks on the battlefield can often disrupt the enemy's morale,' I lectured. 'I think myself they withdrew when they saw us coming, and the fact that we couldn't find anybody to fire at simply proves that there wasn't anybody there firing at us.'

I walked round to *Alert* and *Angler* and told them the same thing, until in the end I almost believed it myself.

Then I saw 'B' Squadron on the other side of the hill, and the shelling having now stopped for a few minutes, I walked across turning over in my mind some witty phrases with which to point out Tommy Tucker's slowness.

They told me Tommy Tucker was dead, his tank having been hit by an 88-millimetre anti-tank gun. Immediately afterwards his Troop Sergeant and Corporal had, between them, destroyed the gun; but it gave me much food for thought.

On the way back to Five Troop I heard another issue of shells coming over and, casting dignity to the winds, I leaped into a shell hole. It was a fairly large shell hole because there were four people in there already. In the reflected light of the searchlight I saw that they were a sergeant and private in the Wiltshires, and two Germans. My immediate reaction was that the two Germans were prisoners, and then I saw that they were still wearing their steel helmets and one of them clutched a rifle and bayonet.

It took me about ten seconds to realise I was sharing a shell hole with four dead men, and then I decided to take a chance on the shelling and make a beeline for *Avenger*.

'Why didn't you wait for a break in this lot, sir?' said Pickford as I scrambled breathlessly into the turret.

'This?' I said, waving an airy hand in the general direction of the erupting earth. 'This is all part of the day's work now. Have to get used to it, you know.'

It sounded good to me, but he gave me a shrewd sideways look as he reached for the cigarette tin again.

How long we sat on that hill I can't remember. I have a distinct recollection of sitting peacefully on a railway line in the sunshine while Alan Biddulph gave an excellent analytical description of the general run of the battle, so we might have withdrawn from there some time during day. But before dark we were back again on Hill 112.

The infantry whom we had so enthusiastically helped in to Bon Repos, had been ordered to withdraw to Hill 112 again and here they sat in defensive slit trenches, gazing down into the valley which had been the scene of our first battle.

Our job now was to sit behind the infantry ready to dash forward if the enemy attacked those slit trenches. And we did this by having one troop up close behind the infantry and the remainder of the squadron at the bottom of the hill ready to be called forward if necessary.

Ten days we stopped there, enduring intermittent shelling and occasionally being troubled by a persistent sniper who sat in one of the tall trees overlooking our little patch of France.

For ten days we lived in our tanks, cooking, eating, drinking, and sleeping. We did almost everything without getting out. And I mean almost everything.

Under the blazing sun the mud quickly turned to dust; and under the impact of this dust we drank a fair amount of liquid. Since our natural functions didn't cease just because we were living inside a round, armour-plated wall with shells bursting around us from time to time, we found an unorthodox use for empty shell cases. They were just the right shape for emptying out of the turret hatch. When more solid relief was necessary there was nothing else for it but to wait for one of the occasional shell-free spells and get out and seek an unoccupied shell hole.

But whenever possible this operation was carried out under cover of darkness. Especially after the case of Jim Steward.

The afternoon was unusually quiet and I was leaning out of the top of the turret getting a much-needed breath of fresh air. Some of the crews had dismounted and were stretching their legs while the slave carrier charged their tank batteries.

I saw Jim climb out of his tank, calmly take a spade from the clips on the engine-hatch, and set off across the hill.

I knew he wasn't going gardening. In those days people sought solitude with a spade for one purpose only.

I breathed a sigh of relief that I wasn't feeling that way myself right then, because the air was deceptively quiet. And since certain functions should be carried out in private I turned my attention to other things.

The wireless crackled and spluttered at my elbow and I wondered if we were flogging our batteries too much. And then I heard Alan's voice on the air and for once he'd lost his air of unhurried calm.

He was sending an urgent and peremptory message for a scout car to take away a casualty, and when I popped my head out of the turret I saw a group of men helping Jim back to the security of his tank.

The short point was that while Jim had been communing with nature he had been shot by a German sniper. He had his back to the enemy lines at that moment and the bullet had penetrated the fleshy part of his buttock, missing all the vital spots and making a not-too-serious wound.

The only lesson to emerge from that incident was that, despite propagandist's edicts to the contrary, the Germans have a sense of humour. That sniper could equally well have drilled Jim through the back of the head, but he chose the larger and (he no doubt thought) funnier target.

By the fifth day we were a grim looking lot. Grimy, unshaven, and red-eyed from lack of sleep.

Catching up on sleep was a problem in itself. We had to be on the alert at sunset and dawn (since these are the two times when attacks are most likely to be launched) and between these two times the hours of darkness were all too short.

Some troops dug pits in which to sleep, running their tanks over the top to act as armour-plated roofs. But the thought of being crushed to death by a slowly settling Churchill was just too much for Five Troop.

Other people dug slit trenches, in which they crouched in fitful slumber to awaken with a start every time a shell landed.

We slept in our tanks.

Looking at the inside of a Churchill some years later I had difficulty in believing we ever managed it. The fighting compartment is designed to get the maximum amount of equipment and ammunition into the minimum amount of space. But we were helped, of course, by the diminutive size of ex-jockey McGinty.

He used to curl up around his gunner's seat in a weird, foetus-like attitude. This allowed Crosby and Hunter to let down the backs of their seats and by drawing their knees up to their waists they were able to lay down.

Pickford used to sit on an ammunition bin, wedge his knees against the front of his wireless set, rest the back of his weary head on the two-inch bomb thrower, and somehow snore.

I was luckiest of all. I had a tiny tip-up seat about the size of a tea-plate. Perched firmly on this, with my feet resting on top of the 75-mm gun, I was able to drop my chin on my chest and doze off quite satisfactorily.

And then it came to be Five Troop's turn to move up the hill closer to the infantry. This, of course, meant no sleep at all and if the experience of other troops was anything to go by it meant a constant running back and forth between the tanks and the infantry, investigating odd noises and making sure they didn't want you.

The laid-down procedure was that if the Infantry Commander wanted the aid of the tanks he would send a runner. But across that bit of ground runners were expendable, and I wanted to make sure I received all the necessary information. I didn't want to look out of my turret and find a large German swinging on the end of the gun with a knife in his teeth.

So I made a brilliant plan with the young Platoon Commander in front of me. We arranged a series of Verey light signals in an elaborate code so that he could almost send me a Greetings Telegram if he wanted to.

I forget what they were now, but there are three types of Verey light: red, green, and white. And sitting in that slit trench in the moonlight we worked out a permutation to delight the heart of a Pool's enthusiast. And the only one I can remember now is that a green light meant 'Enemy tank approaching'. Two green lights meant two tanks, three meant three or more.

I remember I laughed nervously and said: 'If you get attacked by a Panzer Division just set fire to the green cartridge box!'

Just as if I had anything to laugh about.

I told Sergeant Atkins and Corporal Robinson what I had arranged and they seemed to think it was a good idea.

'What do we do if the enemy attack in strength, sir?' said Corporal Robinson.

Sergeant Atkins gave him a withering look and before I could reply he said: 'Go and drive 'em back, of course.'

'But supposing they're too many for us?' persisted my Troop Corporal.

I knew just how he felt, and I replied: 'Then we call up the rest of the squadron.'

Corporal Robinson thought about this one for a bit, and then he said: 'But supposing they're too many for the squadron?'

This sounded to me like what the Manual of Military Law calls 'spreading alarm and despondency'. So I told him not to be funny, the

Germans hadn't got that many troops facing us. And those aeroplanes we could hear overhead were almost certainly ours.

Hardly were the words out of my mouth before there came a loud crack in the sky and a dazzling green light illuminated the scene.

'Christ! We're off!' I said. 'Action!'

I flung myself into *Avenger*, kicked the crew into wakefulness and snatched up my headset. But before I could order Crosby to start up, another green light burst in the sky. And then another, and another until the whole of our front seemed to be a mass of green lights drifting down from the clouds.

I decided Five Troop were about to achieve immortal fame by taking on a complete armoured division, and reached for the microphone to tell Alan so.

'Hello, William Five,' I said. 'I think the enemy may be attacking in strength. Have received information that a considerable amount of armour is advancing towards us.'

'Well, good luck, John,' came Alan's laconic reply. 'We got troubles, too. Let me know what you can see yourself.'

'Wilco, out,' I said.

As I put down the microphone it struck me that our infantry were being suspiciously quiet. I would have expected their slit trenches to be alive with firing and noise. But apart from the steady sending up of showers of green lights, there was no sign of activity.

And then there was a violent explosion from some way behind me, followed by another and another. Far too heavy and loud to be shelling, it took me a few seconds to realise they were bombs. And soon the roar of the aircraft overhead grew louder and louder as stick after stick of bombs crashed into the ground some distance away.

This is part of the preliminary softening up for the attack, I thought. The first assault wave will hit us as the aircraft depart.

But the aeroplanes were still coming in, so I knew I had a few minutes in which to act. The bombs were still some way off, though I could see one or two dropping near the rest of the squadron at the bottom of the hill and I knew what Alan meant when he said he had troubles, too.

With considerable lack of enthusiasm for the project I climbed out of *Avenger* once more and scuttled up the hill to find my infantry subaltern. I located him smoking his pipe peacefully in his trench, from time to time standing up to peer across the moonlit valley below.

'What's the idea of all the green Verey lights?' I demanded with some heat.

'Not ours, old boy,' he murmured, between puffs of strong tobacco. 'Germans.'

He stood up and pointed with the stem of his pipe down to where, several hundred yards away, I could make out faint flashes as more and more signal flares went up.

'Oh,' I said, and then after a while, 'what do you think the idea is?'

Again using his pipe as a pointer he jerked the stem backwards over his shoulder.

'This bombing raid, I expect,' he said. 'Those green lights are probably the code to mark the limit of their own lines, and the Jerry pilots have orders not to bomb until they pass the green lights.'

Then I had another of my brilliant ideas.

'Why don't you fire up a few?' I said. 'Then they won't bomb you!'

'What?' he said. 'And have you getting all het up thinking enemy tanks are approaching?'

There didn't seem to be any answer to that, so I crept back to *Avenger* and the rest of the night passed in peace for Five Troop.

But not for the rest of the squadron, who were supposed to be resting. Although the raid was primarily aimed at an ammunition dump some distance away from the tank harbour, the other troops came in for one or two spare bombs. And because none of them suffered a direct hit there were no casualties. We learned that night that the old Churchill could take quite a lot of punishment from near-misses, and without batting a revolver port.

As a result of having been Guard Troop (although in fact we had had a less hectic time than the rest of the squadron) Five Troop were relegated to reserve for the next day. All this meant was that in the event of an enemy attack we would be the last troop to be committed against them. But as the enemy hadn't attacked yet it didn't seem to make much difference. I might have known there's a first time for everything.

The day after the Air Raid we were sitting peacefully in our tanks, wondering how much longer the Powers That Be were going to keep us on 112, when Mike Carter (who was Guard Troop) sounded the call to arms. The enemy were attacking, and we sallied up the hill to beat them off.

It didn't turn out to be the desperate struggle we expected. The Germans seemed content to stand off in the valley and blast at anything which showed itself on the skyline. Being in reserve we didn't see anything of them, but we could see Mike Carter's troop blazing away over the crest and we could hear his somewhat puzzled voice reporting over the air that these enormous great Tiger tanks managed to hide themselves remarkably well.

That was the point at which Mike's tank seemed to sit back suddenly on its rear bogies, and tongues of flame shot out of the engine compartment. Four figures leaped out of the tank into the clouds of black, oily smoke which were now pouring from their burning vehicle.

A few minutes later three of them came stumbling down the hill, supporting the fourth. Mike's big, burly form wasn't amongst them and I feared the worst for a few moments until I saw Mike standing on the back of his Troop Sergeant's tank directing some return fire.

In Five Troop, hatches were gingerly opened and we stared in breathless awe at the burning tank. This was the first time we had seen the phenomenon casually referred to as 'brewing up'; although we were due to see a lot more.

The blazing hulk vibrated with the crash of ammunition exploding in the bins, and feathery plumes of white smoke arched out of the open hatchways as the smoke bombs caught fire.

Vicious spouts of earth spurted from the hill crest, to be followed by the diminuendo whine of an armour-piercing shell ricocheting off the ground.

It was some comfort to know that the Germans could miss, too.

We had a reserve squadron standing by, and Alan seemed to think it was a pity they should miss the fun, too; so he sent out a call for reinforcements.

'Hello Baker,' he said. 'Would you send up another shilling?'

Shilling was the simple code-name for a squadron; individual tanks were known as pennies, and troops as sixpences.

We thought these code-names were darned clever; fox the enemy every time. We learned.

People were now being understandably cautious about driving up over the skyline so Alan got out of his tank and to everybody's dismay calmly walked up to the top of the hill and studied the scene below through his binoculars. I tensed myself and waited for him to collapse in the traditional crumpled heap; but he didn't. Instead he walked firmly back to my tank and climbed up on to it.

'There's just one tank I can see, John,' he said. 'And it's got with it a sort of staff car with a long radio aerial. If you go out to the left and creep gently up to the top you may be able to get a shot in his flank.'

I opened my mouth to answer but before I could say a word I was interrupted by Alan's voice coming out of the headphones slung around my neck.

'Hello Baker,' said Alan's voice. 'You needn't bother about that shilling now. It won't be needed.'

'Roger, out,' replied the voice of the operator at RHQ.

Alan and I stared at one another in incredulous amazement for a couple of seconds, and then he grabbed my microphone and said:

'Hello Baker. Ignore that last message. It wasn't me – it was the enemy.'

That explained the radio car, of course, and as soon as Alan had jumped off my tank I took the troop round to where he had indicated. But the birds had flown.

McGinty, to his evident satisfaction, blazed off a few rounds into every clump of bushes which looked as if it might have sheltered a tank or a car, but we never saw any results.

'Hello Baker Five,' called Alan over the 'A' set. 'Any luck?'

'No,' I replied. 'I think they have withdrawn.'

'Of course they have,' said a smug voice in my earphones. 'You're wasting your ammunition, Baker Five. I told you that other shilling wouldn't be necessary.'

Since the provision of asbestos sheeting would make the cost of this book prohibitive, I won't print my reply.

After ten days of this sort of thing we were pulled back for two days' rest; two days far from the continual shelling and out of range of snipers; two days in the sunshine with nothing more annoying than the decomposition of a dairy herd in the next field; two days of shaving, bathing, writing letters home, sleeping long and peacefully and checking over the tanks.

One of the odd things which emerged from that period was the business of Watches, GS, TP.

You should know that each tank radio set had a fitting on the front of it specially designed to accommodate a watch. The watches were the normal pocket timepieces, but being made to army specifications they were good. Not very elaborate, perhaps, and not made of any precious metal; but they maintained a degree of accuracy good enough to run a railway – and a pre-war railway, at that.

Under peacetime accounting procedure these watches were treated as if each was worth a king's ransom. To lose one was tantamount to resigning your Commission and it was rumoured that Ordnance had a permanent Court of Enquiry specially skilled in unearthing 'lost' watches. Even if a watch was broken all the bits had to be produced, together with a certificate from a qualified instrument mechanic to the effect that all the component parts were accounted for.

It was almost as bad in war; in fact the only way an army watch was allowed to end its natural life was by being destroyed in action. The magic words 'destroyed in action' were apparently accepted as a good enough reason for the absence of anything from an army corps downwards.

So it was not surprising, therefore, that five Troop Leaders blandly reported they had lost their radio watches in action, and what a pity it was.

Alan smoothly commiserated with them, but I noticed he didn't put in for any replacement watches, and nobody seemed to have any difficulty telling the time. But as far as I know those watches are still ticking steadily on, telling the time in offices, shops, and factories all over the United Kingdom.

The man who first said 'all good things must come to an end' has been quoted often enough, so once more won't hurt him.

When our forty-eight hours' rest was over we moved up to the front again. Not, we were relieved to find, to Hill 112 but to the remnants of a little village just around the corner from it.

And here again we sat just below a skyline; standing by or in our tanks day after day in case the enemy chose to attack that sector. But he didn't. So, applying the old principle of Mahomet and the mountain, we went to him.

Five Troop looked a bit distrustful when I told them that our objective was to be our old friend Bon Repos again, only this time coming in from a different direction. I allayed this distrust as soon as I explained that this wasn't to be an attack to capture the place, but merely a raid to seize a few prisoners. In other words, no hanging about down there. Straight down and straight back. No funny business getting lost in smoke, and no trouble at all.

I never did find out which of them said 'Oh yeah?' but he was quite wrong. No doubt to the planners' unbelief, everything went according to plan.

Five Troop had a definite target this time. A farm and out-buildings on the right edge of the hamlet. And the idea was that we should keep it so peppered with machine gun fire that nobody in there would attempt to take part in the battle until the raiding party had safely returned to their own lines.

Again there was a lot of smoke about, and again it was one of those sunset sorties. We cursed the smoke a bit, because there was no nice road to guide us to Bon Repos this time. But when, for a few minutes, the smoke cleared away and we found ourselves exposed to the full view of a long range of enemy-held hills, we felt as naked as three nudists at a mission meeting, and almost as embarrassed.

However, it gave us long enough to get our bearings on the farm which was to be our target and after sending *Alert* out to the extreme right to act as longstop in case anybody tried to leave by the back door, *Angler* and *Avenger* started in to use up as many belts of ammunition as we could.

If you're the sort of person who operates an electric riveting gun inside boilers for a living, you would have felt completely at home in *Avenger*. With all hatches closed the two Besas made an incredible din.

The smell of hot gun oil intermingled with the acrid cordite fumes and made our eyes shed streams of tears. All the fume-extraction fans were going, of course, but they weren't designed to cope with such a terrific burst of firing.

In the end we had to open the hatches and allow the cool night air to sweep in.

In the village itself the infantry were getting on with their task in admirable fashion, and I could see Duncan Watson's Troop sitting on the crossroads firing with gay abandon into all the bedroom windows.

And then the shelling, which had been sparse and spasmodic until then, began to increase in intensity as the enemy brought down a heavy concentration on the hamlet itself, without apparently being unduly worried by the fact that a considerable number of his own troops still occupied it. So it was with some relief that we heard Alan's voice telling us to come back now, it was all over.

I think everybody must have got the order at the same time, because the pockmarked landscape was suddenly full of soldiers, tanks, carriers, prisoners hurrying along with their hands in the air, and a wildly driven jeep.

Here and there were standing knocked out and burned-out tanks, relics of previous battles over this ground. In one or two cases their crews lay stiffly beside them, having been probably machine gunned to death as they baled out from their wrecked vehicles.

Instinctively I turned my eyes from these unpleasant reminders of what might be in store for us, and then I looked at one of them again. It was moving slowly towards Bon Repos, its turret swinging lifelessly to right and left. But it wasn't a Churchill; it was a Sherman.

'Hell,' I told the crew. 'The Brigadier's taking part himself now. He'll probably turn us all round to have another go, just for the ride.'

Brigade Headquarters were equipped with Sherman tanks because of their greater speed, and it wasn't until I drew nearly level with this Sherman that I saw it bore on the front the sign of a Division which should have been right over the other side of Caen.

'Now what the devil are they getting mixed up in our battle for?' I asked the crew. And hoping it wasn't the Divisional Commander I leaned out of the turret and made a rude gesture to the Sherman as we swept by.

It just trundled steadily on, heading for Bon Repos, and I turned my attention again to the problem of navigating our way back to harbour.

Not that it was much of a problem; there were so many vehicles and people going that way it looked like the Brighton road on a summer Sunday evening.

Back in harbour we were unloading our empty belts and cartridge cases when Charles Geoffreys, our tame Intelligence Officer, came along.

'Hello, John,' he said. 'Have a good shoot?'

'Pretty good,' I said, pointing to the empty cartridge cases. 'Didn't see any results, though.'

'No? Oh, well. Didn't see anything of a spare Sherman from X-Division trundling around, did you?'

'Yes, I did,' I said. 'Nearly collided with the wretched thing. It was heading happily for Bon Repos when I saw it last. Who was in it, anyway?'

'Germans,' grinned Charles. 'It's one they managed to salvage and put on the road again. The infantry have reported it tonight, but I wanted to get some tank confirmation. You didn't take it on by any chance?'

'No,' I said. 'But I called the commander a rude name.'

'I hope he heard you,' said Charles. 'Well, I'll put the anti-tank gunners on to it, and if he shows his nose on this sector again he'll get a hot reception.'

'I'll keep a special look out for him next time we run down there,' I said.

'You won't be going down there again,' said Charles. 'We're off tomorrow to the Villers Bocage area. We're in for some real Armoured Division stuff – pursuit of a retreating enemy across unspoiled country.'

FIVE

BY THIS TIME things had begun to move in Normandy. The Americans had broken out of the Cherbourg Peninsula and on the right flank of the British Army a similar (but smaller) break-out had been achieved.

And our regiment had been chosen to pursue the fleeing enemy.

And 'A' Squadron had been chosen to lead the regiment.

And which troop do you think was picked to lead the Squadron?

When I broke the news to Five Troop I got a very mixed reception.

'So we'll be right at the point of one of those arrows they draw on the maps in the newspapers, sir?' said Pickford.

'Right at the very sharp end,' I said.

'Ah've often wanted to see one o' them things on t' ground,' said Westham, shaking his sandy head.

'Are we expecting any enemy resistance, sir?' asked Sergeant Atkins.

'That's one of the things we hope to learn,' I said.

'Ullo, we're off again,' said Smith 161. 'Learning the flippin' 'ard way. Cor, strike a light!'

'Anyway,' I said, 'it'll be a relief to know that there won't be anything in front of us except enemy. We won't have any bother about our own side getting in the way.'

How little I knew.

By the time we reached the Start Line just outside Villers Bocage the road looked as if it led to Wembley on Cup Final day. Men and vehicles jammed the road as far as the eye could see.

Patiently Alan explained to me that although Five Troop was leading the pursuit, in front of us would be a Flying Squad outfit from the Reconnaissance Corps, the Recce Troop from RHQ, the Gunner OP (who wanted to see where his battery's shells were landing) a couple of platoons of infantry (just in case), a section of sappers (in case we met any mines) and I'm not sure he hadn't got an ENSA party up front as well (just in case we got bored).

Despatch riders dashed frantically up and down the column, scout cars buzzed back and forward like angry beetles, and Five Troop took up its position for the headlong dash which didn't look as if it would ever get started.

But it did. After many false alarms, and after much revving up of engines and hoarse shouts of command, the column slowly rolled forward and we prepared ourself for some excitement.

We'd had more exciting rides on the ranges – especially the day *Angler* got a runaway gun.

Nothing disturbed the tranquillity of the afternoon as we patiently followed the tail of whichever vehicle happened to be in front.

At first we did the thing properly, keeping our guns trained on likely-looking defence posts, gingerly creeping around corners in case an anti-tank gun barred the way, and generally doing a textbook 'Advance to Contact'. But after a while it became difficult to keep up a tense alertness, especially after we found the infantry riding on the back of *Avenger* were having a quick hand of three-card brag.

After a while we came to one of the inevitable hold-ups. In the distance we could hear the linen-tearing sound of a Spandau in action, and for a moment I thought Five Troop was going to have something to do. But then word filtered down from the head of the column that the road had been mined, and the Spandau fire was coming from a different part of the front.

We were parked outside a grey, cement-faced house and bearing in mind one of our earlier lessons about picking up useful information from the local inhabitants, I clambered down from the tank and walked up the short gravelled path towards the front door.

Dutifully I knocked on the peeling woodwork, but the door swung open to my touch so I entered the drably papered hallway.

'Anyone at home?' I shouted in English. There didn't seem anything else to say.

I waited a little while and then gingerly opened a door on my right. On a plain deal table stood four bowls of soup, and scattered about the room were odd items of German uniform and equipment.

That made me think for a bit, and in the end I summoned my courage up to its highest point and drawing my revolver walked softly across the room and examined the table.

The soup was warm, and beside one of the plates a grey finger of cigarette ash indicated that the occupants of the room had been gone at least fifteen minutes.

And then I had the paralysing thought that maybe they hadn't gone at all; maybe they were hiding in the house at that very moment. A tall, mahogany cupboard looked certain to contain at least a couple of stalwart Wehrmacht privates, and I kept it covered with my revolver as I backed out of the room.

This, I thought, is a job for the infantry. That's what I'm lugging them around on *Avenger* for; house-clearing is 'the-cat-sat-on-the-mat' stuff to them.

I ran down the gravel path, intent on interrupting the brag school, but as if my arrival had been the signal to move off, the carrier in front of *Avenger* suddenly revved up, crashed its gears happily and started to chug down the road.

Quite the last thing I wanted to do was to be left behind on this 'pursuit of a disordered enemy' so I decided that the soup-eaters (if they were still in the house) could safely be left to the tender care of someone at the tail of the column.

On we chugged, a steady ten miles an hour, until we came to a brand new set of notices saying 'VERGES UNCHECKED' and saw some significant holes in the roadway.

'This must be the spot where the mines were,' I told the crew. 'Keep to the road, Crosby. This is no time to get a track blown apart.'

'OK, sir,' said Crosby, and promptly swung *Avenger* to one side to overtake an inverted carrier.

The carrier was, of course, the one which had made the discovery that the road was mined. I leaned out of the turret anxious to see what sort of effect a Tellermine had on an infantry carrier.

I nodded gratefully to the benevolent spirit that looks after half-witted Troop Leaders, and dropped a bit lower in the turret for the rest of that journey.

The earphones crackling about my neck told me that all was going well at the head of the column. The enemy on our particular bit of front had apparently thought it wiser to retreat across the River Orne. But on our right, where Bob Webster of 'C' Squadron was leading the advance on a parallel road, they were meeting odd Spandau parties in what the communiqués blandly called 'pockets of resistance'. I gather Bob had quite an annoying trip. Every time he got his troop into a decent firing position, the enemy withdrew from the game and scurried back a bit further.

But we rolled peacefully on, and we began to see why Kent had been chosen for an invasion training ground. The orchard-dotted hills and the winding hedge-lined roads looked exactly like the country around Stone Street. Every minute we expected to round a corner and find a board proclaiming 'Teas, Light Refreshments, and Minerals', or to come in sight of a swinging sign saying 'The Ship and Shovel'. But we didn't. I don't know what the Calvados equivalents are of these signs, but we didn't see those, either. In fact we just had a nice ride in the country until we came in sight of the River Orne. And that started something.

Our bank of the river was peaceful and quiet and for the first time since leaving our original little field we were able to get out the tank bivouac and stretch our limbs in peaceful sleep.

The river here flowed along the bottom of a deep gorge, and the enemy on the other side seemed a long way away. But you never can tell with these things, so we duly posted guard tanks here and there.

Avenger was one of the guard tanks, which meant that throughout the hours of darkness the turret would be manned by a gunner and loader, both wide awake. These were not necessarily from Five Troop, and although we didn't very much care for the idea of aliens sitting in our turret, it was better than sitting up all night ourselves.

The first pair of sentries arrived just as we were settling down for the night, and with a contemptuous disregard for our paintwork they scrambled up the side of the tank into the turret.

'Hey! Watch what you're doing!' I said indignantly. 'We'll be using that tank for a long time yet.'

Which is just one more instance of my speaking too soon.

It is given to most of us to have some outstanding characteristic in which we are better than our fellow men. My brother, for instance, can flick a matchstick a greater distance, and with a greater degree of accuracy, than any man I know. Smith 161 could find aces in a face-down pack of cards with a facility which would have smacked of dishonesty under less keen eyes than Five Troop's.

My little party trick was revolver shooting.

And I learned this, too, the hard way.

Many years ago a painstaking sergeant in the Royal Tank Corps taught me how to use a revolver. This was in the leisurely days of 1936, when they trained you as a soldier for nine months before they admitted you were just beginning to learn. This particular sergeant was a humorous soul who used to take a chair leg with him to the 30-yards range. He would stand behind me (and other unwilling recruits) and would use the chair leg with good effect if I didn't hold the revolver butt in the correct manner, or if I pulled the trigger instead of squeezing it in the laid-down fashion. There must have been something in this method because we finished our training able to fire our revolver with considerable effect at thirty yards.

And it was a source of delight to Five Troop when I used to pick up the kitty at officers' revolver shoots on the ranges. I used to be very proud of this knack of mine.

Used to be.

Some people have fame thrust upon them, and this fancy business with the revolver resulted in a certain amount of fame being thrust upon me. I heard it whispered that the troops called me 'Deadshot Dick', and whenever they were talking about revolver shooting I would hang around on the outskirts of the group, pretending to be studying something in the middle distance. But much to my chagrin, I never had any concrete evidence of this nickname.

Until the night after the Orne crossing.

And the way of it was this.

The morning after our breath-taking dash to the Orne, Alan gathered us together and said that during the night the infantry had made a small bridgehead beyond the river. We were to go across and help them to break out of this bridgehead. And since the steep, wooded sides of the river gorge were pretty nearly impassable to tanks, the sappers were that moment building a Bailey bridge on the site of a stone bridge blown up by the retreating Germans.

It was believed that a pretty hefty number of Germans were located beyond the river, and the big idea was that our little operation would draw them away from the First Canadian Army who were advancing down the far bank of the Orne from Caen.

'More to the point if the Canadians drew them away from us,' grumbled Johnson. But I told him he couldn't always have a carefree drive like the previous day's, and if other people always had to do the actual fighting the rumour would get around that the enemy were avoiding us. And then, what would he say?

He told me, but I let it pass.

Because of our strenuous day leading the advance to the Orne, Five Troop were in reserve for this operation. Which meant we tailed along at the back until Alan remembered about us.

And then just as we were getting ready to move off a truck came roaring up from RHQ. Vaguely I wondered what it had brought, but Sergeant Atkins came running up to me, his thin face heavy with worry.

'Can you grab that truck before it goes back, sir?' he said.

'I expect so,' I said, climbing down from the tank. 'Why?'

'It's Worrall, my co-driver, sir.'

'What's the matter with Worrall?'

'He's been sick all night, sir. And this morning he looks like death. I think he'd better go back to RHQ for a bit of a rest.'

'But what'll you do without a co-driver?' I said.

He shrugged his shoulders.

'Better without one at all, than with Worrall in the shape he's in.'

'All right,' I sighed. 'I saw him yesterday munching apples in the front of *Alert* all day. If that's the cause of his trouble I'll give him more than belly ache.'

'So will I, sir,' said Sergeant Atkins darkly, as he turned away.

I walked up to where the truck was standing by Alan's tank, and a familiar Cockney voice hailed me.

'Wotcher, sir! Ow's the best troop in the regiment been gittin' on wivaht me?'

It was Farrell, minus appendix but as full of beans as ever. He was beaming all over his face as he told the tale of how he had cajoled and bullied his way right through all the reinforcement units up to the line.

'I know, Farrell,' Alan was saying patiently. 'But you can't get six men into a tank. Not and keep it in action, anyway. So be a good chap and go back to RHQ until we get a vacancy.'

I saw Farrell's face fall, and he drew a big, deep breath. Fearful of what he would say to Alan's well-meant suggestion I hastily broke the news about Worrall's sickness, and two minutes later Five Troop were roaring a ribald welcome to the little, swaggering man.

He took a dim view of the fact that I wouldn't turf young Hunter out of his seat in the front of *Avenger*, but with very good grace he condescended to act as co-driver and front gunner for Sergeant Atkins.

And then Alan shouted: 'Stand by to move!'

It was then about nine o'clock in the morning, and a very fine August morning it was, too. The birds sang lustily as we dropped down the steep and narrow road leading to the Bailey bridge. On the wooded banks towering behind us batteries of artillery (including lots of anti-tank guns) were being dug-in. I pointed this out to the crew.

'Those boys up there have got a grandstand view,' I said. 'If any enemy tank pokes his nose out of cover the other side of the river, he'll be picked off like a target on the pellet range.'

Which was all very comforting to think about, but it didn't turn out quite like that.

Over the Bailey bridge and up the not-so-tall bank the other side, and we found ourselves in the little hamlet of Brieux. The infantry had dug themselves in and we spread ourselves around the bridgehead perimeter and waited for things to happen.

It was very rolling country, dotted with small woods, cottages and deep valleys, all of which made visibility very tricky. Short bursts of firing told that some activity was going on somewhere, and from time to time a beaming infantryman would appear leading a couple of tousled prisoners.

We found ourselves a nice position behind a ridge of ground, so that only our turrets were visible to the enemy, and waited for orders. On the air I could hear Alan giving his orders to the other four troops who were to do the break-out with the infantry and all seemed to be settled except the actual time of start. I couldn't quite figure out the delay but it had something to do with the infantry wanting to consolidate a corner of the bridgehead before they launched themselves forward again.

But we were in reserve, and apart from trying to remember what everybody else was going to do in the forthcoming battle, I just kept my eyes scanning the countryside for likely targets.

And then to my surprise I saw one. About a hundred yards to our right six German soldiers suddenly stood up in the waist deep corn, and began to run away from us. *Alert* was right in my own line of fire and I was scrambling frantically for the selector knob to call up Sergeant Atkins on the 'B' set when I saw his turret swing sharply round.

'He's seen them,' I said to the crew. At least, I meant to, but Corporal Robinson told me afterwards that he heard this excited statement over the 'B' set.

I waited for *Alert*'s turret machine gun to rip off a few hundred rounds of ammunition. Instead I heard a solitary 'crack' followed by a loud stream of Preston profanity from Henry Westham. In the stillness which followed the single explosion, we could hear Long, *Alert*'s gunner, wrestling with the mechanism of his Besa, urged on in no uncertain manner by his tank commander and Henry Westham.

'Fire!' roared Sergeant Atkins.

'Crack!' went the Besa, doing a good imitation of a rifle.

'Driver start up!' yelled Sergeant Atkins, and I guessed he was going to advance to give Farrell a crack with the hull machine gun. Because of the ridge behind which we were sitting, Farrell, of course, had not been able to see the target yet.

And then a most astonishing thing happened; the six Germans turned about and came walking towards us, vigorously waving white handkerchiefs. We couldn't believe our eyes and wit great suspicion we watched them getting nearer and nearer until they were standing beside our tanks, looking up at us trustfully and still waving like mad their grubby pieces of white cloth.

Everybody seemed to be wanting for me to do something, so throwing caution to the winds I leaned out of the turret and pointed in the direction of the nearest infantry post.

'*Gehen sie das Weg*!' I said hopefully.

I'm not quite sure what I expected them to do, but nobody was more surprised than I when they dutifully trotted in the direction indicated.

Five Troop had taken its first prisoners. And from that day onward

Long, the gunner on *Alert*, was known as 'One Shot Long' – a soubriquet guaranteed to place his blood vessels in dire peril every time it was used.

The rest of the day wore on and we saw no more targets. The promised break-out had still not materialised and the only stir of interest was caused when a helpful RAF plane reported that the Forét de Grimbosgq, right opposite our position, was pretty well packed to bursting with enemy tanks and troops.

But I pointed confidently to the wooded heights behind us, and the masses of guns ranked in the trees, and told Five Troop to stop worrying.

Maybe I should have worried a bit more myself.

Eventually it was decided that the battle to enlarge the bridgehead would be launched at sunset, and the tanks taking part would be 'A' Squadron and 'C' Squadron. The remainder of the regiment were still on the other side of the Orne, helping to thicken up the umbrella of anti-tank guns.

Sunset, as I have pointed out, is one of the favourite times of launching an attack. Unhappily, it is a favouritism not confined to the British Army; the Germans, too, decided that that August sunset looked a pretty good time to launch an attack.

Now, in most military operations one side is usually attacking and the other, funnily enough, defending. The side which takes the initiative launches the attack, and their opponents sit tight in their defensive positions and try to fend off the onslaught. And after that may the best man win.

But when two sides simultaneously decide to attack, and both launch themselves forward from their defensive positions at more or less the same time – well, you get a battle of the River Orne. Like this.

The first indication we had that things might possibly go amiss was when we heard a well-known, very frightening, multiple shriek. It started with a series of explosions and high-pitched whines, then made a chromatic descent down the scale to end in a sequence of violent detonations. It was the German multi-barrel mortar, known fondly to the troops as 'Moaning Minnie'.

Instinctively we tensed ourselves and waited for the stuttering detonations which always followed a barrage from Moaning Minnie, but for a change the whines ended in a series of harmless-sounding plops. Sergeant Atkins looked across at me, and I looked back at him, and we both shrugged our shoulders.

Another chorus from Moaning Minnie rent the dusty air, and again it was followed by a noise like a lot of children's balloons bursting. And then I glanced over my shoulder and saw that the high ground beyond the Orne was swiftly and methodically being curtained off with dense white smoke.

'Hullo, Five Able and Baker,' I said over the 'B' set. 'Don't look now, but there's an awful lot of smoke going down behind us. Looks like we're being isolated from that curtain of steel I told you about. It's the usual prelude to an attack, but it may be just the enemy trying to confuse us.'

I tried to sound hopeful, but I didn't feel it.

Then we came in for some desultory shelling, which gradually increased as the minutes wore on and the sun sank lower behind us.

Soon the shelling and mortaring were pretty thick, and Five Troop had their engines running, ready for anything. Reports began to filter back that on one of the sectors some of the infantry thought they saw enemy tanks, but by that time our attack was just about to commence. The other four troops had left their defensive positions and were forming up with their allotted infantry, planning lines of advance and working out mutual targets.

This was the stage at which the 12th SS Panzer Division, supported by a company from a Heavy Tank Battalion, decide to wipe out our bridgehead.

The ground vibrated from the shelling and soon ominous clouds of flame-tinged black smoke rose up against the darkening sky. The crash and scream of armour-piercing projectiles echoed over the bridgehead, and incoherent reports over the 'A' set told of the bloody battle in progress, and the tale of death and destructions stalking about the fields around Brieux.

Duncan Watson's Troop Sergeant reported that his Troop Leader's tank was blazing furiously, and that the crew had been machine-gunned to death when they tried to bale out. Incoherent with rage, Mike Carter told briefly that both his sergeant and corporal were aflame, but his message was hard to decipher because his voice was drowned by the crash and stammer of his own guns.

Calmly and methodically Alan rallied the squadron, and told me to bring Five Troop up on the right of Brieux to see if we could catch the enemy in the flank.

'Wilco, out,' I said, and looking at Sergeant Atkins and Corporal Robinson. I received nods of the heads to show that they had picked up Alan's message.

That was about the last voice we heard over the air that day. Just as we climbed over the top of our ridge and advanced suspiciously forward, a loud shriek from the headphones nearly blew in my eardrums.

Cursing fluently, Pickford hurled himself at the radio set and juggled with the controls, but after a few minutes he shook his damp head and switched to IC.

'It's jamming, sir,' he said simply. 'The enemy have got on to our frequency and are transmitting a constant oscillation.'

Luckily the jamming didn't apply to the 'B' set, but I soon confirmed from *Alert* and *Angler* that their 'A' sets were out of action, too.

So we were on our own. And this time we really were up against a Panzer Division, plus a Heavy Tank Company.

The Panzer Division might not have been so bad; they were equipped with Panther tanks and by playing a fantastic game of 'touch' it was sometimes possible to catch them sideways on and knock them for six. But the Tigers of the Heavy Tank Company were a different kettle of fish altogether. I believe there were odd spots on them where the armour was thin enough to allow a 75-millimetre shell to penetrate, but these spots were harder to find than a needle in any haystack I've seen.

We came to a fold in the ground, and here we halted to see what we could see. And what we saw was this.

Ahead of us were the ruined houses of the village of Grimbosq, and crossing a field to the right of the village were a string of tank turrets. For a minute I couldn't make this out, and then I realised they were motoring down a sunken road. I don't know how many there were, but we loosed off a few round at them, without seeming to do any good, and then an awful lot of enemy turrets started swinging round in our direction.

'Enough's as good as a feast,' I murmured. 'Put down smoke.'

The three of us fired our tiny two-inch smoke bombs, and under cover of this vest-pocket screen we swung around in a wide left-hand circle, finishing up behind a ridge some five hundred yards back and left of our firing position.

I trained my binoculars on the spot we had just left, to see fountains of turf being thrown into the air as scores of armour-piercing shells tore through the remains of our smoke and into the ground.

A few disorganised remnants of infantry went scurrying past us, and from them I gathered that the slaughter in their particular company had been terrible.

We saw a group of German infantry advancing in battle order, and gave them a longish burst of machine gun fire, but they swiftly dived for cover and a few moments later more AP shells were screaming about our ears.

So back we dodged again, and then as we drew level with the hamlet of Brieux again I saw Alan's tank parked near the crossroads. This was a heaven-sent chance to try and find out what the situation was, so committing *Avenger* to Pickford's care I ran across to Alan's tank.

'Hullo, John,' he said quietly. 'Bit sticky, isn't it? Duncan and Hobby have had it, and quite a few chaps in "C" Squadron. I'm just swanning around trying to get the battle organised, but they've rather caught us with our pants down.'

I was to remember that phrase later.

'Any gen?' I said.

'It's these bloody Tigers are the trouble,' he said. 'The Panthers keep well behind 'em, but I believe we've managed to brew up a couple of the sods. As far as I can gather there's one particular Tiger being a thorough nuisance. He just ambles forward rolling everything before him and ignoring all we can chuck at him. See if you can do a right flanker on him.'

'Thanks, pal,' I said, cocking an eyebrow at him. 'And then what?'

He thought about this for a minute and then said: 'I think it will probably finish up with us fighting with our backs to the Orne. I can't see a hope of getting any ammo or petrol tonight, so if you run dry and have to bale out, make sure your tank isn't any good to the enemy when you leave it.'

By now there was hardly any light left at all. The first thing McGinty said to me when I got back to *Avenger* was that looking through his telescope was like looking through a keyhole of a dark room. But I didn't answer him.

Dead ahead of us, and trundling slowly across our front, was an enormous Tiger tank.

And then I saw that for about half his height he was protected by a thick stone wall, and was advancing along the far side of it. He hadn't seen us, and to try and engage him through that wall would have been asking too much of our 75-millimetre guns.

Fascinated I watched the Tiger swing left at a crossroads and head down towards the bridge. Somebody had told me that those things have 32 different gears, and even above the din of the battlefield I fancied I could hear the German driver ringing the changes up and down his gearbox as he manoeuvred his monstrous vehicle around the corners.

'Now what the hell is he up to?' I muttered to myself, and then like a burst of white light in my brain I suddenly thought of a wonderful plan.

The Tiger was, I surmised, going for the bridge. The way I reckoned it, that's what I would have tried to do in his place. Once astride the Bailey bridge, the rest of the attacking force could reduce the bridgehead at their leisure, for there was no other way for vehicles across the canyon-like sides of the Orne.

The road leading from the crossroads down to the bridge passed between a little row of detached cottages. It seemed to me that if I could lie in ambush for him in one of those gaps between the cottages, I could pump shells into his side as he rumbled past. But time was precious; already he was nearer to the cottages than I was, and the planning of a troop action would have taken vital seconds.

'Driver advance!' I yelled, and there must have been some urgency in my voice because instantly Crosby had *Avenger* rumbling forward.

'Drive left... OK.... Speed up... Now, flat out for those cottages!'

Tracks clattering madly we rushed across the open ground. Head and shoulders out of the turret I turned to look back at *Alert* and

Angler, and held up my hand in a Highway Code halt sign. I hoped they would gather from this that I wanted them to stay where they were – this, rightly or wrongly, was to be a one-tank show.

'Driver left… Halt! Gunner, stand by!'

We were in position, about forty yards from the road. The Tiger had not yet gone by, but a little way up the road to the right I could see the cottages vibrating from the passage of the super-heavy tank.

'It'll all depend on you, Pickford,' I told the perspiring operator across the turret from me. 'The quicker you can load, the more shots we'll get off.'

He nodded to show he understood, and McGinty cuddled closer into his telescope.

I saw the front of the Tiger's track starting to cross the gap – and then I was staring straight down the barrel of an indecently long 88-millimetre gun. He hadn't been going for the bridge at all; he had been coming after us.

The tank commander of the Tiger must have thought we were still in our defensive position some way back, because in the brick-dust and smoke he didn't see us at first. My entrails turned to ice as I stared at the heavily armoured front of the Tiger. And then I yelled 'Fire!'

McGinty fired, and even before the gun had run back into its mounting, Pickford had slammed home another shell and the breech had clanged shut.

'Fire!' I yelled again, and this time I watched the white-hot tracer from our gun smack straight into the front plate of the Tiger, and go soaring up into the sky like a penny rocket.'Fire!' I yelled again.

'They're bouncing off, sir!' shouted McGinty, as he fired for the third time. I knew of course that our little gun wasn't supposed to be able to penetrate the front armour of a Tiger, but I thought that at that incredibly short range it would be bound to have some effect.

I decided to have one more crack at him, and if he didn't brew up then, to put some smoke and get to hell out of it. If he'd let me. And he didn't!

McGinty had just got off the third round when the Tiger gunner recovered from his surprise. I was peering forward through the gloom when suddenly, and without any noise that I can remember, a sharp spike of yellow flame stabbed out of the muzzle of the 88mm gun in front of us.

Sparks flew from the front of *Avenger*, and she reared back on her hind sprockets, the nose lifting slightly off the ground.

A sudden heat singed the back of my neck and a rapid glance over my shoulder showed flames and smoke pouring from the engine hatches.

'Bale out – round the back of the tank!' I hollered, and snatching off my headset I dived from the turret straight to the ground.

Crosby, Pickford, and McGinty joined me as a second shell crashed through the length of the tank and into the engine compartment.

Feverishly I looked around for some sort of cover, and a shallow, saucer-like depression in the ground some distance away was the only thing I could see.

'Into that hole over there. Move!' I said, and keeping bent double we ran across and into the hollow.

Then I realised one of us was missing.

'Where the hell's young Hunter?' I said.

'E's 'ad it, zur,' said a white and shaken Crosby.

'How do you know?' I rapped, standing up.

'I went to 'elp 'im out, and 'e 'adn't got any 'ead, zur!'

'Christ!' I said, and looked back at *Avenger*. She was blazing furiously from stem to stern, and even as I looked one of the petrol tanks exploded with a blinding white flash.

I crouched down again, and it was at that moment that my braces chose to break and it looked as if I was about to achieve military immortality by exemplifying the phrase 'being caught with one's trousers down'.

Pickford lent me one of the safety pins he used to keep his chevron on his sleeve, and sitting there in that hollow with the enemy practically at our elbows I carried out some essential maintenance.

I knelt up to spy out the land again, and McGinty touched me gently and wordlessly pointed to my leg. My denim trousers were slashed across the thigh and on the exposed white flesh a long, thin, gash was slowly oozing blood. I hadn't noticed it until then, and even when McGinty pointed it out I still didn't feel anything. Perhaps that was because at that moment a rapid burst of fire crackled over our heads from the Tiger's supporting infantry. It looked as if they'd got us bottled up in that hollow and I really feared the worst. But I reckoned without *Avenger*.

A kindly gust of wind blew a thick column of black smoke from the burning tank, straight over the ground in a beautiful smokescreen leading towards the river.

'Come on,' I said. 'This is no place for us.'

The dense columns of smoke from the burning tank gave us enough cover to get away from that spot and into the comparative shelter of a low, brick wall. I glanced quickly around. The last rays of the setting sun shone redly above the high ground bordering the Orne.

Mindful of the fact that my crew had been cooped up inside the tank all day, and therefore had no idea of direction, I said to Pickford: 'I'm going to find *Alert* and *Angler*. Just keep heading into the sun until you come to the river, and once across the river you're OK.'

But finding the other two tanks of my troop was easier said than done. With commendable presence of mind, Sergeant Atkins had taken command of the troop as soon as he saw *Avenger* blow up, and had taken his own tank and *Angler* around in a wide sweep to engage the enemy from another flank.

Ten yards from the brick wall it became abundantly clear that there were a lot of Germans between me and two-thirds of my troop. And if I didn't do something about it, there looked like being another lot between the other third and the river.

So I returned to the wall and collected my crew and together we edged our way in what I hoped was the direction of the Bailey bridge.

We found the road leading down to the bridge, and were making our way along the hedge which bordered it when suddenly there came a crashing from the hedge some way in front of us, and two hefty German infantrymen pushed their way through, carrying a Spandau machine gun between them. They were so close that we heard one of them swearing in German as the hawthorn spikes caught at his clothes.

In the same instant we saw why they had crashed through the hedge; an infantry carrier, loaded with grim-looking soldiers of the

Norfolks, clattered up the road going towards Brieux. This heartened me considerably, for it pointed to the fact that the two merchants in front of us were not part of a larger body, but just two of those engaging types known as 'infiltrators'.

They hadn't seen us yet, and hoping to be thrice armed by getting my blow in first I shakily drew my revolver and blazed three rounds off at the two Germans. They looked around and saw us for the first time, and their faces were almost comical in their expressions of bewildered panic. Nothing daunted, I let them have the other three rounds in the chamber of my revolver, and with a loud wail of dismay they dropped their Spandau, bolted back through the hole in the hedge, and legged it like mad across country.

Filled with elation at my unexpected victory I blew down the muzzle of my revolver in approved cowboy fashion and stuffed it back in my holster.

'That fixed them!' I said with a Western drawl, and it wasn't till I'd started to swagger forward again that I realised I'd missed a target as big as a couple of barn doors. Deadshot Dick, indeed! I pulled in my legs and pushed on towards the river.

The general battle for the bridgehead was now in what the military commentators call a state of fluidity. To our right and left I could hear the firing of German Spandaus, but here and there the slower and more deliberate firing of Bren guns told of bitter resistance being offered to the enemy.

A full moon now rode in the August sky and by the light of this, and in the fitful glare of burning tanks, we came to the top of the steep bank of the Orne.

I looked down at the dappled water, and could see little spurts shooting up from the surface, just as if it was raining. Only it wasn't raining.

'Come on: we'll cross under the bridge,' I said. And so we slipped and slithered diagonally down the bank until we came to the Bailey bridge, and beneath the protection of this we crossed the river, with the cool water swirling about our waists.

On the far side of the river a solitary tank of 'B' Squadron stood, doing a Horatius act in pregnant silence.

The commander of this tank couldn't tell us any news, except that quite a lot of de-horsed members of 'A' Squadron had got back across the river and were now making their way back to RHQ.

I asked if we could help him in any way, but he shook his head and seemed only to want to get rid of us.

That was a reception we kept meeting: I took my tired crew along to the nearest infantry post, and offered our services as temporary infantry, if the situation was pretty bad. But we were politely thanked and sent on our way.

At RHQ everybody was too busy planning the restoration of the situation beyond the river, and after a few words of formal commiseration, we were sent on our way to the Tank Delivery Squadron – a sort of mobile home for spare tanks and spare crews, but one which served a vital purpose in providing reinforcements when most urgently needed.

We were tank crews without tanks, and nobody wanted us.

SIX

TIRED AND DISHEARTENED we toiled up the hills rolling back from the Orne. My wet trousers clung coldly to my legs, and the scratch across my thigh was beginning to ache. I was dirty, sore-eyed, half-deafened by the noise we had gone through and bitterly miserable over the death of gay, enthusiastic young Hunter. Yet I thought that death had come to him kindly; like a playful child tiptoeing into a room while your back's turned, and suddenly switching out the light. I judged that the first shell had entered our front plate opposite his neck, cutting off his life in an infinitesimal fraction of a second.

And I wondered dully what had happened to Sergeant Atkins and Corporal Robinson. I wondered whether I had been right to sally forth in single combat, instead of keeping the troop together as a troop. Usually I am pretty good at being wise after the event, but now the event was over and I was still no wiser than I had been before.

Through the fog of self-analysis my brain picked up the conversation behind me and when I looked around I saw the pocket-sized McGinty trudging along with his hands thrust deep into his pockets. He was talking to 'Bing' Crosby.

'Bouncing off, they were,' he said bitterly. 'Bouncing off like peas off a flippin' drum!'

It seemed to me that Five Troop morale was in danger of sinking to an all-time low, so I dropped back and joined in the conversation.

'What's the matter, McGinty?' I said.

He kicked a stone idly and muttered under his breath. Then he said: 'Didn't somebody in Parliament the other day say that our tanks were every bit as good as the Germans?'

'I believe he did,' I said. 'But it's not the sort of thing you can generalise about like that. Some of our tanks are better in some respect than some of the German tanks, and vice versa.'

'What have we got that will knock out a Tiger?' he said.

'The seventeen-pounder Sherman,' I said. 'And the Firefly SP gun. Besides, we've got the RAF on our side with their rocket-firing Typhoons. They make a hell of a mess of a Tiger.'

But he wasn't convinced.

We had collected quite a few stragglers at RHQ, and as we plodded through the dust McGinty and I became the centre of an attentive group of dirty, dishevelled tank crewmen.

'And what have we got that'll keep out an eighty-eight, in the same way that they can keep out our seventy-fives?' was the next question.

I racked my brains but couldn't think of anything off-hand, and I wished I had one of those clever articles from the 'ARMY QUARTERLY' in which ballistic experts proved by numbers that we had better tanks and guns than the enemy.

'Look,' I said gently. 'You're a gunner, and you know that a hell of a lot depends on the angle of impact. An armour-piercing shell will bounce off water if it hits it at the right angle.'

'A seventy-five will bounce off the front of a Tiger from any bloody angle,' he said stubbornly.

McGinty had always been pretty punctilious about his 'sirs', and I could tell this thing had really upset him. His next remark confirmed this.

'Next time we meet the bastards I'm going to bale out and climb into their turret with a bayonet. Do a damn sight more good!'

'That's no way to talk,' I said sternly. 'Pull yourself together, man, God! You've got a thick wedge of armour plate in front of you – well, fairly thick, anyway. It'll keep out a hell of a lot of stuff the Germans try to throw at us, so don't get a what'sit about the wretched eighty-eight. What about the poor bloody infantry? They go into action with nothing but their uniforms between them and all kinds of unpleasantness!'

'Yes, sir,' said McGinty quietly. 'But what would the infantry do if they were sent into action with rifles which wouldn't penetrate the enemy's uniforms?'

'If I know anything about our infantry, they'd go into action just the same, doing the best they could. And that's what we'll do too, as soon as we get the chance,' I said.

Even to my ears this sounded a pretty pompous remark and I was glad the argument was brought to an abrupt halt by a yell from an adjoining field. It was Pat Baker (who had taken over second-in-command of the squadron after Jim Steward had been wounded) together with another large batch of stragglers, including, to my huge relief, Corporal Robinson and his entire crew.

But Corporal Robinson had grievous news.

'I think Sergeant Atkins has had it, sir,' he said. 'I saw him brew up but I couldn't do anything about it because I was up to my ears in a battle myself. I believe he's caught a pretty bad wound, and I've heard that his crew flogged all over the bridgehead until they found a stretcher so they could carry him out, even though Westham and Worrall were wounded, too.'

We marched stolidly on towards the Forward Delivery Squadron, and he told me how Sergeant Atkins had led him from the perilous position in which I had last seen them, to well inside the defended perimeter of the bridgehead. And he told how, bit by bit the enemy had reduced odd sectors of the bridgehead by flinging bitter attacks at them again and again.

'I don't know what hit *Angler*, sir,' he confessed frankly. 'I was taking on a couple of Panthers who were dodging in and out of Brieux, and the next thing I knew something caught me in the flank and we brewed right away. Judging by the bang it made as it went in I should say it was a bazooka, but I didn't see any Jerry infantry near us.'

I told him about our meeting with the infiltrators, and he said maybe *Angler* had met its end at the hands of a couple of similar characters, but he seemed too mentally stunned to take part in any detailed post-mortem.

Pat Baker, too, had news. In his low, cultured voice, like a BBC announcer describing the stage settings during an opera, he told how Alan and he had fought a rearguard action until their two tanks were almost falling backwards down the sheer sides of the Orne ravine. And how Alan had then calmly destroyed his own tank and set about collecting survivors of the squadron and taking them across the river.

'Where's Alan now?' I said.

'He stayed at RHQ to meet stragglers,' said Pat. 'He arranged for Sergeant Atkins to be evacuated, and the rest of his crew, too. They were in a pretty rough way.'

'I'll bet they were, too,' I said.

Better soldiers than Pat and I would have formed up the de-horsed tank crews and made them march to the FDS, but we were both full of our own thoughts, and the long line of straggling survivors were allowed to make their own way along the signed route we were following.

The Forward Delivery Squadron, bless their hearts, made us warmly welcome. Despite the fact that it was an ungodly early hour, they fed us and gave us a hot drink, tended to my scratched leg and found us somewhere to sleep.

It was a stifling hot night so we needed no cover apart from a blanket. Pat and I saw the men roll in their blankets and settle down in the lee of a hedge. And then we did likewise.

And then began one of the most frightening episodes of the whole day.

Suddenly, through the starry silence of the night, a raucous voice cried:

'Joe! Hey, Joe! Joe, where are you?'

There was a spine-chilling, unearthly quality about that disembodied voice, and I felt the skin on my back starting to twitch.

'Joe! Joe! Answer me, you silly sod! Christ, Joe! Where are you?'

I raised myself on one elbow and looked at Pat. He was sound asleep.

And then another, squeakier voice joined in.

''Ave we got any dog buscuits left, 'Arry? This is a right bloody muck-up, I must say.'

I sank back on to the rolled-up jacket I was using as a pillow. It was the over-wrought tank crews talking in their sleep. But although I now knew what it was, it was still an awesome experience to be there and hear these mechanical voices recounting episodes from their subconscious minds.

'I reckon we should get the freedom of Canada for drawing this lot off,' said a drowsy voice from the end of the group.

'Gimme that bit o' waste, Sam. No, not that one you clot. The other!'

And so it went on, occasionally punctuated by ribald bursts of song.

And then I heard Lance-Corporal Pickford.

In a crystal-clear, disdainful voice which crushed my ego like an eggshell, he said, 'Deadshot Dick!'

The next morning things began to sort themselves out. There was much to be done: new tanks to take over and prepare for action. New kit to be collected. Replacements to obtain for casualties. And as we worked we heard that the 12th SS Panzer Division (plus their Heavy Tank Company) had failed in their task of eliminating the bridgehead.

We heard, for example, how Mike Carter had found a largish hollow, and turned it into a citadel, collecting into it all the leaderless infantry he could find, plus the few battle worthy tanks in his bit of the bridgehead. And how he launched savage counterattacks from the hollow, at one time standing on top of his turret with a Sten gun hurling abuse at the enemy as he mowed them down.

(Personally, the sound of Mike's bull-like voice from the top of a turret would be enough to scare me, without the Sten gun).

And we heard how, on another part of the bridgehead, a Captain in the Norfolks, supported by a single Troop Sergeant's tank from 'C' Squadron, had fought a bitter and determined defensive action all through the night, going over to the attack as soon as dawn broke.

And we also heard how, thanks to the southward advance of the Canadians from Caen, the majority of the enemy had to withdraw from the bridgehead, allowing 'B' Squadron to cross the river next morning and, despite a lot of unpleasant hazards from mines and snipers, restore the bridgehead to its former area.

And then another regiment went in, and the advance went on.

A few days later we were back on the other side of the Orne, and we came across the reddened, burned-out hulk that had been *Avenger*.

Sadly we shook our heads, and climbed over the ruins pointing out to one another where the shells had finished up.

Suddenly, with a puzzled look on his face, Pickford produced a length of string from his pocket. He tied one end of it to the hole in the front mantlet where the first shot had come in and killed young Hunter. And he tied the other end of it to the hole in the engine bulkhead door where the shell had burst through and started the blaze.

The string passed through the co-driver's narrow compartment, through the tiny space below McGinty's armpit where his right arm stretched out and down to the pistol-grip of the gun, through my groin and into the bulkhead door.

We stared at this phenomenon for a few minutes and couldn't make it out at all. There was no doubt about the fact that I had been on my pedestal when the shot entered; there was equally no doubt about the fact that my groin was quite unpunctured; yet the string which traced the path of the shot was there before our eyes as mute proof that I ought to be grievously wounded.

Even if I squeezed myself as far over to the left as possible, the shot would still have carved a hefty lump out of my right leg; and as far as I could remember I was standing up fairly straight.

The whole thing was so incredible that when I chanced to be at Brigade Headquarters later that day I sought out the ammunition expert and told him of the astonishing behaviour of the Tiger's shell.

'Nothing amazing about it, old boy,' he said professionally. 'An armour-piercing shot does unpredictable things once it has penetrated a piece of armour plate. The spin on the projectile causes it to deviate from a true straight line. I've known a shot enter a tank hull and charge round and round inside, chewing up the whole crew. You were just lucky, that's all. Yours made a curved path through the air and by-passed you.'

And then I thought of the gash across my thigh.

'It didn't quite miss me, come to think of it,' I said. 'But I don't want them any closer.'

And I nodded a grateful acknowledgement to the same benevolent spirit who had defused the anti-personnel bomb outside Villers Bocage.

Five Troop re-joined the regiment somewhere west of Falaise, where we found them in a pleasant hay field busily reorganising themselves after the depredations of the Orne and subsequent minor operations.

The officer who had given me the rocket for not saluting at Westgate was back as our Commanding Officer, his predecessor having been evacuated as a result of a mortar wound.

A complete squadron came to us from one of the disbanded Churchill regiments, and was henceforth known as 'C' Squadron.

Bob Webster joined us and took over Hobby's old troop, and Harry Langton arrived to take Duncan Watson's place.

Corporal Robinson pinned up a third stripe and became Five Troop Sergeant, and a young and cheerful laddie known as Watson arrived as our Troop Corporal.

We were given a fortnight in which to lick our wounds and prepare for the fray once more. As soon as Five Troop heard that we had a definite promise to remain in that nice field for two weeks, they started to pack their kits straight away, since it is axiomatic that such a promise is hotly followed by orders to move. But this time no such orders arrived, and for fourteen days we busied ourselves preparing the new *Avenger*, *Alert* and *Angler*, and in exploring the surrounding countryside. We found a little farmhouse where, for a few francs, we were given the most gigantic and feather-light omelette I have ever seen. This did much to convince Five Troop that maybe, after all, there was something in all this talk about French cooking. And it also helped to raise their morale.

But what did their hearts a great deal more good was a tour of the area known as the Falaise pocket. Here the fleeing Germans had been trapped in a ring of steel and pounded mercilessly by our guns and the rockets of the RAF. It was an unsavoury sight, but McGinty's eyes glinted happily as he surveyed the scorched and shattered Tigers and Panthers with which the roads were littered.

After spending a day picking our way over brewed-up enemy vehicles, and shuddering slightly at the mounds of dead men and horses slowly being cleared away by unhappy looking POWs, we returned to our field full of confidence once more. There couldn't be much wrong with an army who could do that to its opponents.

Fourteen glorious, sunny August days and nights.

I beg your pardon – thirteen nights. It rained one night, and again I learned a few facts. The hard way, I mean.

It was about this time that our rear party from England finally caught up with us, bringing such luxuries as batmen, camp kit, best battledresses, and so forth.

I welcomed my camp-bed with open arms. The earth had provided me with a good enough bed in many ways, but I have never claimed to be one of those tough, manly characters who throw wide their chests and proclaim that there's nothing they like better than to roll in a blanket (preferably a thin one) and curl up to sleep on the bosom of Mother Earth.

Give me a camp-bed every time. Or nearly every time.

The first time I erected the camp-bed in the tank bivouac I came in for a certain amount of raillery from the crew.

'That bed of yours takes up 'arf the bivvy, sir!' said Farrell. 'You want to let us up on there, an' you come dahn 'ere!'

'In future I shall give my orders from up here,' I said, stretching out on the bed. 'What they call high level decisions.'

'What, noa satin sheets and silk pyjamas, zur?' grinned Crosby.

'I shall wear pyjamas tonight,' I said simply. 'And if there's any rudery from you lot we'll do a bit of track changing in the morning!'

A groan went up from *Avenger*'s crew when I mentioned this most-hated-of-all maintenance task.

'The sooner they open up the Officers' Mess again, the sooner I'll be able to turn over in my sleep,' McGinty said *sotto voce* to Pickford.

This was a bit of clairvoyance on his part, but he didn't know it; next day the Quartermaster produced a small tent for use as officers' sleeping quarters. And nobody cheered louder than Five Troop.

The camp bed turned out to be just too long to fit completely into the bivouac. About six inches protruded beyond the eaves of the canvas. But I didn't mind that – it only meant sleeping with my knees drawn up a little way, I thought.

It was delicious to be able to have a real bath. Well, fairly real, anyway; it was a canvas portable affair, but a considerable improvement on the groundsheet-lined holes in the ground we had used previously. And after my bath I put on my much maligned pyjamas and settled down in my lovely camp bed.

Some people have it that after you've slept on the ground for some time, you can't get used to sleeping in a bed again. Don't you believe it. I got used to sleeping in that bed in five minutes flat.

It was the early hours of the morning when I was awakened by the sound of rain on the bivouac roof; heavy rain, too. But I knew we had a sound, waterproof shelter so I rolled over on my bed and drifted peacefully off to sleep again, to the soporific effect of the drumming of rain about my head. But not for long.

I was awakened again by the horrid suspicion that I was damp. In a panic I seized my torch and shone it on the bivouac roof; it was intact and bone dry. Warily I reached out and felt the top of my blankets. They, too, were bone dry.

'Imagination,' I thought. 'Not used to sleeping in a comfortable bed.'

And I closed my eyes once more and listened to the rain.

Next time I woke up I was quite sure I was damp; in fact I was exceedingly wet. Yet again my torch revealed a perfectly dry bivouac roof and dehydrated blankets on top of me, and then I realised that the wetness was underneath me, and that I was laying in a pool of cold water.

'Damn! The bivvy's flooded,' I muttered, and shone my torch down to the floor. The four members of my crew were snoring lustily, rolled in dry blankets and laying on sun-baked grass without a trace of water.

I was just beginning to have suspicions that somebody was being funny with a jug of water, when I saw the foot of my camp bed. The six inches which were sticking out beyond the side of the bivouac were making an excellent catchment area for the rainwater pouring down the roof. And my weight on the canvas mattress of the bed was turning it into a boat shaped receptacle; so that the rain hit the roof of the bivouac, rolled down on to the foot of the camp bed, and then rolled back underneath my blankets. And my back, behind and legs were soaking wet.

No sooner had I made this discovery than Farrell sat up in his blankets and stared sleepily at me.

'Wassermarrersir?' he said.

Briefly and pointedly I told him, and then waited for the peals of laughter. But he didn't laugh.

Instead he was instantly wide awake, and he said:

'Chuck that ruddy fing ahtside, sir. Ere, wake up you blokes; I want a blanket from each of yer. Mister Foley's flippin' wet.'

Despite my protestations they salvaged the dry blankets from the top of my bed, pitched the bed unceremoniously out into the rain, and ten minutes later I was wearing my shirt and pants and crawling into a nest of blankets. On the ground.

'Oh well,' I thought, as I settled down yet again. 'I'll catch it from the humorists in the troop tomorrow. The Troop Leader who put the foot of his bed out into the rain – hell! It sounds like a Bateman cartoon.'

But I was wrong. Next morning Crosby started up his engine and dried my pyjamas in the hot blast from the rear air vents, while the other two tanks did the same with my blankets and camp bed.

I suppose this is where I ought to say something about hearts of gold beneath rough exteriors. So let it be said.

* * *

'Dear Mrs. Atkins,' I wrote.

By now you will have received officially the grievous news of Tom's death as a result of the wounds he received in action. This letter is to tell you how terribly upset we all were when we heard the news, and how very much we shall miss him in the troop. You know better than I what a tower of strength he was in emergencies; but as his Troop Leader and, I hope, his friend, I would like you to know that he was one of the most popular NCOs in the regiment and the troop thought the world of him.

I feel sure that, at this terrible time, you would not wish to know all the harrowing details of exactly how he came to be wounded, but I can assure you he fought bravely and well that day, and had it not been for him and others like him the history of the war may well have taken a different course, and things might have gone badly for England.

I know I speak for the whole troop when I ask you to accept our deepest sympathy in your grievous loss. If there is anything I can do at all to help you during this trying time, I do hope you will let me know.

Yours very sincerely.

I read it over and didn't like it very much, but there didn't seem to be any words to express the gloom which had fallen over Five Troop since we heard that the indomitable Sergeant Atkins had died. It was just not conceivable that his tall, sparse figure would no longer stalk amongst

Five Troop, alternately encouraging and brow-beating the men into achieving the results we wanted. I found it hard to believe that never again would I look back over the tail of *Avenger* and see his thinly chiselled features and pencil-line moustache above the turret hatch of *Alert*.

But I heaved a sigh, signed my name to the letter and stuck down the flap.

Footsteps approached me over the grass, and I looked up to see Alan's bulbous form rolling towards me.

He sat down on the grass and lit one of his inevitable cigarettes, and for a time we talked about the squadron and Five Troop in particular. And for the hundredth time we went over the disastrous Battle of the River Orne.

'I don't want any more parties like that,' I said. 'But I expect we'll have some.'

'*You* might, John,' he said with a grin, as he stood up and brushed the bits of grass off his trousers. 'I'm off to command HQ Squadron tomorrow.'

We were all sorry to see Alan go, but we agreed he deserved a change. The enemy had been shooting at him ever since the first advance to Benghazi, and now it was time he had a slightly less hazardous job. He went to Headquarter's Squadron, charged with many important administrative jobs such as getting petrol and ammunition up to wherever the tanks needed it. And he never once failed us in this.

To command our squadron in his place came Ian Bates, a very different sort of man but very likable, too. He was tall, tanned, brown-haired, and spaniel-eyed, and with a warming, lopsided grin. He seemed to be very slightly round-shouldered, and as he mooched around Squadron Headquarters he gave you the impression of being slow – until you remembered his reputation as a rugger wing three quarter.

Our fourteen days was nearing its end when another member joined the squadron – Jim Steward, back once again with his wound mended, as far as any of us could see, none the worse for the sniper's joke.

So we were all set for another brush with the enemy – and it wasn't long coming.

On our maps we had watched the Allied armies sweeping forward triumphantly, and Five Troop were already talking hopefully of being home for Christmas. I told them I thought they were being a bit optimistic, but they pointed out that they were always careful not to mention any specific Christmas.

And on our maps we noticed that the advancing forces were by-passing certain heavily-fortified places; and we judged that the reduction of these would be our next task.

We were right. And it was to be Le Havre.

But Le Havre was some distance away from our field at Falaise, and speculation was rife as to how we would get there. The favourite bet was that we would be carried on tank transporters and although this was undoubtedly the most comfortable and easiest method of getting a regiment of tanks from one place to another, we were all hoping that we would be allowed to move on our own tracks. Even the drivers were keeping their fingers crossed about this, although it would mean a long, dirty, and tiring day for them.

Just why this should be, I don't know, but I remember Crosby's face lighting up like a torch when I told him we would be driving to Le Havre under our own steam. And I warned him it would be hard work.

So it was, but as the miles rolled by beneath our tracks we hardly noticed them because for the first time we were experiencing the tumultuous welcome which the people of France extended to their liberators. We felt a bit guilty about this, since tanks other than ours had done the actual liberating, but the French people didn't seem to mind so we didn't either.

The pavements of villages and towns were packed with wildly cheering people, showering us with flowers and fruit and bottles of wine. Once we were held up at a crossroads in Rouen and with a happy disregard for the celibate life the men had led since landing in Normandy unselfconscious young ladies swarmed all over the tanks and crews.

On top of *Angler's* turret, Trooper Cooper had a mademoiselle kissing him on either cheek, and he was blushing as furiously as a schoolboy being seen off at a station by an over-amorous mother.

So it was with some relief that I saw the column roll forward again. It had seemed like hours, yet in fact it had only been a few minutes.

Nevertheless, a fortnight later I was censoring letters from Trooper Cooper to an address in Rouen.

Ragged urchins kept pace with the tanks, screaming 'Chocolat! Cigarette pour Papa!' and the good-humoured troops showered them with boiled sweets, the unsweetened chocolate from their rations, and ribald remarks about how they would only give cigarettes to their fathers (or possibly their elder sisters).

And so in due course we came to a village a few miles east of Le Havre, and here we swung into a field on top of a hill, wondering what the next day held for us.

And there, for the first time since leaving Lee-on-Solent, we slept in a building. True, it was only a stone floored, single-roomed building; but it was a pointer towards better things to come.

SEVEN

THE ASSAULT ON Le Havre was to be more the sort of thing for which we had trained. Quite different from our 'pursuit' from Villers Bocage.

At the risk of this sounding like a military textbook (which Heaven forbid) it would be as well if I explained that there are two jobs for which tanks are considered to be the right tools. One is the short, set-piece attack, in which you are given an objective not very far away but pretty heavily defended. The other is the disorganising, long sweeps behind the enemy lines, playing havoc with his bases and lines of communication and generally getting as far as you can, as fast as you can.

The first of these jobs was the sort of thing we liked, because each of these tasks requires a different technique, different equipment and, I maintain, a different personality on the part of the tank crews.

Personally, I would much rather be shown a hill, say, a thousand yards away, and told that once I'd reached the top of that hill the job was over – although the ground between was stiff with defence works and hateful devices to stop us reaching that hill.

I have an inherent loathing of dashing madly through enemy-held territory for mile after mile, never knowing which bend in the road conceals an anti-tank ambush, and expecting any moment to hear that you've been cut off from your own supplies and the enemy were just sitting back waiting for you to run out of petrol.

This is a gross case of over-simplification, I know. But it will give you the rough idea.

And, of course, it's only fair to tell you that I've met lots of chaps in Armoured Divisions who take exactly the opposite view, and who would much rather do a mad dash across Europe than plough their way slowly and steadily through a heavily defended locality.

So there you are.

And there we were, sitting on a hill outside Le Havre and wondering how hard we would have to persuade the garrison to surrender.

Hardly had we switched off our engines before Ian Bates called the Troop Leaders together and told us we were going for a short walk to examine the enemy defences.

I asked if this was with the enemy's consent, and were we expecting any Germans to arrive to examine our Churchills, but it only seemed to draw a forced laugh from the other Troop Leaders. And then I saw one of the Defence Overprint maps and understood why.

These Defence Overprint maps were magnificent things produced by the Ordnance chaps practically as you went into battle. They were large scale maps of the battle area, and clearly printed in blue was the location of every field-gun, anti-tank gun, minefield, rifle and machine gun pit, barbed wire entanglement, and concrete obstacle. The blue printing pointed out where the anti-tank ditches ran, and where the concrete dugouts were situated. They described the state of the ground, and practically gave you a weather forecast.

They were a great help, but sometimes a bit frightening.

The one for Le Havre seemed just a solid mass of blue, and although we had been banking hopefully on the fact that most of the town's defences ought to have been sited to cover a seaborne attack, it looked from the map as if the enemy had known all along just which way we would come.

However, we fell in in single file behind Ian and made our way towards the town.

It was hilly country, and we dropped down into valleys and climbed up hillsides until at last we stood in a small copse on top of a hill. Here we got down on our bellies, discovered that tank suits were not strictly designed for crawling on the ground, and wriggled painfully forward until we reached the front edge of the wood.

Below us lay a large plateau guarding the eastern outskirts of the town. And in our binoculars we could see just what we would be up against the next day. It looked pretty formidable, and I thought we were in for another sticky party. So did the others, and we were all a bit thoughtful as we made our way back to the tank harbour.

I was discussing with Tony Cunningham ways and means of getting across that plateau when suddenly the sound of voices raised in song made us stop dead in our tracks. A lot of people were doing a lot of singing, and we just couldn't make it out at first. And then we found that, in order to pass the time, the Padre had organised a session of community singing and in the middle of the harbour the tank crews were gathered roaring 'Nellie Dean' at the tops of the voices and seeming to enjoy themselves no end.

I forgot how many songs we listened to them sing, but by way of the more sober numbers they were gradually led to 'Abide With Me', and the twilight sky echoed to a full-throated chorus sung with great gusto and, to my astonishment, considerable feeling.

I don't think the troops were feeling particularly religious at that moment, it just happened to be a good song that most of them knew the words to, and to which some of them could sing the harmony. But with great shrewdness the Padre ended the programme on this note and the crews dispersed quietly to their bivouacs.

It had been a long and weary day so I decided to leave until the next morning our usual troop gathering at which I told them our tasks in the battle. And I thought it would be as well to leave them to sleep with the peaceful strains of 'Abide With Me' echoing in their minds.

Yet when I walked up that way some twenty minutes later I found they hadn't gone to sleep. Sitting on a jerri-can, McGinty was holding a large, black book in his hand, and was talking earnestly to the troop, and they were leaning forward expectantly, drinking in every word he said.

This set me back a pace or two: it looked as if the hymn singing had had a more profound effect than I thought. Though quite the last person I expected to find as a lay preacher was ex-jockey McGinty.

'Life's full of little surprises,' I breathed. And I stepped into the shadow of one of the tanks to watch McGinty at work.

From time to time he would devoutly consult the big book, and holding up an admonitory finger would read several passages from it.

In the end my curiosity got the better of me, and I stepped cautiously forward to hear what he was saying.

'You can't lose,' he said. 'It's an absolute certainty, this system. Try again; pick a date, any date, I don't mind. What? 24th June. Right!'

He thumbed his way through the book.

'Here you are,' he said. '24th June, racing at Kempton Park. The first race was won by an outsider; second by the favourite; so was the third. Here you are – the fourth race! Won by Blue Lagoon, second favourite at six to four!'

He closed the book with a bang.

'All you've got to do,' he said dogmatically, 'is to go on doubling your stakes until you win. Then pack up and go home. Never a race meeting goes by without a second favourite wins one of the races. You can't lose – it's a wonderful system!'

I tiptoed away. I might have known the sort of prayer meeting Five Troop would hold.

That night we were awakened by a deep and terrible rumbling in the distance, and by the roar of labouring aircraft engines in the sky. From the top of our hill we could see the reflected light of bombs bursting in and around Le Havre, as wave after wave of RAF heavy bombers passed over the unhappy town. It was all planned to make our task easier the next day, but I couldn't help thinking it was a painful way for the French to be liberated. Yet it did some good, and after Le Havre was all over we speculated about what the job would have been like without the preliminary softening up from the clouds. We decided it might have been much worse than it was.

The first reports next morning sent our hopes soaring. The attack by the other troops was going well but slowly. Mines were sown thickly everywhere, and clearing them was a painstaking but time-spending business. Yet the enemy were not putting up much resistance and slowly but surely the perimeter of the garrison was shrinking.

Up on our plateau the infantry (a Scottish Regiment) were reported to be getting on famously. They didn't need any tank support, one of their liaison officers said. Well, well, we thought. The bombing must have done an awful lot of good.

But despite these optimistic reports it was decided that 'A' Squadron should go up on to the plateau, if only to see these infantry who didn't need tank support.

We found them pinned to the ground in helpless groups, machine-gun fire from concrete pillboxes sweeping the ground from side to side.

This was something we knew something about. Keeping a weather eye open for those anti-tank guns we had plotted on our maps, we swung into action firing high-explosive shells from our 75mm guns.

Sergeant Robinson's tank, equipped with a six-pounder instead of a 75mm, fired belt after belt of Besa, and before long little white flags were fluttering from the pillbox slits.

The infantry dashed forward with their bayonets and winkled the prisoners out of their blockhouses, and the Company Commander came across to my tank.

His language was understandably disgraceful when I told him we had heard he didn't need any support. Ian must have told the infantry CO the same thing, because I could see Ian standing beside his tank, grinning his lopsided grin as the grey-haired infantry Colonel said what he thought about the liaison officers concerned.

But after that we got on just fine.

We found that the plateau was really a rolling hilltop, so that visibility was limited to a few hundred yards. Every time you thought you'd reached the top, you found another stretch of ground rising away in front of you.

The previous night's bombing had left huge craters everywhere but it had also destroyed a lot of the defence works. Anti-tank guns there were, but the bombing had written off their protective machine gun posts. And in some cases the bigger guns had been bombed, leaving the Spandau pits unharmed.

We very soon reached a working agreement with the infantry; we would take care of the machine guns for them, if they would sort out the anti-tank guns for us.

And it worked like a charm.

We would roll slowly forward until a burst of unpleasantness met us, and then we would turn our combined guns on to whatever was causing the trouble. Sometimes we had to put down a hasty smoke bomb, and retire a little way down the hill; and sometimes the infantry would dive into the bomb craters while we fired shells at the pillbox until the little white flags began to appear.

On my right Tony Cunningham had the bad luck to come on an anti-tank gun and Spandau post together and in action. But by cunningly using his smoke thrower and guns alternately he managed to persuade these particular Germans that the war held no future for them.

At last we reached the top of the hill and were able to spread out and allow a couple more troops to pass through and continue the good work. The plateau, we knew from our maps, ended in an almost sheer drop to a riverside road. Over the radio we heard that scores of Germans were scrambling down this drop, away from our advance.

It was too bad for them that another tank regiment was waiting to meet them on the road. Unlike McGinty's famous system – they just couldn't win.

And then we thought it was all over. Grinning Scotsmen were hurrying prisoners out of the trenches and blockhouses. In the distance we could hear the crackle and explosion of demolitions being carried out in the dockyard area, and we could also hear a stiffish battle being fought by the troops attacking the town from the north.

It was with a curious sense of elation that I realised we had done the job we set out to do, and it hadn't been anything like as bad as we feared it might be.

Inside the turret we grinned at one another and wiped our faces on cordite-dirty handkerchiefs. And then through my periscope I saw my particular Company Commander walking towards *Avenger*, beaming all over his face.

I flung up the turret hatches and leaned out.

'That's about the lot, isn't it?' I said.

'I think so, thanks very much,' he said. 'I think there are one or two odd bods here and there who are laying low hoping to do some dirty work later on, but we'll soon sort them out. There's only one thing; I'm not too happy about that little stone place over there… '

He turned and pointed to his left, and at that moment a deafening bang smacked my eardrums and a red hot hand seemed to slap my face.

My ear caught the cupola ring as I jerked my head sideways and dropped down into the turret. Instinctively I clapped my hands to my face, and when I took them away they were covered in blood.

'Christ! I've had it this time,' I choked.

For a brief instant Pickford stared across the turret at me, his eyes wide with horror, then like lightning he whipped the first aid box out from behind the wireless set and flicked it open.

McGinty peered around at us in complete disbelief. Not a moment ago I had told him it was all over bar the shouting.

He grabbed his microphone and said: 'Who did it, sir?'

With a bloody hand I pointed shakily in the direction of the little stone shack to which the Infantry Company Commander had pointed, and at once he swung the turret around and opened fire with his Besa machine gun.

With a wad of cotton wool Pickford started gently to wipe my face, but I took it from him and cleaned myself as best I could.

Then I saw Pickford staring at me, holding a wound dressing in his hand.

'Whereabouts are you hit, sir?' he shouted above the roar of McGinty's gun.

'Well, dammit all man, you're looking at me! Can't you see where I'm hit?'

He peered closer and then shook his head.

'No, sir. Where do you feel the pain?'

And then I realised there wasn't any pain – just a general overall soreness. Gingerly I touched my face all over, and found that it was still all there and there was no sign of a wound anywhere. The blood had stopped flowing from where ever it was flowing from, and that was that.

I got up and looked out of the turret again.

'You all right?' shouted the Company Commander.

'Damned if I know!' I said. 'I'm still alive, anyway!'

'Sniper I think,' he said thoughtfully. 'Look!'

He pointed to the flap of my turret hatch, and I saw an irregular shiny patch where a bullet had flattened itself about an inch from my nose, splattering my face with bullet-splash. (When I went to shave the next morning I found hundreds of tiny fragments of lead in my cheeks. Each one must have made a pin-point of blood as it went in, producing in the mass a most gory – but quite harmless – effect).

'Funny things these snipers,' shouted the Company Commander conversationally. 'He could see all of me, but only your head. And he had to try for your head. A couple of inches to the left and he'd have had it, too.'

'Well, I should think *he's* had it now,' I said, as another empty Besa belt dropped from McGinty's gun. But just to be on the safe side we drove over there and looked into the tiny redoubt.

It contained a German paratrooper – and goodness knows what he was doing in Le Havre – and he was very dead. I cut off his parachute badge as a souvenir and we drove back off the plateau.

I was getting more and more indebted to the benevolent ghost who takes care of half-witted Troop Leaders.

Much to everybody's delighted astonishment we were given another fourteen days' rest after Le Havre, but this time for quite a different reason. The speed of the Allied advance across Europe was such that everything on wheels had to be mobilised to keep the supplies rolling forward. Everything was still being carried from the beaches of Normandy, and as the lines of communication grew longer and longer, more and more lorries were needed.

We watched all our regimental transport depart from us, and at one time we were told that it might be necessary to drain off the petrol from our own tanks, to keep the advance moving.

Scattered around the delightful countryside near Bosc-le-hard we settled down to a fortnight as spectators of the war. Our Squadron was based on a largish farm, and a long, wooden hut provided sleeping quarters for four of the troops.

Five Troop were herded into a stone-floored annexe.

This, I thought, was no way to treat Five Troop. Merely because of the accidental numbering of the troops from 1 to 5, my lot came in at the tail end of everything. We were pretty used to this by now, but I wasn't going to stand for them being pushed into a cattle byre while the rest of the Squadron lorded it in a wooden building with a nice oak floor.

Pink with indignation I stormed up to Ian and Jim, sitting in the little out-house which did duty as a squadron office, and said my piece.

'You can't do this to Five Troop, Ian!' I said. 'It's not on! Shoved into a ropey old, windowless shack while the rest of the Squadron relax in the lap of luxury.'

He tried to look worried, but didn't make much of a success of it. Finally he grinned and ran his fingers through his overlong hair.

'Come off it, John,' he said. 'You can't get a pint into a quart pot. And there just isn't room to get five troops into the wooden hut. So stop making a fuss about it.'

'I'm not making a fuss,' I said. 'I'm just taking a proper interest in my men.'

'Oh?' said Ian.

'Yes! Welfare and all that,' I added lamely.

Jim Steward looked up from the sheaf of signals he was trying to sort out.

'Well, what do you suggest we do instead?' he said.

This was a real flanker; even as I pushed back my beret and sat down I knew I'd made a tactical error in not finding alternative accommodation first. But Ian came to my rescue by standing up and saying: 'Well, let's go and look at Five Troop in their horrid squalor.'

I led the way across the farmyard towards the stone building which housed my rabble. I saw that from somewhere or other they had procured a door to hang on what had been bare hinges half an hour ago. But even then I didn't suspect anything until I pushed open the door.

The stone floor was covered by all the tank sheets, under which had been laid a solid packing of straw. Electric light blazed down from six headlight bulbs strung across the ceiling and wired to a block of tank batteries in a corner of the room. A pair of headphones were relaying a concert of light music from one of the beams, and lounging on improvised couches, looking like oily illustrations from *The Arabian Nights*, or swinging from hammocks made of camouflage netting, Five Troop were peacefully reading Western magazines or writing their never-ending letters home.

'Oh!' I said, and before I could say anything else Smith 161 and Farrell pushed past me, carrying between them a windowframe fully fitted with glass. And this they proceeded to fit into the empty window aperture at the end of the room.

''Ome from 'ome, eh, sir?' said Smith 161, cheerfully.

Ian and Jim looked at me significantly.

'Living in horrible discomfort, eh?' mused Jim Steward smoothly. 'Well, well; what a shame.'

I stammered something about perhaps we could make do with this room after all, but Ian was thinking about something else.

'They've brought out a complicated scheme for when the war ends,' he said, as we crossed the farmyard again.

'Oh?' I said.

'Yes. They call it the Age of Service Release Scheme. Something to do with leaving the army by groups.'

I wondered what he was getting at. I wasn't left wondering long.

'I want an officer to explain it to the squadron,' he said.

'Oh.'

'Somebody who takes an interest in the men.'

'Oh.'

'Welfare and all that,' he said blandly.

'Oh!'

And that's how the Squadron got a Welfare Officer.

Alan Biddulph's petrol and ammunition lorries came back to us eventually with tales of long hauls from the beaches of Normandy up to the Arnhem corridor, where the Airborne boys were doing their stuff with great gallantry. It made us feel very much out of things and for the first time since we landed I began to notice a certain restlessness in the troop.

So we were all rather glad when one day Ian broke the news that we were on the move once more. And this time we were going up into the Arnhem corridor, north of Eindhoven. Like a lot of rowdy schoolboys breaking up for the holidays Five Troop stripped down their electric lighting and hammocks of camouflage netting, rolled up their blankets and groundsheets and stowed them on the tanks once more. Crosby actually rubbed his hands with glee when he heard that we were moving up to the Belgian frontier on our own tracks, and thence on transporters as far as the Albert Canal.

'Be noice to feel the old bus on the road again, zur,' he drawled. 'We'm gittin' too fat sittin' back 'ere listenin' to the war on the woireless.'

So off we went again, and again we experienced the second-hand joy of being cheered enthusiastically by people and hailed as liberators of enslaved towns.

The cheering even continued after we had reached the Belgian frontier and driven our Churchills on to the huge sixty four-wheeled trucks.

These powerful vehicles saved us a lot of valuable track mileage and it was a pleasant change to sit perched up on the tank, being carried smoothly along without the din of the engine and the tracks, and without the worry of wondering if the engine was going to stall on you and whether or not you were on the right route.

I often wondered what would happen if one of the transporters broke down. Would we wait patiently for the breakdown to be put right, or would we be justified in unshipping our tanks and carrying on under our own steam, like an energetic terrier following the local hunt? But I never had to make this decision: every time we had to be moved anywhere on transporters these little-publicised giants of the RASC met us at the appointed place, took us smoothly to our destination, and then vanished down the lines of communication again to pick up another load of tanks somewhere.

Brussels was in darkness when we passed through it, in the early hours of the morning. The crew had settled down to sleep, either in the tank itself or in the little cabin built on to the back of the transporter towing vehicle. I dozed in the turret of *Avenger*, but the gentle rhythm of the big tyres, and the slow roll as we rounded corners, were so different from *Avenger*'s usual method of progression that I couldn't get to sleep properly. Besides, we had just been grounded for a fortnight and there had been no recent shortage of sleep.

There was a sharp promise of frost in the late September air and I was grateful for the woollen sweaters and scarves which were beginning to arrive from all sorts of knitting groups in England. Some of the men found little notes of good wishes pinned to these garments and I always insisted on them writing a letter of grateful acknowledgement in these cases. Except Trooper Cooper. He wrote enough letters as it was.

There was a blue sparkle about the wide streets of Brussels as we motored slowly through it. The deserted avenues bore only a few late revellers, and these hardly turned a glance in our direction. And then I heard a faint cheer from the head of the column; a cheer which was taken up and echoed all along the line as each transporter passed a certain road junction. I shook off the drowsiness to see what the troops could find to cheer about at four o'clock on a frosty morning, and then I saw two red-capped military policemen, immaculately attired in glistening white blanco and beautifully smooth uniforms. They were pacing the pavement as steadily and as purposefully as if they were marching down Aldershot High Street on a Saturday night.

McGinty stirred sleepily in the turret.

'What's to do, sir?' he yawned.

'A couple of military policemen,' I said.

'Blimey! They've changed our route,' he said. 'They must be sending us via Catterick!'

This was gross slander, of course. We had seen military policemen, their scarlet crash helmets spattered with mud, calmly directing traffic in the forward areas with shells bursting all around them. And always they came in for this cheer from the troops. I tried to find out why this was so, whether it was a cheer of admiration or a cheer of sarcasm. But no one I asked could tell me; they just scratched their heads and said well, they had always done it because everybody else seemed to.

I remember thinking drowsily about this as the long line of heavily loaded transporters carried us through the outskirts of the Belgian capital and then the next thing I knew was that we were halted in the sunshine and tank engines were being started up.

I peeled off my pullovers and scarves and climbed down to check on the unloading of the tanks.

We were on a long, straight road with a few isolated houses on one side and a low, red-brick buildings on the other. As far as the eye could see the country was as flat as a billiard table, and I thought with dismay of trying to fight a tank battle in this sort of country, where the enemy could see you coming from several miles away.

It was while I was lost in this disturbing thought that I noticed an alien aroma in the air; a scent reminiscent of First Class railway compartments and opulent business men. A perfume of cigars.

'Nevah, in the history of human conflict,' droned sonorous tones from the turret of *Angler*, 'has so much, been owed… '

It was Smith 161, smoking a large cigar and giving a passable imitation of a Churchillian speech. And Corporal Watson was smoking a cigar, too; and so was nearly everybody else in the troop.

It seemed that the red brick building was a cigar factory – fact which hadn't escaped the notice of Five Troop. Soon a long line of black berets was vanishing into the open doorway of the factory and, more to placate any angry executives than in the hope of collecting a box of cheroots (well, that's what I told myself at the time), I hurried into the building.

In the entrance hall of the factory a fat and beaming Dutchman was distributing boxes of cigars to all and sundry. In halting English he spurned all offers of payment, and as soon as somebody told him I was an officer he took me affably by the hand and insisted on escorting me on a conducted tour of the factory.

This was fine, but outside in the road I could hear the transporters driving away, and the Churchills starting their engines.

'Thank you very much,' I said hastily, edging my way towards the door. 'But I must go now – the tanks – you know – wait for no man, or something – '

But it was no good. The benevolent cigar manufacturer was not going to lose the opportunity of walking around his factory with a real, live British officer, so willy-nilly I was paraded through long rooms where round-shouldered Dutchmen sat at long benches, rolling cigars by hand with unbelievable dexterity.

From outside on the road came the clatter of tracks as the tanks moved forward, and in a frenzy of alarm I dragged my host to a window and showed him the tanks moving off.

We saw Five Troop happily parked on the grass verge of the road, making obvious arrangements for the brewing of tea.

'Zo! Iss oll right, no?' beamed the fat man. 'You com mit me in der packink house, is it?'

I closed my eyes and followed him wearily, already turning over in my mind what I was going to say when charged with absenting myself from the line of march without due cause or reason.

I'm sure the 'packink house' was fascinating, but I can't remember a thing about it now. But I can distinctly remember being given a monumental box of gigantic cigars before being ushered out of the front door, my fingers limp and powerless from having been gripped too warmly and too often.

And I remember, too, having to thrash our engines into a white heat in order to catch up with the tail of the regiment.

But we did it, just as darkness was falling and we were entering Eindhoven.

West Country soldiers were battling grimly to reach the isolated Airborne troops at Arnhem, and stretching north from Eindhoven a narrow strip of land reached up to form the famous Arnhem Corridor. Twice the Germans had managed to cut this umbilical cord, and twice they had been forced to withdraw again. Our job was to man a section of this corridor and help to keep it intact.

Yet before we left Eindhoven we were to witness a scene which would bring home the gratitude of the Dutch people far more than any cheering, flower-throwing crowds.

We parked our Churchills on either side of a wide road on the outskirts of the town. The houses bordering the road were neat and well-kept, but not unduly pretentious.

Ian and Jim went off to find billets in the town, but before leaving they said it might be a good idea to erect the bivouacs just in case they didn't have any luck.

At first sight there wouldn't appear much that anyone can say in favour of sleeping on pavements; but if you think about it a bit it's a considerable improvement on a wet, shell-torn field. So Five Troop were quite cheerfully putting up the bivouacs and swapping good-humoured badinage with the Dutch children. And then I felt a nervous touch on my arm. I looked around and saw a large, homely, blue-eyed housewife. She was middle-aged, comfortably plump and looked for all the world like an advertisement for somebody's starch, complete with sparkling white apron.

She pointed a stubby finger at the crew, wrestling with the main sheet.

'Vot is dey doink?' she said.

'For sleeping,' I smiled. 'Schlaffen!' And I place my hands together against my cheeks in the traditional international sign for slumber.

For a minute I thought she had interpreted it as an improper suggestion. She backed away with eyes ablaze, her complexion growing pinker every minute.

'Here?' she cried. 'On der floor?'

I nodded pleasantly. That did it! She flew away in a cloud of petticoats and high-pitched Dutch, hammering on every door and jabbering madly to the householders. Doors were flung open and a host of men and women surged out on to the road, swarming in amongst the tank crews and gesticulating fiercely towards their houses.

By the time Ian and Jim returned with the news that they had found a cinema in which we could sleep for the night, every man had a bed in one of the nearby houses – complete with clean sheets and pillowcases. I daren't think how many of the good folk of Eindhoven spent that night in armchairs or on sofas, but every man in the regiment was accommodated like a king.

I found myself in the house of the motherly soul who had organised the accommodation. The bed looked inviting and the sheets smelled of lavender. But before I was allowed to go to bed she asked me if I would like a cup of tea.

I stood in the middle of the spotlessly clean living room wondering if I ought to be polite and say no thank you. The chances were they were short of tea, but the kettle was singing on a trivet and a tray was laid with cups of eggshell china and little plates of cakes. It had so obviously been prepared long in advance that it would have been churlish to refuse. So I lowered my haversack to the floor, smiled in what I hoped was a winning manner and looked around for the least clean chair in which I could park my grubby self.

It wasn't bad tea, at that. A bit weak, perhaps, but then I'd been used to army tea, which is likened to a most obnoxious fluid if it doesn't stain the cup brown. And as we sat and sipped our tea more and more people crowded into the room. The rose-patterned teapot seemed to become the ceremonial centre of the evening; conversation stopped abruptly every time my hostess reached out for the teapot. But we talked about the war, and I told them about the raids on London and other places, and in this way the evening passed until I felt I had justified the production of the best china and I began to make a move towards bed.

It was not until the next morning that things were explained to me. We were stowing our gear on the tanks and talking about the excellence of our several bedrooms the previous night, when a young dark-haired man stopped beside *Avenger* and smiled at me. I remember seeing him at the tea-drinking ceremony the previous night and, in fact, had addressed most of my remarks through him, for he spoke very fluent English.

'Good morning,' he said cheerfully. 'Did you enjoy your tea last night?'

'Yes, indeed,' I said. 'Very nice tea.'

He nodded and turned to walk away; then he hesitated and came back to me.

'The housewife bought that tea five years ago,' he said quietly. 'It was the last in Eindhoven. And she swore she would keep it for when the English came, because the English so love tea. Goodbye!'

He waved his hand quickly and strode away. I thought how near I had come to saying 'No, thank you,' and mopped my brow in relief.

But before we rolled out of Eindhoven we broke several different kinds of regulations by thrusting upon the reluctant housewife several tins of best bully beef.

'It's pretty rough,' commented McGinty. 'But it's not so rough as all that. So what's she crying for, sir?'

Our stay in the Arnhem corridor lasted but a week; and although 'C' Squadron on our left did a short and successful attack on a German position opposite their location, for us the stay was enlivened only by one 'Stand to' (which came to nothing) and by the issue of fresh rations.

Until then we had existed on the pre-packed composite rations and very well we had fared too. But one day out of the blue we were given meat, vegetables, bread, fat, and all the bits and pieces to prepare ourselves a more conventional meal. And just for the fun of the thing it was decreed that cooking would be on a troop basis.

'Who can cook?' I said to Five Troop. 'No one? Well, you are a helpless lot. Let me show you.'

Five Troop were only too willing to be shown, and they settled down with evident relish to watch what they hoped was going to be an entertaining programme. But I didn't like the way Farrell started counting the reserve compo rations in the back bin of *Avenger*.

It was evident that to cook a proper meal required a proper source of heat. A tank pressure stove wouldn't do – at least not for Five Troop.

'We will build a field oven,' I said calmly, and set a couple of them on to digging a short, narrow trench.

'And we want a flue, too,' I said. 'What can we use for a flue pipe?'

Now it happened that at that time 75mm ammunition came encased in round, hardboard tubes. Each tube had a narrow collar at the end, so that one could be slipped on top of another, thus making a pipe of almost indefinite length.

'The longer the flue-pipe the greater the draught,' I said authoritatively, as we erected a pipe like a flagstaff.

Then we dug over the soil in the bottom of the trench, thoroughly soaked it in petrol and laid an empty ammunition box over the top of the trench to act as an oven.

'Give me a match someone,' I said. 'Hey! Where are you all going?'

They were wiser than I. When I threw a match under the oven and in to the petrol-soaked trench there was a loud WOOF! and the hardboard chimney disintegrated into its component tubes, scattering them all over the Squadron area, and causing our attendant infantry to leap into their slit trenches and don their steel helmets.

The steel ammunition box just missed my head, thereby convincing me that maybe I wasn't an expert heating engineer after all.

Nothing daunted, I rallied Five Troop again and said perhaps the pressure stoves would do for today. But I would show them how to cook – the principle was the same, anyway.

I looked at the raw rations and wished Troop Leaders didn't have to be such super know-alls. And then my eye fell on a bag of rice. That, I thought, was my salvation. Nothing to rice-pudding. Just milk, water, butter, and rice. Easy.

I filled a dixie with rice, milk, and water, and put a knob of butter on the top. With much professional lecturing I gingerly placed the dixie on a low flame and sat back to await results.

I think it was about five minutes before I had to borrow the dixie from *Alert* to take the rice overflow. And perhaps a quarter of an hour before we needed the one from *Angler*.

By now Farrell was shamelessly opening tins from the compo rations, whilst Pickford went around the other troops seeing if anybody wanted any extra rice.

Ian leaned on the back of *Avenger* and with a perfectly straight face said: 'Didn't you know rice swells when you put it in water, John?'

I swallowed hastily.

'Of course I did,' I said. 'Didn't I tell you it would?' I went on, glaring at Five Troop.

Without batting an eyelid they chorused 'Yes, sir!'

EIGHT

IT TURNED OUT that our next bit of business was to be Armoured Division stuff again, but by this time we had reached that convenient state of mind which always expects the very worst and is highly delighted when it turns out to be just ordinary bad.

From the Arnhem corridor we moved west to take part in a drive north towards Tilburg. We formed a combined force with some infantry, a Reconnaissance Regiment and some self-propelled anti-tank guns. The whole outfit was under the command of our Brigadier, and since his name was Clarke they called it Clarkeforce.

The job amounted to a twenty-five-mile attack over the flat billiard table of the Dutch countryside, against an enemy rearguard screen of self-propelled anti-tank guns and infantry strong points.

It looked as if anything could happen – and it did.

In the little Belgian town of St. Leonard we stood by our Churchills in the cold, frosty light of an October dawn. We yawned sleepily and sucked down our rum-laced tea. A mile up the road in front of us another Churchill regiment was going into action with the object of capturing a small village. And the idea was that we would leap-frog through them and on to another village. And so on.

The other regiment did not have a very easy time of it, and it was late afternoon before we got the signal to start the advance.

We motored over the recently won ground, past burning houses and vehicles, past tired, grimy tank crews making rude gestures to us as we clattered by, and out into the open country beyond.

With a minimum of words (for the amount of verbal traffic on the air was deafening) Ian spread us around a bit and we rolled forward.

It didn't seem like a real battle somehow; there was no barrage of shells from our own guns; no whistle of enemy shells bursting amongst us; in fact if it hadn't been for the crackle of burning buildings we might have been on Stone Street.

The country was flat, as I have said, criss-crossed with narrow lanes and dotted with isolated farms. Here and there a twin line of poplars denoted a paved road and little groups of trees were splashed at random over the landscape.

Sergeant Robinson was keeping *Alert* steadily rolling forward on my left, and a couple of hundred yards away on the right Harry Langton seemed to be shaping all right with his new troop.

Head and shoulders out of the turret I scanned the country for signs of the enemy, but the only movement came from a group of grey-green lorries about a mile away on our left front.

I yawned – and looked again. And then I snatched up the microphone and nudged McGinty with my knee.

'Seventy-five traverse left,' I yelled excitedly. 'Steady... on! Fifteen hundred... transport... FIRE!'

For some reason which we never went into, Sergeant Robinson chose that moment to speed up. *Alert* plunged forward, right into my line of fire. I saw the white trace of the AP shot skim past the front horns of *Alert*, and then I reached for the control switch and put it to 'B'.

'Hello, Five Baker,' I said. 'Get out of the daylight! There's some enemy transport on your left!'

'Roger, out!' said Sergeant Robinson, and I saw his turret starting to swing round. But it was too late. The lorries had disappeared into a wood, leaving one of their number burning as a tribute to McGinty's marksmanship.

'Well done, McGinty,' I said over the IC. 'It should have been HE, really, but AP seems to have done the trick all right.'

'On the move, too,' said McGinty, smugly.

Ian came up on the 'A' set then and wanted to know what I'd been firing at. So I indicated the column of smoke on the horizon. But he couldn't reply because at that moment one of the Reconnaissance Troop came up on the air to report the discovery of an undamaged bridge across a river which barred our path.

This was wonderful news. We had taken it for granted that the enemy would blow up all the bridges, and we had made lengthy plans for crossing the river using special devices. And the news of the intact bridge set us sweeping forward at a great pace.

It looked as if we really had caught the enemy off-balance this time. The Reconnaissance Troop just in front of us captured two German staff cars, bundled the bewildered occupants back in an infantry carrier, and took the two well-upholstered cars in tow. But it was not until we reached our objective in the village of Wuestwezel that we realised just how unexpected our attack had been.

We grouped the tanks around the centre of the town – a crossroads, as usual – and occupied several of the houses and buildings nearby. It was nearly midnight, and we had long settled down to sleep, when a great commotion was heard from the police station on the edge of the town.

It turned out that a German soldier had bicycled slowly past an astonished sentry, unsteadily dismounted at the police station, and marched in to hand in his late pass. When he saw a grinning British tank sergeant sitting behind the desk, instead of the usual *Obergefreiter*, he was foolish enough to try and run away. But already two privates of the Duke of Wellington's regiment were tossing up for possession of his bicycle, and he was patiently led away to a camp from which late passes were never issued.

We were all laughing heartily about this when Ian came slouching out of the darkness with news which killed the laughs cold.

'The Brigadier wants us to advance,' he said.

'When?' I asked.

'Now!' said Ian.

'What? But it's pitch black!'

'I know. And it's starting to rain. But if we wait until morning the Germans will have had time to get themselves organised again.'

'Oh hell. Why doesn't somebody tell the Brigadier that tanks can't operate at night,' said Tony Cunningham.

'I know,' said Jan, shrugging his shoulders in the darkness. 'The gunners won't be able to see a blasted thing.'

'So what do we do?' asked Harry Langton.

'We stand by to move!' said Ian flatly.

Looking back on it now, the Brigadier was quite right of course. But at midnight in Wuestwezel, with the rain getting heavier, we cordially agreed he'd gone mad.

Five Troop were far from enthusiastic about the idea. I pointed out to them that it was a road advance; all we had to do was bash straight along the road north from Wuestwezel, until something stopped us. With great delicacy we didn't discuss exactly what was going to stop us.

We heard the tinny roar of the Reconnaissance Troop starting the engines of their little tanks, and they were already moving past us when Ian came running up.

'Start up!' he yelled. 'John, you can lead. But you'll have the Recce Troop in front of you!'

'Right, Ian,' I said miserably. Then turning to Sergeant Robinson I added: 'You'd better go first; Johnson's got the best night vision in the troop.'

I was about to offer to change tanks with him, and let him follow on in *Avenger*, but he didn't give me a chance. While I was still wondering how to make the offer without hurting his feelings, he was up into his turret and *Alert* was clattering northwards.

The road was narrow and bordered on each side by a ditch and a thick belt of trees. Here and there a little house fronted the road, but we could see none of this.

There was no moon and, as far as I remember, no stars. It was one of those incredibly black nights when it seems to make no difference whether you have your eyes open or shut. The rain sliced down out of the inky sky, cutting the skin like slivers of ice. Never have I felt so completely lost as during those first few moments of the advance from Wuestwezel. I could just barely make out the glow of *Alert*'s exhaust in front of me, and from down in the driving compartment Crosby's rich voice kept up a steady commentary alternating between hope and despair.

'Reckon we'll 'ave none o' they dodgin' tic-tacs tonoight,' he muttered. 'Finish up in one o' they ditches loike as not. Ar, 'seasy for you to talk, Mac. You doan 'ave to steer this ruddy thing – 'Ere, where's old Johno takin' *Alert*, for Gawd's sake? Caw! Now 'e's gorn. D'you see where *Alert*'s to, Mac? Ar, there she be… '

And then a crackle of glowing red tracer bullets above our heads set the ball rolling. It was the Recce Troop, involved in a battle around an enormous tree which the Germans had felled across the road.

Dimly I could see the vague shapes of infantry hurrying past *Avenger*, as we juddered to a halt. The battle was only a couple of hundred yards ahead by the sound of it, but for all the help we were able to give it might as well have been in the Antarctic. I got out of *Avenger* and felt the tail of one of the Recce Troop's tanks. It was almost impossible to find out what was going on, and then I heard that the enemy had been driven off or captured, but the tree still barred the way, and that it was too big for his little tanks to get over or round.

I knew what that meant. And I was right.

'Hello, Baker Five,' said Ian's voice. 'See if you can shift it.'

'Wilco, out,' I said, with a hollow laugh. The idea of fiddling about with tow-ropes and Churchill tanks, in that wet blackness, trying to haul a forest giant out of the way, was not my idea of a quiet evening's entertainment.

I made my way forward until I met Gerry Hodgson, the Recce Troop Leader. His glasses glinted in the darkness and his eager voice was bubbling over with enthusiasm.

'Hullo, John,' he said, as if we had just met in Bond Street. 'I reckon one of your Churchills will shift this easily. Come on.'

We stood beside the tree – at least it felt as if we were – and explored it with our hands.

'I think it would be a good idea if we took a look at it,' said Gerry, with brisk enthusiasm. And as he spoke he shone his torch over the tree.

Instantly a shot rang out from somewhere up the road, sending up a shower of splinters from the obstacle in front of us.

'Ah, well. Perhaps not,' said Gerry, switching off his torch.

So there we were. And as far as I could make out it looked a pretty formidable task shifting that tree without being able to see it. But in the brief light of Gerry's torch I had noticed that the tree tapered, which seems to be a habit of trees; and at its narrowest point it looked as if a Churchill might get over it, even if we couldn't tow it out of the way.

I got back on the 'A' set and told Ian this.

'Hullo, Baker Five,' said Ian. 'Roger. If you can get across and clear the road ahead for a bit, we'll be able to get a working party up to the tree. Have a go. Over.'

'Baker Five. Wilco out.' I said.

Then I went and hammered on the front of *Alert*, and made urgent signs for Johnson to join me in the road.

'Can you see that tree?' I said.

'Yes, sir,' he said simply.

'Reckon you can get *Alert* over it?'

'I think so. Have a crack at it anyway, sir.'

'Right!'

Then came the problem of what to do once we were across the tree. And since we wouldn't be able to see anything to fire at, I decided to fire at everything.

'We'll go flat out up the road,' I said to Sergeant Robinson and Corporal Watson. 'Fire your Besas at the edges of the road all the way. You take the left of the road, Sergeant Robinson; I'll take the right. And you, Corporal Watson, take whichever side seems to be giving most trouble. All right?'

'All right, sir,' they said in unison.

'And don't forget,' I added. 'Besas blazing like mad!'

I had unknowingly coined a catchphrase. For years afterwards, if anybody in the regiment wanted to describe a state of chaos they said: 'Oh, yes: it was besas blazing all right'.

I expected the tree to test our Churchills to their limit, but it didn't prove to be a very formidable obstacle after all. The forty tons of armour-plate crushed the branches of the tree into a compact mass, and the heavy tracks got a satisfactory grip and heaved up over the top.

Once across, we opened fire and set off into the unknown. The six machine guns blazed away and so intense was the darkness that the light of our tracer bullets seemed to illuminate the whole scene. The relief at being able to see something was indescribable. We rattled along the road, pumping bullets into the hedges and grass banks, and by the rosy glow of the tracers we were able to make out vague shapes tumbling out of our path.

A blaze of sparks streaked across the road between the back of *Alert* and the front of *Avenger*, and I guessed it was a bazooka fired by a German hiding in the ditch. But Corporal Watson had seen it, too, and when I twisted my head round I saw his turret Besa traversing round and pumping bullets into the spot from which the sparks had come.

More and more tanks were now joining us at our side of the tree and I was beginning to feel quite exhilarated. The bazooka that missed had given us all a boost of morale, and I felt that so long as we kept moving at a good speed there was a distinct hope that others would miss, too.

And that was the point at which Ian came up on the air and told me to halt.

We halted and stopped firing, and waited for the fun to begin. But as the minutes ticked by and nobody shot at us I began to wonder if, after all, our headlong dash had frightened the enemy away.

I gave the signal to switch off engines, and listened.

Distorted voices crackled from the radio; rain hissed on the hot exhaust pipes; but apart from that the night was silent.

A voice hailed me from the road. It was Harry Langton wanting to know the time. As if it made any difference what time it was. But just for the record it was 2.30am.

From conversations on the air I gathered the tree was proving obstreperous. Even some of the Churchills were getting stuck on it, and probably because of this the next order I got was to turn into the nearest field and form a tank harbour.

To this day I don't know how we managed to find a field in the blackness. But by 3am the tanks were drawn up in a square and by 3.30 the tree must have been cleared because soon after that Alan Biddulph's lorries were pulling into the harbour with petrol and ammunition. By four o'clock we had finished our essential tasks, and were munching biscuits and bully beef and swilling compo tea.

And at 5.45 we received the order to stand by to move again.

From that point onwards the enemy fought a skilful rearguard action. There were no tenacious battles; he would site a self-propelled anti-tank gun in an excellent position and camouflage it well.

The first thing we knew about it was when armour-piercing shells started whistling amongst us. Traditionally, we put down smoke, mounted a short attack to deal with the gun, and by the time we got the attack launched he had quietly stolen away to another position a mile or so back.

But not always.

One day we were temporarily halted on one of those awful Dutch roads which run along the top of an embankment. Silhouetted against the skyline we felt like clay-pipes at a fair waiting to be shot at.

Luckily there was no cover for an enemy gun for at least two thousand yards, and that was in a wood on our left. Yet we had evidence that they were in that wood, because from time to time a piece of the road surface would disappear with a demoralising crack.

Every tank commander scanned that wood through his binoculars, but the camouflage was perfect and the Germans were using flashless ammunition. So everybody fired at where they thought the blighter was. Which made the odds something like fifty-four to one. And that stopped the gun all right, but nobody ever did decide just who knocked it out.

And then on another day the enemy SP left it a little too late in withdrawing from his hiding place. He managed to brew up one of the squadron tanks, but a few seconds later he was burning himself.

But the most gratifying episode to happen during the first few days of the advance was just outside the village of Nieuwmoer. Ian's own tank was on the road heading for the village, while the other troops were spread out over the adjacent fields. We heard a sudden fusillade of AP shells from the centre of the village and heard Ian on the air saying he was being fired on by an SP gun sitting on the usual crossroads. He fired back, and took some evasive action, and a couple of hours later Tony Cunningham got a shot in the SP's flank which put paid to its military career.

And that night in harbour we gathered around Ian's tank and pointed in awe to the seven dents in the front of his Churchill, where the enemy shots had failed to penetrate.

'See?' I said to McGinty. 'We can keep them out, too.'

Until that moment I don't think he had really believed my profound statement that some British tanks were better in some respects than some German tanks. And vice versa. Especially the vice versa.

But he gingerly fingered the gashes on the front of Ian's tank, and went away to polish his telescope.

If this book can be said to be a history of anything, it is a history of Five Troop. Not of the squadron, or of the regiment. If anybody wants to know what happened in other troops, or in other squadrons, it's all recorded painstakingly in the War Diaries and lodged in a Records Office somewhere.

And as Clarkeforce slowly forged its way northwards Five Troop religiously shot at things which were supposed to be shot at, managed to avoid casualties within the troop, and never once got lost.

But this isn't to say that there wasn't any excitement. Each day brought it's tale of brewed up Churchills, and enemy guns; men on both sides were killed, wounded, and taken prisoner. Ian Steward was carried away with his second wound of the war when a high explosive shell burst near his tank. Unfortunately he was sitting on the side of the tank at the time. Determined snipers brought death to one or two unwary tank commanders. Once the enemy launched a counterattack, but it was a half-hearted affair which he broke off before he'd got it properly launched.

And all the time we plodded on northwards.

But nothing noteworthy happened to Five Troop.

Until we reached Brembosch.

Brembosch was nothing much to look at; just a dead flat piece of ground, with isolated groups of farm buildings here and there. I never could make out why the enemy wanted to defend the place, but he did. In fact, he went so far as to build an anti-tank ditch right across the landscape. There was a certain amount of trouble getting over this obstacle but in the end we managed it and started to advance.

Sometimes things get a bit confused on a battlefield; and when you've only got one crossing over an anti-tank ditch it gets a bit like the first jump at Aintree during the Grand National.

After a good deal of juggling I found myself somehow or other alongside the tank of 'C' Squadron Leader.

We did an 'After you, Claude' act for a little while, and then he rolled forward over the temporary crossing. At that moment a cloud of dust raced to meet us from the far side of the ditch, a cloud which suddenly halted to reveal the Brigadier's Sherman tank.

The Brigadier shoved his dusty head out of the turret, took one look at 'C' Squadron Leader cautiously trundling forward, and then he bellowed: 'Go on, Tubby! There's nothing up there!'

I really did fear the worst then.

And five minutes later Tubby's tank was knocked out and he was carried back, wounded.

Nobody saw where the shot came from, and in moments like that you're apt to take shelter behind anything you can. Out on our right was a thickish sort of hedge, and somehow or other I shepherded Five Troop into the lee of it. Not that the hedge would have stopped anything, in fact if anything it prevented us seeing the battlefield properly. But I suppose there's something of the ostrich in all of us.

So we inched forward in the shadow of this hedge, keeping our eyes peeled for anything which looked like trouble. We were not alone: in front of us Tony Cunningham was taking his troop along the hedge too, and behind us one of our SP guns was tailing along looking as if he had just come for the ride.

And then there was an unpleasant bang from behind us and the SP gun went up in flames.

This was bad: the SP's seventeen-pounders were precious to us, and their numbers were gradually being whittled down. But it was clear that the shot came from beyond the hedge, so throwing caution to the winds I stood up on top of the turret to see if I could spot the blighter. And I could.

About a thousand yards away a low-slung German self-propelled gun was hugging the cover of a small copse. Its grey-green colour blended beautifully with the trees and if it had not been moving I doubt if I would have seen it.

It was changing its firing position, so I knew we had a few minutes' breathing space. Quickly I pointed it out to Sergeant Robinson and Corporal Watson, and with one accord we traversed our guns to the right, sweeping aside the top brushwood of the hedge.

McGinty quickly picked up the target and just as I was about to bawl 'Fire!' I heard three rapid explosions on my left. Tony Cunningham had seen it, too, and opened fire. A second later six tank guns were throwing armour-piercing shells at the target.

The commander of the enemy gun was quick off the mark. Before anybody had time to fire a second shot he had surrounded himself by a screen of phosphorous smoke. But he was pinned in that copse. He couldn't move – and we could wait.

But we were impatient, that was the trouble. We kept firing into that little smoke cloud, lacing it back and forth with AP shot. I dare say we indulged in what the finance kings would call 'an uneconomical expenditure of ammunition,' but after twenty minutes' steady firing the smoke screen thinned out and drifted away. Through our binoculars we saw that the SP was brewing nicely, and there was no sign of life in its vicinity. Not that we expected any; if the crew had any sense they were laying in the nearest ditch waiting for the schemozzle to die down.

Tony and I tossed up for that one.

But I think it was a little hard that he should paint the swastika on the end of his gun with black paint borrowed from Five Troop. I don't think McGinty ever forgave me; for a long time afterwards he was muttering darkly about double-headed pennies and things.

That night we settled down around the usual crossroads, and made plans for the next day's advance. Clarkeforce was going well and the end of our twenty-five-mile trip seemed to be in sight. Our objective was now firmly established: to cut the road leading from Bergen-op-Zoom to Breda. And it looked as if we would do it.

There was a sliver of moon out that night, and as we formed the tanks into a ring of steel I felt peculiarly comfortable. All guns were traversed outwards, and inside the ring was a strange sense of security.

I was talking quietly to the troop when Ian came up and leaned on *Avenger*.

'Got your map?' he said.

I nodded and reached into the turret for it.

He took the map from me and made a ring round a group of farm buildings about half a mile to the right of our harbour position.

'The Brigadier's a bit worried about that spot, John,' he said. 'It's empty now, but the enemy could move a couple of SPs in there during the night and make things hot for us in the morning.'

'So?'

'So I want you to take your troop out there and see he doesn't!'

I gulped and stared wildly around. The bare idea of driving out to that farm in the darkness gave me the willies, let alone stopping there all night!

'I see,' I said, for want of anything better. 'Well – see you in the morning, I hope.'

The troop had been listening to this in stunned silence. After Ian had mooched away I turned to them and said:

'Well, we're going out on our own. Any questions?'

Sergeant Robinson cleared his throat.

'We'll have to take it in turns to be guard tank, then, sir?' he said.

'I don't know,' I admitted. 'We'll see what it's like when we get out there. I dare say we'll all be on guard, all night.'

But we weren't. In fact, once again we had a better time than the rest of the outfit.

Knowing that if we went cross-country in the dark we would almost certainly get lost, and probably finish up in a German Ration Dump or something, I decided to follow the road to our little farm. This meant pushing on a good deal further than the area we had cleared of the enemy, for the road ran north for some distance before sending off a side-track to the farm.

For a few moments I toyed with the idea of doing another 'Besas blazing' charge, but in the end I decided it might be better to try and creep up on the thing.

Imagine, if you can, a thirty-odd ton tank, trying to do 'softlee, softlee, catchee monkey' act. Well, that was us; crawling at nought miles per hour through the dark lanes towards this isolated farm.

It felt as if we were making enough noise to wake the dead, and we probably were, but if there were any Germans about they decided not to get mixed up with us.

It seemed as if the low hedges on either side of us would never stop passing, and even Crosby called up on the intercom to ask if I was sure we were on the right road.

I was far from sure, as a matter of fact, but I tried to get a ring of confidence into my voice as I said 'Of course I'm sure. The turning off to the right is just about here.'

To my eternal astonishment I had hardly uttered the words before the road off to the right appeared in the faint moonlight, and it was with an audible sigh of relief that we swung down it and away from the enemy.

The farm turned out to be three buildings in the shape of a capital A, and having heard that all-round defence is a thing to be aimed at, I stationed one tank at each corner of the triangle. And then we switched off our engines and waited.

Somewhere in the darkness to the left and behind us lay Clarkeforce, in harbour. And everywhere else as far as I was concerned lay the enemy.

We tiptoed about and spoke in hushed whispers as we unshipped the tank spotlights. In the turret of each tank a man kept watch, eyes and ears alert for the slightest sound from the darkness.

But when the sound did come we all heard it clearly. It was the unmistakable noise of tracked vehicles bearing down on the farm.

'Someone coming, sir!' whispered Corporal Watson hoarsely.

'Not tanks, anyway,' I breathed. 'Too light. Get everybody mounted.'

He glided away into the darkness and I climbed up on to *Avenger*, to stare down the lane along which we had recently travelled. If they were Germans they were in for the shock of their lives, because I had a 75mm gun and two machine guns trained down that road.

I didn't know whether to be pleased or disappointed when I saw the shape of a British steel helmet above the top of the hedge, but when I quietly spoke to a British infantry sergeant he nearly jumped out of his skin.

'Cor flip!' he said. 'I didn't know you wus 'ere, sir. I wus tol' to bring my platoon and a section of Vickers out here for the night. The Brigadier wus a bit worried about this farm.'

'So I heard,' I said. 'What have you got?'

What with Bren guns, a two-inch mortar, some Vickers machine guns, and a happy assortment of Stens and rifles, I was able to get down to the all-round defence business with some effect.

But that was not all; half an hour later three towed anti-tank guns came lumbering down the lane, commanded by a young Second-Lieutenant.

'Hullo,' he said politely. 'I had an idea I might find some of you chaps out here. My CO said... '

'I know,' I said. 'The Brigadier's worried.'

'That's right,' he grinned. 'Well, we seem to have a pretty formidable force here now. I shouldn't think he need worry anymore.'

We talked a bit about where the anti-tank guns would best be sited and then I got on the 'A' set to Ian.

'Hello, Fox Five,' I said. 'Am in position, and have been joined by friends from forty-five and fifty-one. All is quiet so far.'

'Hello, Fox Five,' Ian replied. 'Roger. Carry on, Foleyforce.'

And that's how the name came to be coined.

And we had a peaceful night, too. But the rest of Clarkeforce didn't. Through the darkness we heard the occasional crack of a rifle and we learned later that one of two determined snipers had made the night seem much too long, until an infantry patrol was organised to chase them away.

The next morning I disbanded the combined force, but not without a tinge of regret. Our tank spotlights would have provided ample illumination for the field of fire, and if the enemy had decided to occupy that farm we might have put up a resistance to rank in the history books with the defence of Stalingrad. At least, that's what I thought as I motored happily back to join the squadron.

Harry Langton was waiting by his tank as we drove past.

'Dead lucky Five Troop,' he called out. 'Get the cushy jobs every time!'

I put my tongue out at him, and he thumbed his nose at me, and we were thus engaged when the Brigadier descended on us, just to see how the squadron was shaping.

Two days later we came in sight of our objective – the road from Bergen-op-Zoom to Breda.

Dawn found us in a spread-out harbour, scattered amongst a group of cottages and farm buildings, and through the morning mist we heard the grinding whine of Alan Biddulph's three-tonners coming up with ammunition and petrol.

The boys who drove those lorries deserve as much praise as the actual tank crews. Protected only by a thin canvas screen, often carrying enough high-explosive to blow the whole squadron to Kingdom Come, they quite happily ploughed their way along recently-won roads and over shell-pocked fields to deliver their vital loads to the tanks.

And this is the sort of thing that sometimes happened to them.

We were rubbing the sleep out of our eyes and unloading the jerricans of petrol, and Five Troop were exchanging good-humoured badinage with the truck drivers.

'Where you bin all night?' said Smith 161. 'We wus expectin' you larst night!'

'Well, stop worrying. Your mother expected you for nine months,' said the tired-eyed driver, giving the rest of the troop a broad wink.

Smith 161 heaved a mock sigh of despair.

'I dunno,' he said. 'You Echelon types. Spend arf yer time swiggin' Cognac with Dutch judies, larfin' like a flippin' drain at us poor sods doin' all the dirty work.'

'Dirty work is all you're fit for,' quipped the driver.

And then the lorry lurched sideways and a billow of white flame exploded from the back.

'Christ!' said the driver. And the rest of his words were drowned in another explosion which sent up a fountain of dirt from the road.

Somebody screamed somewhere, and Ian yelled 'Action!' in a voice which could be heard above the crackle of the blazing ammunition truck.

I grabbed the truck driver by the arm.

'Come on,' I shouted in his ear. 'You'll be safer in a tank when this lot goes up.'

'That's all right, sir,' he said. And before I could stop him he wrenched his arm free, hurled himself into the driving seat of his truck, and drove the blazing vehicle a hundred yards down the road before bailing out and scooting back to the harbour area.

Some of the tanks on the north side of the harbour managed to get a couple of shots at the marauding SP which had done the damage, but he didn't hang about long.

And then when the noise and confusion had died down Ian gave out the orders for the final attack towards the road.

A railway embankment hid all but the rooftops of the village of Wouw, but on the left was a tall windmill which reminded me so irresistibly of Stelling Minnis and the 'attacks' along Stone Street that I automatically looked around for Sergeant Atkins.

I couldn't take my eyes off that windmill, and I wasn't the least bit surprised when Ian said Five Troop were to take the left flank, using the windmill as a guide.

We made a brief nodding acquaintance with the Scottish regiment who were doing the infantry work, and then off we went.

By now we had acquired a certain amount of cunning in the use of smoke, but laying the stuff seemed to take up an awful lot of time and attention. I remember we left the shelter of some buildings, firing our little smoke mortar and occasionally thickening it up with smoke grenades hurled from the turret. From time to time I kept an eye on the infantry, but they were plugging doggedly forward like plough-horses homeward plodding their weary way. And it was not until we reached the railway embankment that the enemy reacted at all, and then he did so with some heavy mortaring.

Craters appeared as if by magic, and the din of exploding mortars drowned the noise of our own twenty-five-pounder creeping barrage.

Here and there infantrymen were folding up like puppets suddenly released from their strings, while others took cover in ditches, shell-holes and behind the long embankment.

These things were bursting quite close to us as we motored slowly along behind the infantry, but it somehow never occurred to me that one of them could land on us. But it could, and did.

Quite suddenly there came a brief flash of orange flame from the front plate of the tank, and a tremendous explosion almost split my eardrums. I ducked down into the turret, to find the inside of *Avenger* a thick cloud of dust and smoke.

'Everyone all right?' I said over the IC.

'What was it, sir?' said Pickford.

'Mortar bomb,' I replied briefly. 'And it's blown every bit of dust out of every crack in the tank,' I added.

'Thought this smelled a bit like Goodnestone dirt,' said Farrell from the front compartment.

But apart from the thick dust which now coated everything inside the tank, we seemed to be all right. I gave the Infantry Company Commander a thumbs up sign, and he nodded. So we launched ourselves over the embankment.

We had agreed that from this point the tanks would lead, and it seemed to me that our best plan lay in getting to the shelter of the windmill buildings as quick as we could.

'Driver, speed up!' I said. And away we went like the hammers of hell. I just had time to call up *Alert* and *Angler* and tell them to keep up with me, and then I had to start looking for likely trouble spots, because the smoke had now ceased.

And then I noticed a broad, poplar-lined road running across our front and it was quite a few seconds before I realised that here was our objective. This insignificant path of tarmac and cobbles was the road we had travelled twenty-five miles to cut. A fierce exultation swept up inside me when I grasped the fact that we had reached the end of our journey, but it was a sensation which was quickly quelled by the sight of a German half-track going like stink down the road away from Wouw.

'Seventy-five traverse left!' I said – but there was no need for any more. McGinty had seen it, too, and he had that turret swinging round like chair-o-planes at a fair.

With a loud clang an empty shell case flew out of the breech as the gun whipped back into the turret. Like a well-oiled machine, Pickford fed another shell into the breech and tapped McGinty's elbow to indicate the gun was loaded.

The first shot had missed, and so did the second, and every moment the half-track was getting further and further away. And then out of the corner of my eye I saw a tongue of flame shoot out of the muzzle of *Angler*'s gun. The half-track somersaulted forward, turning nose over exhaust, and a group of tiny figures in field-grey scurried to the side of the road and disappeared into the landscape.

And then we were at the windmill, and the infantry were across the road.

It was hard to keep the smugness out of my voice as I called up Ian and told him that the road was successfully cut, but I still think it would have been a good idea to have painted a large pair of scissors on the side of my turret.

Judging by the noise coming from Wouw, the rest of the regiment were having a tough time clearing the enemy out of it. But soon we saw the heartening spectacle of columns of enemy prisoners being led away from the town.

Harry Langton, I heard afterwards, played a perilous game of hide-and-seek with an enemy SP, before manoeuvring it into a position where one of our own SPs was able to brew it up.

But from where we were, acting as longstop on the road beside the windmill, it was difficult to see anything. So I had the bright idea of climbing up to the top of the windmill and viewing the scene from there.

The windmill seemed to be deserted, so I climbed up the floury, winding staircase until I reached a window near the sail axle. Yet even from here the landscape looked deserted. A pall of grey smoke hung over Wouw, and away to the left I could see the rounded outlines of some Canadian Ram tanks sweeping up towards the road.

And then my eye caught a flicker of movement in a hedge about eight hundred yards beyond the road. Trembling with excitement, I focussed my binoculars on the spot and saw that it was a very nicely camouflaged enemy SP. And it was right in line with *Alert*'s gun!

I looked down from the window, and it was plain that Sergeant Robinson hadn't seen this tempting target. And although I yelled myself hoarse he couldn't hear me because he was wearing his padded earphones.

And that was where a sack of flour came in handy. My immediate idea was to attract Sergeant Robinson's attention by dropping the sack of flour on top of his tank. And then I thought this was trying Officer-NCO relationship a bit too far. So I heaved it out of the window so that it fell on the cobbles beside *Alert*, landing with a satisfying thud and sending up a white cloud of flour.

That did it all right! Sergeant Robinson mouthed an imprecation and looked up to see who was playing silly beggars. Grimacing at him, I mimed the action of removing my earphones, and he tumbled to it at once.

In a few brief words I pointed out where the target lay, and he swung into action immediately. I paused only long enough to see that the SP was withdrawing from the hedge, and then I flung myself down the spiral staircase to join in the fun.

I couldn't get down those stairs fast enough, and every second I expected the place to be shaken by the blast of *Alert*'s gun. But he hadn't fired when I arrived breathless in the cobbled yard. And then I found out why.

The most lurid language was emerging from *Alert*'s turret; it sounded as if the tank commander and gunner were having a competition to see who could swear longest without undue repetition.

Sergeant Robinson was winning easily when a 75mm round came flying out of the turret and on to a grass verge. He leaned out of the turret and spat on the shell bitterly.

'Of all the thousands of rounds I've fired through this gun, I have to wait until now to get a misfire!' he snorted. And then he took up his competition again.

It was too late then, of course, for although we both took several shots at the retreating SP, it was nearly a mile away and well out of our reach.

We harboured that night in Wouw itself, and although their town was sadly battered and scarred, the inhabitants turned out to cheer us as we clattered through the streets. It was just like France and Belgium, except that this was no second-hand acclamation. We really were the liberators this time, and it was strangely satisfying to look at the genuine delight in the eyes of the people of Wouw, a delight which was plainly visible even through tears.

And they still welcomed us, even after the Germans put down a carpet of HE shells on the town that night. Despite the fierce battle which the regiment had fought for Wouw, its spired church had remained standing proudly throughout the fighting. Yet that night a lucky shell from one of the German heavy guns reduce the lovely church to smouldering ashes.

In a way it was our fault; if we hadn't been in the town the Germans might not have shelled it. Yet, as I say, the people still made us warmly welcome.

Five Troop couldn't understand it, until I reminded them gently that our country hadn't been occupied by the Germans.

NINE

FROM THE TIME Clarkeforce ended, it was thirteen weeks before Five Troop fired another shot at the enemy. But we were kept fairly busy, just the same.

We had the feeling of being pawns in a mammoth game of chess – being sent across miles of Europe to act as a threat to the enemy's flank, dashing back again to fend off an enemy threat to our flank. I believe the CO sent a cryptic message to the commander of another armoured regiment going in the opposite direction to us, saying: 'Just castling.' And that was how we went on.

From Wouw we went to Breda, where we lived in a jam factory for a few days. This provided a bit of variety for the rations, and we passed the time concocting various puddings of army biscuits and strawberry pulp. Then just as we got the knack of it we were moved to Oudenbosch, where we lived in a sort of monastery and, because there was a fitted stage there, I was given the job of producing a Regimental Concert Party.

So many things went wrong that the show was a howling success, but luckily we received orders to move to Budel before a repeat performance could be arranged.

There was a definite task at Budel; the capture of the town of Blerick, on the Maas. But it was a two-squadron job, and we sat back and followed the battle over the radio. Sounded a good party, too.

From there we were switched to Brunssum and were all teed up for an attack on the Siegfried Line, with the weather getting colder and wetter all the time.

And it turned out to be the weather which postponed that battle. Reconnaissance reports said that the ground was just too boggy for tanks to get across, and that it would need at least three days' hard frost before any tank movement was possible. So we moved in with the good Limburg folk of Brunssum and sat around waiting for three days' frost.

By the middle of December people got rather tired of waiting for the cold weather, so we rolled on to the big transporters again and set off for Tilburg, to do a spot of training with a division we were scheduled to support in another battle somewhere or other. But somewhere in the middle of Holland we were overtaken by a despatch rider with a message which caused the transporters to turn around and head off in a totally different direction.

Von Runstedt was coming through the Ardennes.

And then, of course, the frosty weather set in.

This time we fetched up in Tongres, once again doing a long-stop act in case the Germans captured Liége or tried to cross the Meuse.

It was in Tongres that we spent Christmas, but I don't remember much about it. That's the sort of Christmas it was. Each morning we would motor gently out to one of the roads leading into the town, and there we would take up our position astride the road and wait for something to happen. But nothing ever did. Unless you count a raid on the town by three Focke-Wulfes.

It was a bright and frosty morning, and Five Troop were more concerned with keeping themselves warm than anything else. Casually we watched three vapour trails up in the sky, and even when they peeled off and dived towards the town we didn't suspect anything. For so long we had been accustomed to having complete mastery of the air, that all aircraft were automatically classified as 'one of ours'.

In the town an American anti-aircraft battery was stationed, and soon the sky was a mass of bursting shells between which the three Focke-Wulfes twisted and turned with apparent ease. The crumps of bombs echoed dully towards us and we were just wondering what the American gunners thought they were playing at when suddenly one of the aircraft sprouted a fan of flames from the engine cowling, and with a crescendo whine started spiralling to earth.

Five Troop cheered loudly, but our cheers were interrupted by a huge ten-ton lorry thundering towards us at breakneck speed. Sergeant Robinson stepped into the road and held up his hand (since we were supposed to check all traffic coming into the town) and with a squeal of brakes the ten-tonner halted and a scared black face looked down from the driving cab.

'Got your trip check, brother?' said Sergeant Robinson, who had acquired the language with remarkable speed and fluency.

'Yessuh, Ah sho' has,' said the driver, handing out a piece of white paper. 'Man, ah's gittin' away from Celles jes' as fast as ah can! There's Germans in that town!'

'What do you think they are; butterflies?' said Senge Robinson, jerking his thumb towards the Focke-Wulfes.

The coloured boy looked up and rolled his eyes.

'Jes' ain't no peace nowheres at all, jes' nowheres at all,' he muttered, as he swung his truck around and roared off in the direction he had come.

Five Troop didn't think much of the American Army that day, but the following morning we heard about the defence of Bastogne and minds were changed with considerable alacrity. We finally decided that the American Army was something like ours, some good units and some not so good. Notwithstanding Napoleon's edict to the contrary, we declared that it takes all sorts to make an army – any army.

A few days later it started to snow, and that was when we were shifted out of the comfort of Tongres and sent off into the Ardennes in pursuit of the now-retreating Von Runstedt.

Transporters took us part of the way, and although at first the scenic beauty was enough to impress even Five Troop, as the day grew on and the snow continued unabated we began to pine for the flat countryside and muggy weather of Holland.

Movement in the snow-covered Ardennes was a nightmare. Our steel-plated tracks just slid impotently off the icy road surfaces and the tanks glided out of control all over the place.

We were very envious of the rubber-shod Shermans who swept past us one day, motoring as happily as if they were on a main road in high summer. But it was a short-lived envy because later that night we passed the same regiment going in the opposite direction, the tank commanders looking like abominable snowmen.

The Sherman engine is cooled by a large fan which sucks air through from the turret. This means that there is always a considerable downdraught going through the commander's cupola, and in a snowstorm this has its disadvantages. A snowflake which is descending quite happily several feet away from the tank, is suddenly sucked out of the vertical and whipped up against the unhappy tank commander.

But sometimes we wondered whether we wouldn't have swapped our steel tracks for their rubber ones, and we would have taken the snow-attracting fan as a makeweight.

The Ardennes was the only place where I've seen a man push a tank. And it was like this.

We were gingerly feeling our way down one of the hill roads, drivers only in the tanks – everybody else walking beside and helping the unfortunate driver as best they could. 'Bing' Crosby did wonders with *Avenger*, coaxing her gently out of the skids and slides, and by featherweight touches on the tiller keeping the massive weight of metal balanced nicely on the centre of the cambered surface.

Behind us came *Alert*, driven by Trooper Johnson, now recovered from his shaking up on the Orne. Beside *Alert* walked Johnson's new co-driver, a big, hefty ex-docker from Liverpool called Riley.

I just happened to look around in time to see *Alert* starting to slide off the crest of the camber. In a fit of angry despair Riley put his beefy shoulder against the side of the tank.

'Get back, ye silly bitch!' he snarled. And to his utter amazement *Alert* dutifully slid back to the required position.

'Jeez, did ye see that?' cried Riley. 'I pushed the thing an' it went!'

'Now I've seen everything,' I said. 'But don't try it again, Riley. If *Alert* hadn't gone back, you'd have been laying under it in that ditch now!'

And that was quite true. At each side of the road ran a deep drainage ditch. As and when a tank got out of control and slid silently to the road verge, it always ended up in the ditch, from where it had to be shifted by the rest of its troop. Usually at considerable expenditure of time, sweat, and self-control.

Each night we slept where we could, and we didn't much care where it was. Barns, cottages, schoolrooms – we flung ourselves down, snow-blind, cold, and weary, with nothing to look forward to the next day except (if we were lucky) five miles of slipping, sliding, skidding and unditching as we travelled uphill and down and then up again.

Somewhere in the Ardennes the Germans were slowly retreating, and at first we used to get hopeful sounding orders to move to such-and-such a village by nightfall in order to put in a dawn attack the next day. But nightfall probably found us only a fifth of the way there, and averaging something like a mile every four hours.

We learned a lot of useful things, though.

For example, we learned that although standing on the engine hatches kept your feet lovely and warm, it fairly wrecked your boots. And for one dreadful day we plodded through the snow with boots which were kept in one piece only by a stitch here and there. By a superhuman bit of organising Ian contacted the Echelon and got new boots for everybody, but even these were no protection against the bitter cold of the snow.

And we learned yet again that the Churchill could take a fair amount of knocking about.

One day, after a couple of ditched tanks had successfully blocked the road, Foleyforce was pushed out across country to see if it was possible to get around the blockage.

The road on which we were waiting wound steeply downhill in a series of tortuous S-bends, and it looked from the map as if we could make a wide sweep out to the right and re-join the road at the bottom of the hill.

It was absolute heaven to be able to get out of bottom gear and put on some speed. We swept across a large field, the tracks throwing up a spray of snow behind us, and after crossing a shaky railway bridge we found ourselves at the head of a narrow lane which led straight down to the road we wanted to join. But it was a drop of about one in six, and at the bottom the lane crossed a stone bridge which spanned a deep gorge.

'What do you think of it, Crosby?' I said, as we stood beside *Avenger* and looked down the hill.

He shook his head doubtfully, but together with Sergeant Robinson and Corporal Watson and their drivers we walked down the lane and looked at the bridge.

Such a short distance it was. Probably we'd have covered it in thirty seconds if it hadn't been for the snow. But at least it was virgin snow, not the solid-packed ice on which we had been skating for the past five days.

'Shall we have a go, sir?' asked Sergeant Robinson.

This, I thought to myself, is what you're paid for, Foley. The ability to make decisions. Oh, hell!

Aloud I said: 'Oh, we'll have a go. Just *Avenger* at first, and only Crosby and I aboard.'

The rest of the troop gathered in the roadway to watch the fun, and I told Crosby to have the side door open just in case he had to bale out quickly.

'Driver advance,' I said. And slowly we crept forward.

For about thirty yards I thought we were going to make it, and then my heart missed a beat as I felt *Avenger*'s tail swinging round in a menacing slide. Crosby felt it too, and he used every trick in the book (and a few more besides) in an effort to get the tank under control again. But faster and faster she was sliding down the slope, gliding to what looked like destruction in the gorge at the bottom.

'We've had it this time,' I yelled into the IC. 'Bale out!'

And I leaped from the turret into a snow-covered hedge at the side of the lane. Then I stood up and looked after the skating tank as it slid faster and faster down the hill.

There was no sign of Crosby baling out.

Seconds that seemed like hours ticked past, and the tank was fast approaching the bridge over the gorge, silently swinging and bouncing from bank to bank. And then at the last second the pannier door flew open and 'Bing' Crosby flung himself clear of the vehicle.

''Ad to stop and turn that master-switch off, zur,' he said, brushing the snow off himself.

In dead silence we watched *Avenger* plunge through the stone wall of the bridge, cascading rocks and mortar everywhere. There came a loud splintering noise as small trees were broken off at their roots, and then a series of diminishing bangs and crashes as the tank bounced its way to the bottom of the gorge.

I don't quite know what I expected to see as we leaned over the shattered parapet of the bridge, but what we did see was *Avenger* laying astride a stream and looking like one of those lead-cast models they use in sand-table exercises.

'Well, she be roight way up, zur,' drawled Crosby.

'Yes,' I said. 'But the REME are going to have a job recovering her from down there. I suppose I'd better go down and get out the maps and codes.'

'Oi'll come with yew, zur,' said Crosby, and together we started to scramble down the precipitous slope leading to the little stream.

We found *Avenger* battered and bent, and the inside of the turret a shambles of ammunition, maps, instruments, and tins of rations. But otherwise fairly sound.

Crosby picked his way into the driving seat, switched on the master switch and pressed the starter button.

Without a moment's hesitation the engine burst into life, and soon the gorge was echoing with noise as Crosby ran the revs up and down.

The IC worked, too, so I put on a headset and spoke to Crosby.

'See how far we can get up the bank,' I said. 'May as well make the recovery as easy as possible for the REME crowd.'

So we backed away from the stream and put her nose at the spruce-covered wall of the canyon.

I never want another ride like that. All the way we were standing on our tail, and there was a distinct chance that at any moment we would topple over backwards. Grenades fell out of the racks as we inched our way up the cliff face, and several times I'd have laid generous odds that we would crash to the bottom again.

If the engine had stalled we certainly would have crashed, but Crosby kept the motor roaring flat out and the horns of the tank jinked from right to left as we snatched our way from one patch of trees to the next.

Three times I raised the microphone to my lips to say 'OK, let's leave it here,' but each time *Avenger* lurched upwards again and we clawed our way a little nearer the top of the gorge.

The rest of the troop had gathered on the stone bridge to watch our progress, and the chasm fairly echoed with their cheers as, with a final burst from the engine, *Avenger* heaved herself over the rim and on to the road.

But I told Ian I didn't recommend that route for the rest of the Squadron. There's a limit to what you can expect even from a Churchill.

We also learned that it doesn't do to have loose tracks in the snow. At least, Corporal Watson learned.

We were about to start our endless journey one morning when I found the crew of *Angler* deliberately slackening the tracks.

'What's the idea?' I asked.

'Well, sir,' he said, in his soft Hampshire voice. 'I've worked it out and I reckon with a slack track we stand a better chance of controlling these slides… '

And he went into a long and involved discussion about track tensions, the packing power of snow, thrust, leverage, and all sorts of things which I only half understood.

'Well, it's worth a try,' I agreed. 'You can always tighten them again.'

As a matter of fact *Angler* seemed to be no better or worse than on any other day. She still slid from side to side as much as any other tank, and she still had to be unditched from time to time.

But by late afternoon we had reached a high plateau and to our intense delight we were able to cram on a little speed and forget the icy roads for a while. We crossed broad fields, deliciously flat, and drove happily along lovely straight rides through pine woods. And as the sun was sinking we were crossing a vast expanse of whiteness – and then *Angler* shed a track.

We pulled over to one side and allowed the rest of the squadron to go by. I wasn't much worried about finding the way – the passage of a squadron of tanks across virgin snow is very unmistakably marked.

'You'd better go on and get the troop billets organised,' I said to Sergeant Robinson. 'We'll stay here with *Angler*.'

In silence we watched the rest of the squadron roar by, showering us with dirt and snow from their tracks. Over the 'A' set I told Ian what was happening, and he gave me the name of the village we were heading for.

'Come on as soon as you can,' he said.

'Wilco, out,' I replied. And then I switched off the set, signalled for the engines to be cut, and climbed down into the snow to inspect the size of the job.

It looked as if *Angler*'s slack tracks had been all right while we were on the smooth road surfaces, but from the moment we started our trek across country, snow had been packing between the track and the top guide rail. Gradually the snow had forced the track away from the guide rail, until during a sudden turn the tank had swung right off one track.

'Couple of hours' job, Corporal Watson,' I said. 'We'll have to break both tracks, chip away all that frozen snow, and then join up the tracks again.'

He scratched his head and looked at *Angler*, helpless in the snow.

'That's about it, sir,' he said.

'Then let's get cracking,' I said. 'Both crews on to it.'

Well, at least it kept us warm. The track plates of a Churchill tank are pretty solid objects, and you need a fair amount of heft to get them where you want them. But we laboured and sweated and wrestled with the things, and didn't notice the sun going down, or the growth of ominous leaden clouds along the skyline.

Soon it was too dark to see what we were doing, so we rigged the tank spotlights and carried on hacking and chipping at the ice-clogged guide rail.

I think it was McGinty who first noticed the noise. He straightened up from struggling with the length of track and cocked his head on one side.

'What d'you make of that, sir?' he said.

I listened, and faintly in the distance I could hear what sounded like an express train going through a tunnel.

'Sounds like a salvo from a battleship,' I said. 'But I don't think it is.'

And then, with a wail like a tortured banshee, the blizzard hit us.

One moment we were working in an unnaturally still silence, and the next we were in the middle of a howling blast of snowflakes. It's the only time I've seen snowflakes moving horizontally, instead of dropping vertically. In the bluey light of the spotlights, the snow was just a foggy, blurred streak, stinging our faces like white-hot rivets.

It was useless to try and shout against the noise of the storm, so I stumbled around shepherding the two crews into the lee of *Avenger*. Here there seemed to be a tiny enclave of silence: a silence which at the same time was strangely airless. We had to suck in deep breaths to get any oxygen from the air at all.

Before then we would have said our thirty-six ton Churchills were pretty large objects, but they were dwarfed into insignificance by the magnitude of the snowstorm which howled about us.

After a few minutes I caught a glimpse of Trooper George's face; it was white and trembling, and his nostrils twitched convulsively. I'd seen those symptoms before – they were the outward indication of an inside paralysed with fear. The blizzard was doing to George what the Germans had so far failed to do, he was very frightened. And there is nothing so infectious as fear.

Standing there in the lee of *Avenger*, with my face buried in the collar of my tank suit, I listened to the shriek of the icy wind and wondered what the devil to do. Dimly I remembered that the antidote to fear is activity, and that the way to stop being frightened is to start doing something, the harder the better.

'We'd better get cracking on those tracks again,' I said. 'Otherwise we'll stay here all night.'

'We can't work in this, sir,' quavered Trooper George.

Inwardly I believed he was right, but I swallowed my Adam's apple and with as much confidence as I could muster I said: 'Don't be bloody silly, George. Get hold of a hammer and start clearing those track guides. Come on, all of you; you've had a damned good rest. The rest of the squadron have got their feet under somebody's table now!'

The wind almost flattened us as we stepped out into it, and I nearly cried with rage when I saw that the blizzard had built a huge snowdrift up against the side of *Angler*, completely burying the track we had cleared. But like men in a nightmare we started the seemingly ridiculous task of replacing the tracks in a whirling world of movement.

With their tank suits zipped right up to the chin, and their waterproof hoods fastened across their faces, the crews looked like figures in an ancient film about arctic exploration, except that instead of dogs and sledges in the background there were the elaphantine shapes of two Churchill tanks.

Eventually the storm eased up a bit, but it was still a pretty fierce snowstorm by British standards. Yet somehow we managed to clear the ice away from *Angler*'s track guides, and somehow we managed to get the heavy tracks back in position and joined up again, and then

Corporal Watson had one of his brilliant ideas.

'We've got that self-heating soup in the bottom of the back bin, sir,' he yelled. 'What about opening it?'

Some of the crew got back into the comparative shelter of the inside of the tanks. Others huddled between the front horns. But each of us had one of those excellent tins of tomato soup, fitted with a centre-tube carrying a quick heating element.

All that was necessary was to touch a small wick with the lighted end of a cigarette and in a matter of seconds we were drinking hot soup and bringing down blessings on Mr Heinz and the shadowy figures of ICI who were jointly responsible for this salvation.

The hot soup gave me a lovely internal glow, but it was not such a penetrating glow as followed a few minutes later when, by some queer trick of acoustics, I happened to hear Bing and Farrell talking in the front compartment of *Avenger*.

'Hope we can foind this village where the rest of the lads are,' said Crosby dubiously.

'That's all right, Bing boy,' said his co-driver. 'It's not our worry, chum. CJ'll git us there all right, you see.'

I beamed happily when I overheard this, and squared my shoulders confidently. And then I walked round to the front of *Avenger* and found that the snowstorm had completely obliterated every trace of the squadron's passage.

We were alone in a vast, unmarked expanse of whiteness.

As if to drive the point home, the snowclouds cleared away and a mammoth silver moon appeared to emphasise the emptiness of the landscape.

I got down on my hands and knees with a torch, and could just make out a very faint depression in the surface of the snow, all that was left of the tracks of sixteen Churchill tanks. But they pointed straight to the moon, so that appeared to be a good way to start, even if it had a faintly symbolic ring.

The snow seemed to muffle our tracks and we rolled across the white landscape to the unusual accompaniment of our engine-noises only. I called up Ian on the radio, but there was no response so I guessed the rest of the squadron were snugly tucked up in bed somewhere.

I kept looking hopefully at my map, but it didn't seem to do any good. Once I thought I'd fixed our position pretty well and then we ran slap into a wood – and there wasn't any wood marked on the map.

We swung to the right and trundled along the front edge of this wood, and then across country again in what I hoped was the right direction. As a matter of fact it was only a question of time before we would get on the right track. If we kept going long enough we were bound to come up against some recognisable feature like a cross roads or a railway bridge, and from here it was just a question of straightforward map-reading.

At least, that's what I kept telling myself as we motored across the featureless landscape, crashing through low hedges and hoping to goodness we weren't heading for any snow-covered frozen ponds.

And then, like twin beacons of hope, I saw the white fingers of a pair of headlights in the horizon. That, at least, indicated a road, and with a glad cry I set off towards the headlights.

To my surprise the lights stopped to wait for us and, my head full of tales about lightning penetration by the enemy, I slowed down and prepared for action.

With the turret unlocked, and all guns loaded, we approached the vehicle waiting for us on the road.

'Shall I give him a burst just to warn him off, sir?' said McGinty.

'Christ, no!' I said, with sudden recognition. 'It's the Colonel!'

It was indeed the Commanding Officer, and as soon as I recognised his square bodied staff car I stopped the tanks and walked to meet him.

'Hello, John,' he said affably. We had come a long way I since my saluting rocket in Westgate.

'Been having track trouble, sir,' I said.

'I thought I recognised Churchill engines,' he said. 'Do you know where your squadron is?'

'Yes, sir,' I said, being careful not to mention that I wasn't quite clear about how to get there.

But I think he must have read my thoughts because he pointed back down the road and said. 'Turn right at the crossroads and left at the next road junction. It's about two miles.'

'That's right, sir,' I said, hoping it sounded as if I knew it already.

He gave me a shrewd sideways look, and walked back with me to talk to the crews.

Things never turn out the way you expect them: not one of the crews was smoking inside a tank!

We had nearly reached the end of our Ardennes travels, but we didn't know it.

Three more days we travelled across the snows, and the last day was the worst of all. The country was truly mountainous; the roads narrow, twisting, and highly polished. We had started before dawn, inching our way along the glassy cobbles, halting interminably whilst ditched tanks were cleared, and plodded on through blustery snowstorms beside our lumbering charges.

Usually we managed to arrive somewhere by nightfall, but on this day the sun set and we sat in the snow eating a makeshift meal of cold sausages and wet bread, washed down with a hot, sweet liquid made from a mysterious substance miscalled Tea Powder. And then we staggered to our feet again and plodded on, lurching and slipping almost as much as the tanks.

It was hell for the drivers, but to replace them with less skilful members of the crew inevitably resulted in the tank sliding straight into the nearest ditch, if not over the edge of a precipice.

The cold penetrated our tank suits and all the woollies we could pack on; feet became numb as we hobbled blindly along, patiently following the waltzing tail of the tank in front. A shrill wind explored my inside with the skill of a qualified surgeon, and several times I was tempted to climb up on the engine hatches and warm my paralysed feet, but the memory of our lost crocodile-jawed boots held me in check.

It seemed a century of darkness before the lights of a little scout car told us we were nearly at the end of our day's march.

Gently we drew to a halt and I stumbled forward to meet Mike Carter (now wearing a third pip and acting as Squadron Reconnaissance Officer).

'All right, Johnny?' he said.

I nodded.

'Right: this way.'

It was pitch black, and we followed the tail light of Mike's scout car along a narrow track of unmarked snow. Then I noticed the absence of drainage ditches, but this fact had hardly registered on my mind before Mike gave the signal to turn off the track and park the tanks beside some snow-laden bushes.

There didn't seem to be a house in sight.

'Not bivvying, are we?' I asked in rising horror.

'No,' said Mike. 'We're all together tonight, thank God, not spread around a couple of villages.'

'What sort of place?'

'Oh, biggish building,' he mumbled diffidently.

I had visions of another stone-floored school of convent and I groaned.

'The SSM is taking the men to their quarters. All officers come with me,' said Mike.

I baulked a bit at this because I liked to see Five Troop fixed up for the night before finding my own sleeping spot. But I was so sore-eyed and weary that for once I decided to leave them to the tender mercies of the Sergeant-Major.

Five Troop leaders trudged through the snow behind Mike Carter. Dimly against the black sky we saw a forbidding looking building and under our feet we felt the rough outline of some stone steps. And then Mike pushed open a large door and we stepped into inky blackness.

'No flipping lights, of course,' growled Tony Cunningham.

'It's the blackout,' said Mike. 'Close the door.'

We closed the door, and he opened a second one. And we stepped straight into fairyland.

Dazzling chandeliers sparkled brilliantly in a long, white and gold corridor. An ankle-deep dove-grey carpet enveloped our snow-covered boots. Overstuffed couches and armchairs lined the walls, and the air was heavy with the rich scent of meaty meals and feminine perfume.

We could only stand and gape, like yokels taking in the lights of Piccadilly Circus, while Mike leaned up against a wall and grinned at our stupefaction.

In a daze I dropped my haversack to the floor and prodded the furniture with an unbelieving finger.

'W-w-what is it, Mike?' whispered Dick Richards.

'It's the Château Royale D'Ardennes,' said Mike. 'Second most expensive hotel in Europe. And it's still partly staffed. Come, I'll show you to your rooms!'

And with a mock bow he led the way through a tall door into a lavishly furnished bedroom, which in turn gave on to a luxuriously equipped bathroom in scarlet marble and gold.

Inlaid sycamore beds were well served with smooth sheets and downy blankets, and the room had a warm and soothing atmosphere. The change from the bitter, harsh coldness of the outside world hit me like an emotional piledriver and for some absurd reason I wanted to cry. And then we recovered simultaneously and a babble of questions nearly engulfed Mike Carter.

For a fortnight we lived in the lap of luxury. Our own rations were cooked in the hotel kitchen, and served with impeccable suavity by a fleet of silent-footed waiters. It mattered not to them that a few days before they had similarly attended German officers (or so we were told); they went out of their way to make us comfortable.

We were able to bathe, and put on clean linen, and regard the snow as a pleasant addition to the scenery rather than a peril to be fought and overcome.

Yet during the previous ten days, when we had slept in damp clothes on stone floors and exposed our bodies to everything the elements could hurl at us, we had remained as fit as the proverbial fiddles. But three days after we entered the Château Royale D' Ardennes we all had stinking colds.

No that that bothered us unduly. As the sole occupants of the hotel we were able to have our colds in comfort and thumb our running noses at the healthier, but less comfortable, people billeted in the adjacent villages.

If you want a description of the Château Royale D'Ardennes you can consult the guidebooks. Originally it had been one of the ancestral palaces of the Belgian Royal Family, and the loftiness of the rooms, for one thing, must have made it a very uneconomical hotel by normal standards. Which probably accounts for its reputation of being the second most expensive hotel in Europe.

Opening a door, for example, was by no means a reflex action in that palace. You didn't automatically reach out and turn a handle: entering a room was practically a ceremony in itself. The double-doors ran clear up to the ceiling, and opening them was a two-handed job really needing a couple of servants in Court uniform.

And that's the sort of style in which we lived for a fortnight. Each day we expected the place to be discovered by some of the little tin gods from higher headquarters, but fourteen days slipped by without the true magnificence of our billets being discovered. And then one day we woke up to see an Army Headquarters' staff car parked outside the hotel, and a Captain in a peaked cap (and an equally peaked nose) carefully examining the hotel and scribbling furiously in a Stationery Office notebook.

It was probably a coincidence but next day we were told to stand by to move again.

By now the snow had stopped, more or less, and in the ice-blue skies the RAF played havoc with the forces of Von Runstedt. We still skated about the place doing our chess moves; standing by here in case of a counterattack; moving there as a potential threat to the enemy flank; but the bright sunshine put a different aspect on matters.

We howled with laughter as one of Harry Langton's tanks went tobogganing down a hill and through a stable, and skylarked about with snowballs whilst waiting for the periodic unditching of one tank or another. And most nights we found sleeping-space in a comfortable, warm building of some sort.

But the Ardennes were to have a Parthian shot at us. On the day we received orders to move back to Holland the sky clouded over again and snow tumbled about our ears once more.

Yet our morale was still high, and Five Troop talked longingly of the lovely flat roads of Holland, and 'Bing' Crosby pointedly cleaned the top-gear section of his gear-lever gate.

There was one fiendish hazard we had to negotiate before we were clear of the hills; a short, steep hill road which swept under a railway bridge. And the only way to negotiate it was to halt at the top of the hill, aim the tank carefully between the railway arch, and then go for it with your fingers crossed and your foot down.

Smith 161 baulked a bit at this.

'This is a bit dodgy, innit, sir?' he said, cocking a sparrow-like eye at me.

'You'll be all right, Smith,' I said reassuringly. 'As long as the engine is driving the tracks, and not the other way about, you'll have control over the tank.'

Which was just fine, but we had to queue up to take our turn at this death drive. One or two tanks got the better of their drivers and slid merrily into the buttresses of the bridge, but luckily they were just glancing blows and the Churchills cannoned off, sending up showers of brickdust.

'Be just about right for us to finish it off,' said Smith 161, gloomily.

'D'ye no' fancy it, Smudger?' said his namesake. 'I'll have a bash at yon, if ye like!'

But this was too much for the pride of Smith 161. He squared his shoulders and climbed into the driving seat.

'Any more for the Skylark?' he shouted, with a brief flash of his usual humour. 'If we don't git through first time we ca always 'ave another bash. Run the pennant up on the aerial, George; then they'll know where to dig for us!'

Corporal Watson looked at me and raised his eyebrows. I jerked my head towards *Avenger*, and he nodded understandingly. And then I climbed up and took his place on the commander's pedestal of *Angler*.

From the bottom of the hill Mike Carter waved for the next one to get ready.

'Driver advance,' I said, and *Angler* inched her way towards the centre of the road. There was a short uphill stretch of about ten yards, and we were using this to get the alignment right.

'Driver left... OK... left again... OK... Driver halt! That's about it, Smith.'

We halted, and I squinted along the commander's sighting vanes to see if it looked possible to do the run without touching the tiller bar.

And then Mike raised both hands above his head and signalled for us to come on down.

'Driver advance!' I said, and held my breath.

Smith 161 gave the engine a preliminary burst of power and then he let in the clutch and we were off. I didn't know whether to keep talking encouragingly over the IC or to keep quiet, and then I decided to see how he managed on his own.

Gradually the hill got a grip on us, and we moved faster and faster down the icy road. The tall span of the bridge seemed incredibly narrow as we clattered towards it – and then I heard the engine note falter and the tail of the tank started to waltz from side to side.

'Watch those revs,' I said warningly. 'Keep them up.'

But it was too late, already we were all over the road and it looked a pound to a pinch of salt that we would crash straight into one of the bridge supports and bring the whole lot tumbling about our ears.

The steel tracks scratched sibilants from the polished road surface, and the more Smith 161 wrestled with his tiller bar, the more *Angler* bounced crazily from one side of the road to the other.

And then I took the bull by the horns and in my best parade ground voice I yelled 'DRIVER SPEED UP!'

It was a hell of a long shot, and I was banking wildly on the reflex action of the driver's right leg. But the years of training which had gone into making Smith 161 a tank driver suddenly came to the fore and the gamble paid off.

There was an instantaneous roar from the engine as Smith 161 instinctively opened the throttle. *Angler*'s nose shot forward and for a brief second she answered the tiller; but that was enough, Smith 161 had her in hand again and in a mounting crescendo of noise and speed we charged under the bridge with inches to spare on one side.

At once the road started going uphill again, and we were able to motor gently along to join the rest of the squadron.

I climbed out of the turret and walked round to the front of the hatch. Smith 161 was heaving himself through his hatchway.

'All right?' I said.

'Cor, blimey!' he said. 'They'd pay pahnds for that ride on 'Ampstead 'Eath on Whit Monday.'

'Well, think of the money you've saved,' I told him.

And then I remembered that *Avenger* still had to come down that slope, as well as *Alert* so I ran back to the bridge.

I was just in time to see 'Bing' Crosby bringing *Avenger* through as calmly as if he had all Stone Street to manoeuvre in.

'What was the idea of weaving all the way down the road like that?' demanded Mike Carter when he saw me.

'Oh, just showing off,' I said airily.

'I thought you were going to pile into the blessed bridge!' he said.

'Mike!' I said, in a voice rich with reproof. 'How could you entertain such a thought. Foleyforce doesn't hit bridges!'

And then I had to dodge wildly as *Alert* bounced off the brickwork and skated sideways under the arch.

But Five Troop were through, and not far away lay the town of Namur where we were supposed to meet our transporters. And when we unshipped our Churchills we hoped to do so in a real billiard table terrain.

We didn't mind the precipitous scenery of the Ardennes, and we could cope with snow and ice as well as anyone. But the combination of the two sent shivers up our spine every time we remembered it.

TEN

I DOUBT IF you'll find Oirschot on the maps of Holland; it's a tiny village somewhere between Eindhoven and 's-Hertognebosh, but a village with a heart as big as any Ardennes mountain. The people took us into their homes and made us warmly welcome for the short time we stayed there.

There were no big buildings in which we could live together, so we were scattered in ones and twos in almost every house in Oirschot. Almost, I said, because even now I can remember the indignant tones of a letter which the CO received from a Dutch housewife, complaining bitterly that no soldiers had been billeted in her house, and all the neighbours had soldiers and please did we think she had been collaborating with the Germans or what because if so she would have us know that the Resistance spoke very highly of her efforts and if some soldiers weren't forthcoming at once she would see the King or somebody... and so on.

Five Troop were in the only row of shops which Oirschot possessed, with their Troop Leader billeted in an establishment known as the Bazaar.

Like every house I saw in Holland it was scrupulously clean, and the bedroom into which I was shown just below the eaves of the house would have done credit to a Hygiene Research Unit.

But everywhere I looked there seemed to be shapely girls. Dozens of them. Not that I'm averse to attractive females; not only do they have their uses but I'm told they do a lot to improve the appearance of a piece of furniture. But there were so many of them that I surreptitiously looked up 'Bazaar' in an Anglo-Dutch dictionary to see just what sort of place I'd landed in.

But it was all very respectable. My first evening in the house commenced with a formal presentation in which the shopkeeper introduced me to his wife, seven daughters and twelve-year-old son.

Despite their years of privation under the Germans, they were a healthy, bouncing happy crowd. And they could all play the piano. All, that is, except the boy. On my first evening in their sitting room he proudly produced a cello-guitar and in halting English told me he was learning to play.

There was much excited chattering in Dutch, and then the boy sat down and slowly stumbled through some of the simpler major chords and dominant sevenths.

I dutifully applauded, but my fingers itched to have a go on that guitar. Years before I had been through the same finger-aching business of learning the instrument and like all mediocre amateur musicians I had one party piece which I'd practised over and over again until it sounded fairly smooth.

May the spirit of Eddie Lang forgive me, but it was *Melancholy Baby* – and to the knowledgeable ones that just about dates my guitar tuition!

However, with the aid of a much-thumbed sheet of music one of the girls was making a pretty good stab at *Whispering*, and a quick glance over her shoulder confirmed that it was in the key of E-flat.

I pointed to the guitar on the table, and then to myself, and made a question-mark of my eyebrows. With enthusiastic alacrity the boy thrust the instrument into my hands and a deathly silence fell on the room.

'They laughed when I sat down to play... ' I said hollowly.

'Please?' said one of the daughters.

I drew a deep breath and launched quickly into the introduction for *Whispering*.

You would have thought it was VE Day or something. The place rang with cheers. Skirts flew in all directions as girls fled to fetch Momma and the neighbours; dusty music was heaped on my lap and the boy leaned over my shoulder excitedly and kept saying 'Ingspots!' over and over again.

Father produced some Schnapps from somewhere and the girls squabbled over just who was going to do the piano accompaniment. They sorted it out somehow, and I found myself perched on a chair looking over the pianist's shoulder and surrounded by a disturbing quantity of young girlhood.

The first two or three numbers were a tremendous success and Anglo-Dutch relations could not have been better. But when I played my party piece the applause nearly brought the house down. And then it occurred to me that well brought-up young ladies shouldn't be shouting 'Wacko! Worrabout Down at the ol' Bull an' Bush!'

With a tingling sensation in the back of my neck I turned around to find all the faces of Five Troop squashed flat against the window.

'Your friends?' asked Poppa.

I nodded dumbly, and soon the well-scoured boards were echoing to the clump of Army boots as the grinning Five Troop self-consciously arranged themselves around the room.

'Er – what about *Home on the Range?*' I asked nervously. And then I realised that Poppa was sternly waiting for me to make the necessary introductions.

'This is my troop,' I said lamely. 'You know, the soldiers who work the tanks.'

'And der names?' asked Poppa.

I looked around, wondering where to start, and then Sergeant Robinson came to the rescue.

He put down the cup of coffee (which one of the daughters had presented to him with a curtsey), leaped to his feet and barked: 'Answer your names – Crosby, Cooper, Farrell, Long, McGinty, Macdonald... '

One by one they jumped up, said 'Sergeant' loudly, and sat down again.

Not to be outdone, Poppa turned to his assembled family and rattled off: 'Greta, Marie, Ilse, Fanny... ' in descending order of seniority.

Thus honour was satisfied and the party was allowed to get under way.

I think we must have made a fair amount of noise because Ian materialised from somewhere or other and wanted to know what the hell was going on.

'I'm Squadron Welfare Officer,' I said. 'Remember?'

He looked quickly around, promptly put the worst interpretation on the scene, and said: 'God! I thought these places were out of bounds.'

Luckily he spoke too quickly for Poppa to understand, and the next thing I knew he had a glass of Schnapps and was loudly demanding *Green Grow the Rushes-O.*

Five Troop seemed to think I was in clover being billeted in a house with seven daughters. But I was never able to find which one of them slipped a large jar of Horlicks into my haversack. In fact, it wasn't until

I remembered the strip advertisement about 'Night Starvation' that I saw what they were getting at.

I explained the error of their deductions, and emphasised the point of my remarks with a bit of cross-country running. But they didn't seem to appreciate it.

For some reason or other we were all sitting around a billiard table when Ian gave out the orders for our move from Oirschot, and a rough outline of our next battle.

I dare say it was only a rumour, but the information got around that, if everything went according to plan, and if we cleared up to the River Rhine, that would be the war over as far as we were concerned. But we'd heard those tales before, and anyway there were an awful lot of Germans between us and the Rhine, to say nothing of the Siegfried Line and the Reichswald Forest. Especially the Reichswald Forest.

From the front of a large wood to the west of the Reichswald we stared through our binoculars at Germany. The ground between was low-lying and looked boggy. Here and there derelict gliders of the Arnhem battle dotted the landscape and the burned-out remains of vehicles told of the battles which had already been fought over this stretch of land.

The Reichswald looked sombre and uninviting, the black trunks of the big trees seeming as solid as if carved from granite.

'There it is,' said Ian quietly. 'That's the objective for the first day. The Germans think the forest is an anti-tank obstacle; maybe it is, too. But you never know till you try. Personally, I think we should be able to operate in there, providing we pick our trees carefully.'

'We've got to reach it first,' said Tony Cunningham. 'Is that the anti-tank ditch, that white thing zig-zagging across by the group of red houses?'

'That's it,' said Ian. 'But the funnies are going to get us over that.'

'Funnies', I may point out, was the generic term applied to those tanks fitted with special gadgets like bridges, ditch-filling fascines, mine-clearing chains, and so on. And very useful they were, too.

It isn't often one can get a grandstand view of a potential battle-field, and when I took Five Troop along to have a look at it they found

MAILED FIST

it hard to believe that the harmless-looking fields and cottages were deserted except for German listening posts covering the mines which were undoubtedly thickly sown below that green turf.

'What I can't understand,' said Sergeant Robinson, 'is why we're starting at half-past ten in the morning instead of the usual crack of dawn or nightfall.'

I agreed it was a very gentlemanly hour at which to start a battle, and I told the troop to get as much sleep as they could because the way I looked at things we weren't going to get much of it once the fun began.

From some mysterious source, known only to himself, Mike Carter had produced some sixty-pound tents for us to sleep in that night. Pitched on a nice level patch of ground, with a soft bed of dry pine-needles under us, it certainly seemed as if we were to spend the night before the battle in comparative comfort.

What with studying the Defence Overprints, seeing that Foleyforce was all teed up and ready to go, and one thing and another, it was about eleven o'clock that night before I finally rolled into my blankets. But I wasn't worried.

'Oh, well,' I yawned. 'I'll probably sleep until nine-ish, a leisurely wash and shave, some breakfast, and then Heigh Ho for the Start Line.' It was a nice dream while it lasted. But at four-thirty the following morning I was nearly blasted from my blankets by a deafening barrage of noise. The ground shook with the fury of the cannonade and the walls of the sixty-pound tent whipped in and out like sparrows' wings.

It was the softening-up bombardment and it lasted until nearly ten-thirty.

We sat up in our blankets, and by means of a mixture of shouting and sign language we agreed that we'd never heard such a noise. Sleep was quite out of the question, so we dressed and went outside the tent. Overhead a solid curtain of Bofors' tracers indicated that even the 40mm anti-aircraft guns were being used to thicken-up the barrage, and the sky behind us was alight with the continual flicker of gunfire.

From the front of our wood it seemed that the edge of the Reichswald was a solid mass of explosions and it appeared impossible that anything could live in that inferno.

'It should be a walk-over by half-past ten!' shouted Bob Webster;

160

but we both knew that the Germans had a peculiar aptitude for emerging unscathed from the fiercest bombardment. Still, it was an encouraging thought.

Dead on the dot of ten-thirty we emerged from our wood and headed for the Reichswald. In front of us the Black Watch moved purposefully forward; little groups of men hurrying over the ground, while others spreadeagled themselves behind what cover they could and fired their rifles and Bren guns calmly and methodically.

We had expected the start to be slow for us, because we were scheduled to wait around quite a bit while the funnies cleared lanes through the minefield. But bit by bit reports came back over the radio indicating that it wasn't the mines which were causing the delay, but the mud.

The smooth green turf quickly churned up into black, track-clinging mud. One by one the Churchills sank on their bellies, their tracks spinning uselessly around in the bog.

There was one road across the battlefield, but this had quite rightly been earmarked for essential wheeled vehicles only. To have put tanks on it would soon have made it as impassable as the rest of the ground.

I called up *Angler* and *Alert* on the 'B' set.

'This is going to be a drivers' battle,' I said. 'Pick your ground carefully, and keep out of one another's track marks.'

'Wilco,' said Sergeant Robinson. 'What about getting out to the right a bit, by the road? It looks a bit more solid there.'

'That's King One's route,' I said, giving the daily codename for Dick Richards' troop. 'But we'll go over there if it gets too bad here.'

And then a violent explosion echoed about the back of my head, and looking over my shoulder I saw Dick's Troop Corporal (or rather his tank) leaning drunkenly to one side, a shattered track and a drifting cloud of yellow smoke betraying the fact that the enemy had mined the solid ground near the road.

'On second thoughts,' I radioed, 'we'll keep away from the road.'

But it was hard going. Bottom gear all the way, and the clinging black mud striving to tug us into the earth. Several times *Avenger*'s engine faltered and spluttered, and each time Crosby managed to nurse the big machine out of the bog.

And then the enemy began to recover from the six-hour bombardment. Eruptions of dirt indicated mortar and artillery fire coming down on our infantry and one or two of them started coming back, stolidly plodding along while holding a bloodstained arm or shoulder. Stretcher-bearers dealt swiftly and efficiently with those who couldn't walk, and still the Black Watch went forward until they reached a group of farm buildings where they were scheduled for a short halt.

We pulled into the buildings with them and I looked around for the Company Commander. He was walking along a bit of a road, quietly smoking his pipe. With his little cane, and his red hackle on the side of his cap, he might well have been taking a Sunday morning stroll down Aldershot High Street, except that vicious little spurts of dust were cracking about his heels.

He raised his stick in greeting when he saw Five Troop, and completely indifferent to the bullets kicking up the dirt around him he strolled across to *Avenger* and swung up to the turret.

'Going very well so far,' he said pleasantly. 'How're your funny-boys getting on with breaching that minefield?'

'They're all bogged,' I said gloomily. 'Look here, aren't you being shot at?'

'Oh, never mind that,' he said. 'It's only got nuisance value. Well, it's a pity you can't get across that minefield. Looks like we'll have to go on without you.'

'Balls,' I said, and hastily added 'sir', because he was, after all, a Major even though it looked to me as if he would soon be a dead one. 'I'll see what the form is on the air.'

I may have been mistaken, but it seemed to me that the Black Watch officer had little faith in our funnies, which was a shame because on the more solid ground to our right, where 'B' Squadron were fighting, the mine-clearing and bridging tanks had done their job perfectly, despite some pretty stiff enemy opposition.

But we decided to wait for a few minutes and, because I couldn't emulate the Scottish indifference to the spasmodic machine gun fire, I juggled the three tanks around until we were in a position to fire at the front edge of the Reichswald, from where we judged the obstinate machine-gunner was operating.

There was no sign of him, of course; I guessed he was probably sitting behind one of the scores of fallen trees we could see. But we blasted away happily at every likely-looking hiding place and the bullets stopped coming our way, so I suppose we must have done some good. But only temporarily.

And then Ian came up on the air to say that we were going to use the road for a little way, and the funnies were in the process of clearing it.

The Black Watch melted into the landscape again, and we picked our way behind them firing over their heads at all the spots which looked as if they might hide the enemy.

Then I heard a noise like a small boy dragging a stick along some iron railings, and a line of sparks dotted the side of *Avenger*.

'They've woken up,' I said, dropping down into the turret.

Inside the turret the noise of the bullets ringing on the armour plate was magnified ten times. I grimaced and pressed the velvet-rimmed headphones tighter over my ears. One of the bullets shattered the periscope block and for a few minutes there was a bit of chaos inside the tank while we tried to remember where we'd stowed the spare blocks.

'This looks a bit ropey to me,' I muttered, as I slid the block into its housing and squinted into it to see if it gave a clear view of the landscape.

It did. In fact it showed a perfect rectangular picture of two men in field grey crouching low as they ran across a piece of open ground and dived into what looked like a heap of fallen branches.

'Load HE,' I said over the IC, and as Pickford unloaded the smoke round we had ready for the minefield crossing, and fed in a high explosive one, McGinty already had the turret swinging searchingly from right to left.

I pointed out the target to Sergeant Robinson and Corporal Watson, and made sure McGinty had it squarely in his telescope.

Then the clanging on the turret wall started again, and I had to really bellow the command 'Fire!'

More by accident than any particular timing, the three tanks fired at once. It was a fairly easy target, and we were stationary, but all the same I felt a tremendous surge of satisfaction as the heap of green branches vanished in a triple explosion and the clanging on the turret wall stopped as if by magic.

Hardly had we got moving again when I saw the Scotsmen having trouble with pencil mines.

Now, these pencil mines are a particularly devilish device which aren't really fair weapons of war. They consist simply of a hollow tube containing a half-second delay fuse, a steel pencil-like bullet, a pressure cap and an explosive charge. These were thrust into the ground, pointing upwards, so that when they were trodden on they waited half a second and then blew the steel pencil towards the sky. The idea of the half second was so that the pencil wouldn't enter the foot, but would penetrate the fork instead. We were told, rightly or wrongly, that they were a German long-term weapon, designed not only to inflict a painful wound, but also to ruin the reproductive powers.

True to plan, we swung right and headed for the road, where we found that the funnies had cleared the mines and bridged or filled in all the craters.

But when we came to leave the road again and rejoin the Black Watch we were in trouble.

'Hullo, Five Able,' said Sergeant Robinson, 'I'm stuck.'

And when I looked back over my shoulder I saw that *Alert* was indeed well and truly bogged.

'Driver halt,' I said over the IC. 'Looks like we're going to have to give *Alert* a tow!'

While I was reporting to Ian what had happened, I saw Sergeant Robinson and big Riley clamber out of their tank and start unfastening the towing hawser. Handling the massive wire rope as if it were cotton, Riley slung it over his shoulder and ran towards the back towing shackle of *Avenger*.

And then he seemed to disappear in a spout of flame-tinted smoke and a cloud of dirt.

'He's hit!' I said instinctively, forgetting I was still on the air.

'Who is?' said Ian.

'Riley. Mortar I think. Can you send 72?'

'Roger,' said Ian. 72 was the codename of the doctor and his crew. They had a half-track for rescuing wounded tank crews and could be summoned instantly by radio.

I put Corporal Watson on to getting the three tanks to form a three-sided square around the wounded man, and Sergeant Robinson and I bent over Riley with the First Aid kit.

The lower half of his right leg was a tattered bloody mess of khaki, tank suit, woollen sock, and raw flesh. I couldn't quite make out what the polished white plastic was in the middle of it, and then I felt slightly sick when I realised it was his shinbone.

I looked at his square, blue-chinned face and the unemotional eyes, like transparent pieces of window glass. Black mud streaked one side of his nose and his usually ruddy cheeks were already going suety from loss of blood.

'Hurt much, Riley?' I asked.

'Only when I laff,' he said, with a dead-pan expression. It seemed incongruous that his muscular frame could have been rendered impotent by an eight-ounce charge of explosive.

'That's probably the shock,' I said. 'It might sting a bit later on, so I'll give you something to keep it quiet for a while.'

He stared woodenly until I took out the little ampoule of morphia, and then he cleared his throat noisily and spat into the mud.

'I don' want that, sir,' he growled. 'Puts ye to sleep and th' next thing ye know ye've no bloody leg.'

'Well, it's bloody enough now,' I said with a forced laugh. And I hesitated with the morphia; but he seemed quite untroubled by pain, and the morphia was fairly limited, so I put it back in the First Aid Box.

'You'll be back in Blighty before morning, Riley,' said Sergeant Robinson. 'Dead lucky, eh?'

A flicker of a smile appeared in Riley's transparent eyes.

'Shake the ol'? woman, that will,' he said. 'Last time I wrote 'ome in a green envelope I told 'er I'd write again from Germany! Jeez! She'll wunder what the 'ell 'as 'appened whenshe gets the telegram from the War Office.'

I straightened up from putting a couple of shell dressings on his leg.

'So you've been sending censorable information home in your green envelope, have you, Riley?' I said sadly shaking my head in reproof.

'I thought that's what they were for!' he said innocently.

And then the MO's half-track crashed through the hedge and the doc was swinging towards us with his satchel.

'How's tricks?' he said, with a broad grin.

'He's worried he's going to lose his leg, doc,' I said.

'Hell, no,' drawled the MO. 'If there's a coupla bits of skin there, we'll fix it up. Be in great shape in a few days.'

He chatted good-humouredly to Riley, his Canadian wise-cracks drawing appreciative grins from the rest of Five Troop. But all the time he was deftly and gently dealing with the shattered leg, and before I hardly realised it Riley was lifted tenderly on to a stretcher and into the half-track, and the heavy vehicle was roaring back towards the Start Line.

Meanwhile Corporal Watson had towed the bogged *Alert* free of the clinging mud.

'We're on the road again, sir,' he said.

'Good,' I said. 'And the Black Watch, no doubt, wondering where the hell we are!'

But we were not being missed all that much. Owing to the bogging, and one or two tanks going up on mines, things had slipped into their usual state of happy fluidity. Dick Richards with his remaining tank, and Mike Carter from Squadron Headquarters, were pitching in with the Black Watch who were now across the anti-tank ditch.

The funnies had made a good crossing over that ditch, but all sorts of vehicles were waiting to cross it, from both sides. Flame-throwing tanks, half-tracks, infantry carriers, jeep-ambulances, were all queuing up to cross the steep-sided obstacle.

Then I looked at the ditch and it didn't seem all that formidable to me. For a short stretch the sides of the excavation had been concreted, and it looked as if a Churchill might get over it with a bit of luck.

I asked Crosby if he thought he could do it, and he climbed out of his seat and walked forward to look at it. In a few seconds he returned giving the thumbs-up sign, and I decided to have a go.

The people queuing at the crossing gave a sardonic cheer as we motored slowly up to the ditch, and when *Avenger*'s nose dropped almost vertically and we slid head first down the concrete I began to wonder if I'd been very wise about this business. If it became necessary to tow us out of that ditch, Ian was going to have some very pointed things to say about Troop Leaders who deliberately drove into anti-tank obstacles. And then we were in the bottom of the ditch and the nose started to lift.

The anti-tank ditch wasn't as wide as *Avenger* was long, so that our nose was going up the far side while our tail was still coming down the other. Since a Churchill tank isn't made to hinge in the middle there came a point where we were completely horizontal, and apparently wedged in the ditch. But on the Churchill there is a handy device known as the 'neutral turn'; it consists of pulling on the tiller bar with the gear-box in neutral, and the result is that one track goes forward while the other goes backwards. (On a smooth surface I have seen a Churchill spin around on its own axis by this method).

With the engine going flat out, Crosby swung the tiller bar to right and left, and *Avenger* wriggled madly like a horse trying to shake off an unwelcome rider. And then the tail dropped lower, the nose rose higher, and to a triumphant cheer from the watchers we clambered out on the far side of the ditch.

By similar tactics *Alert* and *Angler* crossed the obstacle, and we set off after the Black Watch again.

They were in a small copse a few hundred yards short of the Reichswald, getting themselves ready for the last dash which would take them over the intervening open ground and into the forest. And, incidentally, on to German soil.

Over the air Ian gave the tanks orders to help the infantry get across the ground, but not necessarily to follow them into the forest, since their objective was simply the enemy trenches on the fringe of the Reichswald or just inside it.

Firing over the heads of the Scotsmen, we plastered the front edge of the Reichswald as they charged towards dark trees. It was like watching one of those old newsreels of World War One. Khaki-clad figures with fixed bayonets charging across open ground; one or two of them throwing their hands into the air and dropping dramatically to the ground, while others quietly folded up as if their bones had suddenly turned to water.

I took off my headphones to see if I could hear from which direction the enemy fire was coming, and my ears were flooded with wild Highland cries which rang above the cacophony of small arms fire. Unearthly yells, which must surely have struck fear into the few remaining Germans in the defensive trenches.

And then the front of the forest seemed to be alive with khaki, weaving purposefully in and out of the tall trees; and soon jeeps and carriers swarmed forward towards the forest, too, and we knew that the Black Watch were firmly established on their objective.

Later that evening, just as the sun was setting, we harboured around a group of buildings about five hundred yards from the forest. Our infantry friends had set up their headquarters, too, and they seemed quite pleased with the way things had gone so far.

I talked to them for a while, and then Sergeant Robinson, Corporal Watson and I stood on the back of *Angler* and discussed the days doings.

'Do you think we'll have a disturbed night, sir?' asked Watson.

'Shouldn't be surprised,' I said. 'You know what the Boche are like about their beloved Fatherland. I expect Adolf is sending priority signals saying the British must be thrown off German soil at once if not sooner.'

'Ah well, here we go again,' sighed Corporal Watson. And he lowered himself into his turret, flipped down his little padded seat, shoved his feet up on top of the gun and leaned his head back against the cupola ring.

'There's something to be said for that, too,' I said. And Sergeant Robinson and I made our way across to our own tanks.

I was right; we did have a disturbed night. But not in the way I meant.

In the early hours of the morning I was awakened by cold water splashing on my face, and when I shook myself into consciousness I found huge raindrops bouncing off the turret roof. Out of a pitch-black sky the rain was streaming down, penetrating every nook and cranny in the tank, overflowing from the drainage channels and dribbling steadily into the turret.

I swore softly and switched on one of the festoon lights to look for a piece of wire in order to clear the runaway holes in the drainage channels.

'Put that bluidy licht oot!' roared a voice from the darkness, and I reminded myself forcibly that the PBI didn't even have a leaky turret roof over their heads.

I closed the hatchway and stared about the dimly lit interior. Huddled around the column of his gunner's seat, McGinty snored lustily, his black beret pushed over one ear to reveal his smooth, straw-coloured hair.

Pickford groaned in his sleep and automatically shifted his cramped behind on top of the ammunition bin. And then with a sudden spurt a needle of rainwater found its way through the bomb-throwing mounting, landing squarely on his chin.

'Mmmnnnff!' he snuffled. 'Christ! What's going on!'

He looked up in disgust at the stream of water, and edged to one side. Then he blinked blearily at me.

'Reckon we got across that mud just in time, sir,' he said.

I nodded.

'Be a proper mess in the morning,' he added lugubriously.

'Won't be too clever in the forest, either,' I said.

From down on the floor McGinty yawned and sat up, scratching his head furiously. Then he heard the drumming of the rain on the turret roof, and his scratching stopped instantly. For a few seconds he held his head on one side in a peculiar bird-like attitude, and then with considerable satisfaction he said, 'This should square things for a rum issue, eh, sir?'

'Depends how long it lasts,' I said.

Pickford reached for a stub-end of a cigarette from inside his beret. 'Sounds as if it'll last a couple of days, anyway,' he said.

In fact, apart from one or two isolated breaks, it lasted nineteen days.

Slowly we fought our way through the interminable Reichswald Forest. And each day the great trees steadily dripped rain on to us, and succeeded in blotting out most of the grey daylight.

The fringes of the forest were shell-torn and shattered, with untidy heaps of dead Germans flung about in grotesque attitudes. Our three Churchills proved very effective de-foresters; trees of quite respectable sizes were pushed flat and we managed to show the Germans that they were just as wrong in counting the Reichswald as an anti-tank obstacle, as we had been in regarding the Ardennes as one in 1940.

We took it in turns to break the trail, sometimes with unexpected results. Like the time we were grinding our way forward with the infantry, and all was suspiciously quiet. A screen of Scotsmen flung out in front reported that the Germans had withdrawn, but that there were signs of self-propelled anti-tank guns on the rides which crisscrossed the forest.

So we avoided the rides and took it the hard way straight through the trees.

Alert was just in front of me, and because of the comparative quiet I was half-way out of the turret, resting my elbows on the turret roof, and my chin on my hands.

Sergeant Robinson put *Alert*'s nose at a tough-looking fir; the engine roared and the tracks skidded in the loose mould for a few seconds. The tree vibrated and shook – and then a German dropped right on top of Sergeant Robinson.

My immediate reaction was that we had flushed one of those tiresome tree-top snipers, and I tugged my revolver from its holster. And then the German rolled stiffly off the turret and fell spread-eagled to the ground, turning sightless eyes to the sky.

He had been dead quite some time, but we never did find out how he came to get up in that tree. And with complete equanimity Sergeant Robinson carried on as if nothing had happened.

'I would have vomited there and then,' I said to him.

He laughed darkly. 'I nearly did,' he admitted. 'But I was so thankful to find he was dead, I didn't much care what he smelled like!'

Sometimes, though, we came to a part of the forest where the trees were old enough and big enough to defy even the flattening powers of the Churchills, and then we had to take to the tracks. The Germans, of course, knew this, and they had guns covering those tracks and sometimes they mined them as well.

Tanks, and lives, were lost as we steadily battered our way through the greenery; but each time Five Troop had to lead we had an uneventful day. More or less.

Wet and uncomfortable, we were doing our 'tip-toeing elephant' act along one of the winding tracks which led through the forest. At each bend we expected to be greeted by a nasty explosion, and have the tank burst into flames beneath us, or at least blow a track. Cautiously I poked *Avenger*'s nose around each bend and, when nothing happened, ambled forward to the next bend to repeat the process.

Suddenly we heard the roar of a jeep coming along the track behind us. It was going much too fast to be anything less than a Brigadier, so I got out my map and rapidly ran over a Situation Report in my mind. But to my surprise and horror the jeep didn't slow down when it reached us, and when I looked at it I saw the PRESS plaque on the mudguard. I recognised Alan Moorehead of the *Daily Express*, and then the car had swung past us and its engine note was dying away in the distance.

I looked back at Corporal Watson behind me and shrugged my shoulders. But there was no sound of an exploding jeep so I deduced the road ahead was clear.

Five minutes later the jeep came roaring back, Alan poring over his map.

'Why didn't you ask him if there was any sign of the enemy, sir?' said Corporal Watson later.

'Don't be silly,' I said. 'That's an exclusive story he's got there!'

Other forces pushing down from the north were clearing the far side of the Reichswald, so we were switched to the low-lying ground on the south of the forest, and here we came up against the much-vaunted Siegfried Line.

At first the concrete fortifications caused us a lot of heart-burning, and with the assurance of hardened campaigners Five Troop said: 'It wasn't the way we did it at Le Havre.'

But the pillboxes of the Siegfried Line were somewhat different from the ones we had met at Le Havre. They consisted of three embrasures, sited to cover 360°. Each one was made of four-inch-thick steel set in two feet of concrete. Each embrasure was interconnected, and there were sleeping quarters in the centre. And usually each pillbox was protected by a belt of tripwires and mines; and each pillbox was in sight of another.

Tough nuts on the whole, but the army being what it is we tried different methods of dealing with these places until we found the best plan. And this was promptly christened 'the drill' thereby earning much praise in high places, and was put into effect in every case.

Laugh if you like, but it worked. And this was the way of it.

First of all we isolated the chosen pillbox by firing lots of smoke to blind its neighbours. Then we fired high explosives at the embrasures, and sometimes this was sufficient to persuade the pillbox crew that the war held no future for them. But if not, we had a very effective weapon in the shape of one of the funnies: they called it an AVRE. Manned by the Royal Engineers it consisted of a Churchill tank, but instead of a gun it had a petard which hurled a dustbin-sized charge of high explosive. This usually succeeded in blasting the embrasure wide open and causing the occupants to lose all further interest in the campaign.

Yet sometimes it didn't, and then we carried out the third movement of the drill which was to bring a flame-throwing tank. This squirted flame right into the gaping hole made by the AVRE, and the effect inside must have been terrible.

There was no fourth movement to this drill; it wasn't really necessary.

After ten days of rain we were beginning to feel the effect. Wet through, plastered with mud, half-deafened by gunfire, we were getting irritable and short-tempered with one another. Only the irrepressible types like Farrell and Smith 161 managed to remain good-humoured, and it was largely thanks to the impromptu antics of these two comedians that Five Troop managed to keep sane at all.

This sort of thing: several times we crossed and re-crossed the unmarked frontier which, in that part of the world, divided Holland from Germany. But it was not until we were going through a small town that we really felt we were in the Fatherland. The town had been cleared by other troops a couple of days before, and we were just making one of those moves from one sector to another.

'What's this striped pole across the road, sir?' said Pickford.

'The frontier!' I said, pointing to the deserted hut which had housed the frontier police and customs men.

I stared curiously at my first German civilian. He was an old man, dressed in shabby serge and an engine-driver's sort of cap. His grizzled face regarded us from above a bushy white moustache as we clattered over the broken frontier barrier. And then I heard *Angler*'s driver's hatch being thrown open, and when I looked over my shoulder I saw Smith 161 leaning out and staring questioningly at the old German.

'We on the right road for Berlin, mate?' asked Smith 161, with a perfectly straight face.

I swear the old blue eyes winked, as the man tugged at his grizzled moustache and said: '*Berlin? Ja, ja! Gerade aus!*'

'I thought the Germans had no sense of humour,' said Pickford, when we got moving again.

'I know,' I said. 'But he can remember Germany before Hitler, and probably before the Kaiser too.'

Yet eventually the steady downpour managed to dampen the high spirits of even the troop comedians. And my own.

This was brought home to me during a silly little night attack with a battalion of the Black Watch – at least, it wasn't silly to the Watch, who had a very tough battle and lost a lot of men. But to my jaundiced eye it didn't seem to achieve very much, beyond a few more acres of sodden German soil and a cluster of slate-roofed houses.

The narrow roads were built up on embankments, crossing black fields which I knew to be quite impossible for tanks. Tony Cunningham was up in the lead, and we could see and hear him blazing away like mad as the Scotsmen inched their way forward to their objective. I felt sorry for Tony, having to fight a battle in the dark, and being unable to get off the roads. One way and another I wasn't a very happy Troop Leader.

The Black Watch had found a small cottage where they set up their headquarters, and around this cottage I parked Foleyforce and waited for orders, the idea being that the Commanding Officer of the Black Watch would get the news from his forward Company Commanders, and Five Troop would go wherever the need was.

But to get to this little cottage had meant a hazardous journey down a narrow track just about the width of a tank. In the deadened glimmer of my torch the banks looked deathly steep, and I couldn't get out of my mind the fate of an officer of 'B' Squadron who had been killed when his tank had overturned down just such an embankment.

I was told later that I looked as black as thunder as I got on the 'A' set to tell Ian that I had reached the infantry headquarters.

'Hullo Fox Five,' said Ian. 'Roger. I propose to come up there. Take your penny to the track junction to act as a guide for me. Over.'

'Fox Five,' said I. 'That's not necessary. It's the first turning on the right. You can't go wrong.'

'Hullo Fox Five,' repeated Ian. 'I say again, take your penny to the track junction. Over.'

I scowled at the microphone in my hand, and took a deep breath.

'Hullo Fox Five,' I said. 'The track up to here is barely wide enough to get along. I'll come and meet you on foot, if you like. But it will take time. Over.'

I could almost hear Ian hurling his headset into the bottom of his turret. Then he came on the air again with the sort of voice which brooks no argument.

'Hullo Fox Five!' he snapped. 'Meet me at that track junction, in your penny. Quickly! Over.'

'Fox Five, Wilco, out,' I said. Then I switched to IC and said, 'Turn the bloody thing round.'

'Bit 'ard turnin' 'er around 'ere, zur,' said Crosby doubtfully.

'Turn the bloody thing around when I tell you,' I snarled. 'Get out of that damned seat, Farrell, and guide him!'

Gingerly we drove along the ribbon of road.

Twice something hit the road in front of us and went whirring away through the blackness, with the horrible diminuendo whine of AP shot.

'We're being shot at by AP, sir,' said Pickford nervously. But whether he was nervous of the AP or my black mood I don't know.

I pushed my wet beret to the back of my head and thought what the hell. There was damn all to fire back at anyway, so I picked up the microphone and said: 'Probably overs from Mr Cunningham's battle.'

Maybe they were, too. But on the other hand they might not have been. And I didn't investigate them or tell Ian about them.

Which just shows you what a little rain can do.

To our incredulous delight the next day dawned clear and sunny. We were having twenty-four hours' rest, parked around a deserted farm to which we had driven after the previous night's battle.

I had made my peace with Ian; great fires were burning all over the place as the crews dried out their wet clothes and bedding; there had been a double issue of rum; and with his usual bland nonchalance Jim Steward had strolled into the harbour back from hospital in England, acting as if he had just been over the road to another squadron.

Luxuriating in the feel of the sun on my face, I strolled away from the tanks and wandered around the farm and outbuildings. At the end of the yard a little wooden building in a wire pen looked as if it might bear further investigation. It was a chicken run, but all the poultry had long since been liberated by the Scotsmen. But the wire netting looked as if it could be converted into a form of permanent camouflage screen, with the judicious application of some leaves and grasses.

Casually I glanced into the hen house – and then my heart almost stopped beating as I saw, nestling warmly in a bed of straw, a delectable, speckled, brown egg!

Now you must know that in those days an egg was a rare thing of great beauty; a prize to be jealously guarded and cooked with care and attention.

Beaming with pride I carried my treasure back to Five Troop, and I was soon the centre of an admiring throng of whistling tank crews. Those who were quicker on the uptake shot away to look for other hen-houses, but Five Troop just stood around making envious remarks.

'How would you like it, sir,' said Pickford, 'Boiled, fried, scrambled or poached?'

'I think I'd like it boiled,' I said. 'With a little brown bread and butter.'

We settled for biscuits and margarine, but water was swiftly put on one of the pressure stoves and brought to the boil.

At least four separate watches were used to time the cooking of this lovely brown egg, while Crosby sorted out a suitable size of socket spanner to use as an egg-cup. One of my cleaner handkerchiefs did duty as a napkin, and then with great ceremony I removed the egg from the water and settled myself for a feast.

With a great flourish I tapped the egg with my spoon – and was rewarded with a resonant and crystal-clear 'Ding!'

I tried again, mounting suspicion in my heart.

'Ding!' rang the egg.

A stunned silence lay over Five Troop, and then Crosby threw back his head and yelled 'It's a pot egg!'

That did it. Gales of laughter swept over the assembled tank crews; people who had been cursing each other the previous day slung their arms around one another and wept tears of merriment. The reaction would have touched the heart of any ENSA comedian – and I sat in the middle of it and stared unbelievingly at the fraud in my hand.

It was a typical example of German thoroughness. Not for them the heavy, glossy object which fools British birds; my pot egg was the right weight, colour, texture, and everything. The designer of that egg had really set out to deceive the poultry, and I'll bet he succeeded.

And the next day Foleyforce morale was as high as ever.

The rain came back again of course. And we fought some queer battles and had some queer experiences.

Like the time we did an attack just south of Goch. It was night time, but the cloud was just right for using Monty's moonlight. This useful effect was obtained by throwing searchlight beams on to low clouds, so that a dim, blueish light was reflected over the whole landscape. It gave enough illumination so that we could see where we were going, but not enough for the gunners to pick up targets in their telescopes. So we used our machine guns like hosepipes, the blue tracer bullets spraying all over the landscape and doing a certain amount of good. But only, of course, when the infantry had told us where the opposition was. They spoke very harshly to anybody who opened fire over their heads at night without being asked.

And that's how we went on for twenty days and nights, and though Five Troop wasn't in the fore (or even engaged in battle) every one of those twenty days, sometimes it was just as tiring tailing along behind the others. And sometimes enlightening, too.

Goch had been captured and our squadron were driving through it to the other side. Five Troop were about halfway down the column when for some reason or other we halted. I was never able to find out just what the hold-up was, but I know I looked casually around, shaking my head in wonder at the tremendous damage which had been inflicted on the town.

Tall shops lay in rubble and houses had been crushed as if by a giant hand.

Nose to tail the big Churchills stood in the rubble-covered roadway, their exhausts sending up thick columns of faintly blue smoke.

I sat on top of the turret listening to the engines drumming away, and staring moodily at a tottering wall bearing the chalked legend '*EIN REICH, EIN VOLK, EIN FÜHRER*' I mentally contrasted it with the sparkling cleanliness of Oirschott, and I yawned as I thought of the snow-white bed, and the boy with the guitar.

And then I shook my head and blinked, because I found myself staring at a guitar.

A sagging shopfront was spilling sheet music all over the road, and the splintered remains of a piano teetered crazily on the edge of a mound of dusty brickwork. But beyond the smashed piano I could see the unmistakable outlines of a guitar, and the sunburst effect on the belly of the instrument glowed even through the covering of dust. The strings were broken, of course, and I could clearly see the thick E-string curling away from the frets and vanishing into the rubble.

'Looting or no looting, this I must have,' I muttered, as I wrenched off my headset. And then with a jerk Crosby let in the clutch and we were rolling down the road hard on the heels of the tank in front.

In an agony of indecision I wondered whether or not to halt the column while I scurried back and collected the guitar, and by the time I had made up my mind we were a long way away from the shop. But I made a mental note of the shop site and vowed to come back as soon as possible.

It happened that we came back sooner than we expected. Once the centre of the town was reached, the enemy wisely decided to withdraw towards the Rhine, apart from one or two fanatical groups who remained in factories and other large buildings, and these did not give the Jocks a great deal of trouble.

Come to think of it, there isn't much you can do with a tank in an attack on a factory. Except stand off at a reasonable range and keep firing at all the doors and windows until the infantry launch themselves upon it.

We did this fairly comfortably. How comfortably can be judged from the fact that, although a tank gunner needs both hands for his job (one to pull the necessary trigger, the other to operate the turret traversing mechanism) I found McGinty quietly chewing an apple while he plastered a factory with HE fire.

And before the sun went down we turned about and headed for our concentration area beyond Goch.

'I want to stop in Goch as we go through,' I said to Crosby. 'I shan't be a second so keep the engine running.'

'Goin' shopping, zur?' Crosby's voice crackled over the IC.

'That's right,' I said. 'Sort of window shopping in a way.'

The first thing I noticed about the music shop was that the piano was now in bits on the pavement, and the sagging shopfront had been scattered all over the road. Where the guitar had been was now just one more crater.

And in the ruins of the buildings I saw little red notices stuck there by the Royal Engineers. They said: 'BEWARE OF BOOBY TRAPS.'

A cold sweat trickled down my spine as I remembered the way that E-string had innocently curled into the rubble.

'I thought you wanted to stop somewhere about here, sir?' said Pickford.

'It doesn't matter now,' I said.

And once again I nodded gratefully to the benevolent spirit of Villers Bocage.

The fighting ended for Five Troop in pretty much the same way as it had begun.

The drums were rolling for the assault across the Rhine, and we were ordered to hold ourselves in readiness just in case.

'Remember Caen?' I said to Sergeant Robinson, as we rolled up our bedding and stowed it on the tanks.

'Do I?' he laughed. 'Thought we were in for it in a big way then. And then they never used us.'

'Hope to goodness they don't need us now,' I said. 'They've got so many troops lined up for this river crossing that if they need any more it'll mean things are going very badly indeed.'

But things didn't go badly. In fact they went so well that we were never even called forward from the village where we were standing on our toes. Indeed, when we did come to cross the Rhine it was a very orderly procession, escorted by military policemen and greeted by smooth looking gentlemen in long sleek cars.

'Who be they then, zur,' said Crosby.

'Not sure,' I said. 'Military Government or something. They look after the civil affairs of the country.'

A long silence greeted this remark, and then he said: 'What'll we be doin' then, zur?'

I couldn't tell him, because I didn't know. We were still a fighting Tank Troop, and fighting was still going on across the Westphalian Plain. We might yet be required to remove the muzzle covers from our guns and tempt Fate and the Germans again.

So we followed the course of the war on our maps, and spoke feelingly about the new German trick of burying an aerial bomb with their mines, so that you didn't just get a broken track and a bad case of concussion, but a tank and its crew blown to smithereens.

And all the time we were clearing up battlefields, shepherding DPs, manning road blocks, and acting as escorts for the long convoys of supplies streaming across the Rhine and moving towards the Elbe.

April gave way to May, and we realised that for us the war in Europe was over. So much so that when the bells rang all over Britain for VE Day, Five Troop regarded it with the usual disfavour they kept for spit-and-polish parades.

Already whispers of another and longer move were going around, and furtive mentions of the word 'Burma' could be heard from inside closed-down turrets. True, the war against the Japanese was going well, but there still seemed a long way to go to Tokyo and it was regarded as a fair bet that we would yet be matching our skill and hard-won experience against the cunning of the little yellow men.

Of course, we didn't know that somewhere across the world clever men were putting the finishing touches to the atom bomb, and starting a chain reaction which hasn't finished yet.

Probably because of the strict ban on fraternisation we tended to gravitate together more than ever, and troops became more and more self-contained families. I dare say the psychologists could explain that the troop *ésprit-de-corps* was a sublimation of the inherent family instinct in all of us, but whatever the cause I know it gave me a warm feeling of gratification as I looked out of a schoolroom window and saw *Avenger*, *Alert* and *Angler* parked in the playground.

Avenger still bore the line of bullet marks across the turret from the first day of the Reichswald battle, and the little splash of molten metal on the cupola flap was still shining evidence of the sniper of Le Havre.

Angler's tracks wanted adjusting, and I thought of how we had battled to do this task in the Ardennes blizzard.

And looking at *Alert*'s turret I half expected the sharp features of Sergeant Atkins to emerge from the commander's hatch.

'Scruffy lot, aren't they?' said Tony Cunningham, standing beside me.

'Oh, I don't know,' I said. 'I was just thinking, Tony. Do you think anybody would want to read a book about what we've done?'

'Not everything you've done,' he grinned. 'There's a law against indecent literature.'

'I like that!' I said indignantly. 'Five Troop have led a blameless existence, let me tell you. Except on leave, of course, and you don't count that.'

'Well, what *have* we done, come to that?' said Tony. 'We've only done our job: nothing very hair-raising like the Commando-types or the Airborne boys.'

'No,' I said slowly. 'That's true. It was just an idea I had that people might be interested in those ungainly, armour-plated worlds down there and the men who served in them.'

Tony shook his head doubtfully.

'I don't think so, John,' he said. 'Not just yet. The British public is about fed up with war and talk of war. Wait until it's history.'

I nodded, and stared at the sunshine winking on the polished muzzle-brake of *Avenger*'s gun, where McGinty was slowly, but quite pointlessly, cleaning it.

EPILOGUE

IT WAS FEBRUARY, 1954, and I was sitting in the War Office watching the Whitehall rain beat down into the courtyard and talking to a young subaltern just home from Kenya.

He was explaining how, in order to combat the Mau Mau terrorists, the Royal Engineers had built log roads through the jungle.

'Oh, yes; I know the idea,' I said. 'Same as they did in the Reichswald. You weren't in that battle, were you?'

He smiled faintly.

'No, sir,' he said. 'But we heard all about it at my prep school.'

'Then that just about makes it history, doesn't it,' I said pleasantly.

ISBN 9781912423071

'Alexander Baron's *From the City, From the Plough* is undoubtedly one of the very greatest British novels of the Second World War and provides the most honest and authentic account of front line life for an infantryman in North West Europe.'

ANTONY BEEVOR

ISBN 9781912423781

In August 1943, Sergeant Craddock leads his battle-weary platoon down Via Garibaldi in Catania, Sicily. Struck by the oppressive heat and alien new surroundings, the men soon settle into this lull in their combat experience. Against this backdrop, the second book of Alexander Baron's War Trilogy meditates upon friendship, loyalty and love.

ISBN 9781912423798

Spanning the Sicilian countryside to the brothels of Ostend, *The Human Kind* is a series of pithy vignettes of the author's wartime experiences. From the days of training to brutal combat, the book depicts many of the men, women – and, in some cases, children – affected by the widespread reach of the Second World War.

ISBN 9781912423163

'Few other novels of the war describe the grinding claustrophobia, violence and lethal danger of being in a tank crew with the stark vividness of Peter Elstob... a forgotten classic that deserves to be read and read.'

JAMES HOLLAND

ISBN 9781912423422

In January 1941 Griselda Green arrives at Blimpton, a place 'so far from anywhere as to be, for all practical purposes, nowhere'. Monica Felton's 1945 novel gives a lively account of the experiences of a group of men and women working in a munitions factory during the Second World War.

ISBN 9781912423507

George Bunting, businessman, husband and father, lives a quiet life at home in Laburnam Villa in Essex, reading about theprogress of the war in his trusty newspaper. But as the Second World War continues into the summer of 1940, this bumbling 'everyman' is forced to confront the true realities of the conflict.

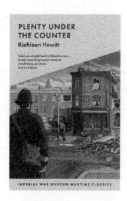

ISBN 9781912423095

'Takes you straight back to Blitzed London... boasts everything a great whodunit should have, and more.'

ANDREW ROBERTS

ISBN 9781912423378

'A highly unusual war novel with several confluent narratives; moving, interesting and of great literary value.'

LOUIS DE BERNIÈRES

ISBN 9781912423156

'When a man has been a soldier and seen action, he writes of war with true understanding, and with authority. When that man writes with with, elegance and imagination, as Fred Majdalany does in Patrol [itals], he produces a military masterpiece.'

ALLAN MALLINSON

ISBN 9781912423088

'A tremendous rediscovery of a brilliant novel. Extremely well-written, its effects are both sophisticated and visceral. Remarkable.'

WILLIAM BOYD

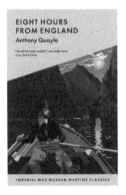

ISBN 9781912423101

'Much more than a novel'

RODERICK BAILEY

'I loved this book, and felt I was really there'

LOUIS de BERNIÈRES

'One of the greatest adventure stories of the Second World War'

ANDREW ROBERTS

ISBN 9781912423385

'Brilliant... a quietly confident masterwork'

WILLIAM BOYD

'One of the best books to come out of the Second World War'

JOSHUA LEVINE

ISBN 9781912423279

'A hidden masterpiece, crackling with authenticity'

PATRICK BISHOP

'Supposedly fiction, but these pages live – and so, for a brief inspiring hour, do the young men who lived in them.'

FREDERICK FORSYTH

ISBN 9781912423651

When Singapore falls in early 1942, the life that Susan Sandyman has lovingly created abroad is shattered. Forced to flee home, she can either succumb to grief or find solace in war work. When a chance encounter with the elusive Air Transport Auxiliary pilots stirs a spark of excitement, Susan's decision is made.

ISBN 9781912423262

'Witty, warm and hugely endearing... a lovely novel'

AJ PEARCE

'Evokes the highs and lows, joys and agonies of being a Land Girl'

JULIE SUMMERS